Your body on my mind
NIKAU & KADEN

AMBRA KERR

Copyright © 2023 by Ambra Kerr

All rights reserved.

No part of this book may be reproduced in any form or by any electronic or mechanical means, including information storage and retrieval systems, without written permission from the author, except for the use of brief quotations in a book review.

This book is a work of fiction. All names, characters, locations, and incidents are product of the author's imagination. Any resemblance to actual persons, things, living or dead, locales or events is entirely coincidental.

Edited by: MadSkillz

Triggerwarning

ONLY READ THIS BOOK IF YOU ARE OF AGE!

It contains graphic sexual scenes, most of which fall into the BDSM category. This is pure fiction and the book states no claims to serve as instructional material for such practices. If you feel the need to explore the subject yourself, do so to the best of your ability – use credible sources. This book is not a fully comprehensive source of information!

This book contains the following Kinks/Triggers:
Collaring, Threesome, Sadism, Outdoor Sex, Impact Play, Anonymous Sex, Toys, Voyeurism, Double Penetration, Dirty Talk, Biting, Breath Play, Disciplining, Slapping, Degradation, Orgasm Control, Honorifics, Knife Play, Blowjobs, Erotic Humiliation, Bondage, Edge Play, Forced Orgasm.

This list may not be complete or in the order it appears in the book to avoid spoilers!

There's only one thing left to say: RIP to your panties (especially @ Jacky)

Prologue

"And you broke up with her just like that?"

Kaden raised an eyebrow at my exaggeration. I knew full well that he *hadn't just dumped* her and that the lady in question was undoubtedly angry with him for more than one reason.

"We're just not right for each other," he muttered, stroking his dark hair as if it bothered him more than usual. "She has other interests. And I need a woman who doesn't get scared when my fingers close around her throat."

As if to confirm, he reached out. His hand closed around my throat in an affectionate gesture. Heat flooded my cheeks. Not because my best friend demonstrated what he meant, but because I could not imagine finding what he was just doing to me exciting.

I cleared my throat. "Maybe all these women are just afraid you'll suffocate them."

Kaden's hands were huge paws, and when a man of his size towered over you and totally dominated you, most women were bound to be afraid. He couldn't expect every woman out there to have the same twisted fantasies he had.

Inquiringly, he gazed into my face. "You're not afraid."

The statement made me smile. "That's because I know you, you idiot."

He lowered his hand, but seconds later I could still feel the pressure on my skin. As if the touch had been burned into my memory. I blamed the prevailing temperatures on the heat that suddenly pulsed through my body. Even for O'ahu it was hot tonight.

"Maybe you should do things a little differently in the future," I added after a few seconds, during which he'd said nothing and instead continued to look at me intensely. The blush in my cheeks would certainly not fade, so I was grateful for the darkness around us. I prayed the moon was not bright enough to betray me.

"You mean you want me to forget what I prefer and do what a hundred other men have tried and failed to do?"

"How can you be sure they're preferences if you've never had a taste of them?"

"How do *you* know they're not *your* preferences if you've never tried them?"

The counter-question made me grit my teeth. Kaden could have any woman our age – and probably plenty a few years his senior. He was devilishly handsome, and looked a few years older than he was. Sun-kissed skin wasn't the only trait of his ancestry. Dark hair curled around his head, despite its shortness. When he moved, he appeared in complete control of his body – and every muscle that moved under his skin put on an impressive show. Most of the time he seemed like a young demigod, and if that wasn't enough to win someone over, his natural charm would. Kaden was personable and knew how to express himself. And when he smiled, or flashed that mischievous grin that revealed that one dimple on his cheek, most women would have licked his bare chest immediately and declared him their property. At least until they found out that he wasn't satisfied with vanilla sex. So far, his quota had been to make a hundred percent of the women run away screaming. That was if he had not already broken up with them. He had a kind of radar for women who were not in tune with him. Unlike him, though, I didn't have the chance to fuck around wildly and find out exactly what he meant by all of his ominous preferences. I didn't have the time – or the interest – for men who didn't even know the simplest basics.

I leaned back with my hands in the warm sand, a sigh on my lips. I tried to come up with an answer that didn't sound like I was trying to tell him how he should choose his next girlfriend.

"We're eighteen, K. I don't think a lot of people our age get to have breathtakingly good sex that satisfies them to the core," I murmured in the end.

He didn't seem too thrilled with the answer. I could imagine him pulling the corners of his mouth down in that dissatisfied way that immediately told everyone he had a problem with what was happening. The word *patience* was foreign to Kaden. If he wanted something, he wanted it immediately. Not in a few years or after an indefinite amount of time.

"What about you? Aren't you afraid of not finding someone who suits you in every way?"

I shrugged before shaking my head, then gazed at the sky and stared at the stars. Everybody dreamed. Pursued goals. Expressed desires. Even if someone claimed to be content with their life as a single person, I believed that, subconsciously, they still felt the need to be close to someone. A need for a life that they didn't have to live on their own. Not because it was a conscious choice. But because there was a deep-seated basic need in all of us that we could hardly escape.

And although I knew this longing, this desire to arrive somewhere and to be at home, I wouldn't say I was afraid that I wouldn't find the right person.

This was nothing more than a romantic notion in our minds that did not exist in the real world.

"Maybe I'll find someone who doesn't suit me at

first sight. But the attraction is so strong that we develop into the people we need to be to have a future together."

"Damn it, when did you become so wise, Nik?"

"Maybe in the time you've spent finding women willing to let you choke them."

He let out a sound of indignation. "It doesn't sound as attractive and sexy as it is the way you put it."

"So how would you like me to put it?"

There was a brief pause, he slid his feet through the sand thoughtfully until he had found the perfect answer.

"It's about freedom. About the thrill rushing through you, making everything feel so much more intense... letting go of control, proving blind trust. It's... fucking seductive."

I swallowed, catching myself in the very revealing thought that there was no way I would let go of control – because, at the same time, it meant I was never going to get what I wanted.

"How do you know?" I groaned nervously, not wanting to give away how long it took me to answer.

"You think I'd do something I don't know? Which I've never experienced myself? That would be a careless thing to do."

Suddenly, I realized how far Kaden had come, how far he'd grown. He wouldn't find anyone our age with the same level of knowledge. Or the open-mindedness that it undoubtedly took to be able to deal with what was going through his head.

"I am sure that one day you will meet someone who will be able to fulfill all of your wishes. And do so with great pleasure," I finally replied.

We hadn't come here to talk about sexual preferences, but that he had tossed another woman to the wind. He was supposed to be sad, a little bit lost. But somehow it seemed to be a typical situation: Kaden always got out of one relationship before he jumped into the next one – only to find out a few weeks later that he hadn't found the right one yet again.

Kaden had slept with more women than I knew men.

"What if I don't?"

I couldn't keep the grin from spreading across my lips. "Then you are in need of a Plan B."

He rolled onto his stomach, automatically moving closer to me. He looked up at me with those stupid puppy dog eyes, which meant I wouldn't be able to refuse him what he was about to say. Regardless of *what* it was.

"You're my Plan B."

I arched my eyebrows in irritation.

"We're going to make a deal," he went on. "If we're both not in a serious relationship by the time we turn thirty, we'll get married. External influences won't be a factor."

More than surprised, I let out a gasp. "You'd ruin your chances of happiness?"

"I'm marrying my best friend. I can't see anything wrong with that, Nikau."

The fact that he used my full name told me this wasn't just some stupid statement he'd made on a whim. Kaden was serious.

Unable to express myself, I suddenly felt immense pressure on my chest.

Kaden burst into laughter. "Huh? I'm not that terrible of a choice. I know my grandma's recipes by heart. I can do the cleaning and the laundry. And most important of all, I know what you like to drink and where you like to eat. Which restaurants to go to when you're in a bad mood or on your period. Your siblings like me, my parents would adopt you if you asked them, and I make you laugh. That's more than anyone else can say. On top of that, I would be married to my best friend. Very few people can say the same."

"To your best friend that's a control freak."

"It doesn't matter."

"But with other women, it does."

"Because they're not you."

"That makes no sense, Kaden. You're telling me that in twelve years you'll suddenly be able to forget a part of yourself."

"Say yes, Nik."

"And then what?"

"Then nothing. In twelve years time, we'll both be happily engaged and some stupid promise won't be important anymore."

"Okay. Fine. If we're both not taken, we'll try each other."

"We'll get married," he countered vehemently. That made me laugh.

But finally I nodded. After all, I couldn't say no to him when he looked at me with those damn puppy dog eyes.

Satisfied, he nodded. "Then we just have to seal the deal."

I looked at Kaden questioningly. Without warning, he drew his knife. The blade reflected the moonlight for a moment and then I felt a surge of adrenaline rushing through my body. Because the next thing I knew, the knife was sliding across my index finger.

I hissed when I felt the cut, but Kaden didn't dwell on my temporary pain. Instead, he took my wrist to press my finger against his warm lips.

His tongue darted out and slid over the wound he had inflicted, hot and wet, before he spread the rest of my blood over his mouth, as if we were about to perform some sort of ritual.

I tried hard to find what I saw disturbing. Repulsive. Strange. Kaden was just an insane man. But the opposite was the case. Instead, I felt a strange attraction to what was happening in front of my eyes. A kind of fascination, because the thought of him handling the liquid that ensured my survival in such a respectful yet captivating way left me momentarily breathless.

Until he looked up at me with a grin and broke the spell. "It looks like we have a deal, Nikau Keahi."

I snorted and shook my head, getting rid of whatever had been building up inside me as I watched the bloody action unfold. "Don't get ideas, Kaden."

He promptly twisted the corners of his mouth into a grin. "But I'm imagining it all, Nika."

Well, the nickname was new.

But it would be a long time before I heard it again.

Nikau

"You're closing up today, aren't you?" chirped Jane, my absolute hated boss, as she whizzed past me with her oversized bag and hurried toward the exit.

The kitchen was under her strict command, but, unfortunately, that didn't mean she cared about leaving her workspace tidy.

I glanced at the clock. Half past ten. Most of the restaurant's guests had already left. A few regulars were still sitting at the bar, and the temporary staff in the kitchen were probably still cleaning up the day's mess.

When I didn't answer her directly, she spun around and gave me that forced friendly smile that showed too many teeth. It made the tiny hairs on the back of my neck stand up. Dramatically, she fluttered her false eyelashes that were far too long.

"Sure, no problem," I replied in a sugary tone. Satisfied, she nodded, pushed the door open and disappeared into the dark night. Cedar Rapids wasn't exactly a pretty town – all of Iowa left a lot to be desired, if I was being honest – and Jane probably only insisted on leaving early because she couldn't wait to get home, put her feet up and let her kids take care of her. At least, that's how it was in my head, because that's how she treated the staff.

I hurried to the back, pushed open the kitchen door and found Samuel bent over the sink, a pile of dirty dishes beside him. Contrite, I watched him for a few seconds. "Let me just get the remaining guests out the door and I'll help you," I called to him, having already turned to leave. Before I returned to the bar, I put on another friendly smile. The muscles in my face ached every night from the constant effort of trying to be polite to all these people.

As soon as I was behind the bar, I tapped on the counter. "Ron, do you need a taxi or should I call your wife?"

Before he had a chance to reach for his car keys, I pulled them in my direction. After the amount of alcohol he had already consumed, I would hardly let him drive home.

"Alternatively, a walk is a good idea. By the time you get there, your intoxication should have worn off, shouldn't it?"

Frowning, he looked at me. "I like you, girl – especially when you're pouring me more booze without saying anything."

I twisted my mouth. "And tomorrow morning you can like me, because I did not just put you on the street," I replied, already reaching for the phone to inform his wife of his whereabouts.

She would probably turn up in her pajamas and drag him home by his ear. A funny thought.

I turned to the other three customers sitting at the bar, gripping their glasses. "What about you guys? Wives you want me to call?"

"We've already chosen our driver," one of them replied, and I nodded in satisfaction.

"Wonderful. Then I'll get the bill ready for you." I turned away with a wink.

"Will you be here tomorrow as well?"

Actually, I was here every day. I had to be. Somehow I had to make a living in this godforsaken place. Iowa wasn't exactly one of those states where you could freely choose your work. You came to this place, took the first job offered, and almost nine years later you found yourself still in the same job, with the same people, and the same problems kept you up at night.

"Maybe. We'll just have to see," I muttered as I tapped on the till.

Riggs lifted his head. "Tomorrow is our dear Nikau's birthday. We could give her a day off from us old farts," he announced, as if proud to have remembered my birthday.

I was worried because I had never told any of these people about my birthday.

Smiling thinly, I passed the bills over the counter and watched as the coins were slammed onto the wood and the men got up. "Have a lovely evening, my dear. I'll have a serious talk with Jane if I see you here tomorrow night."

Amused, I nodded. "Sure. Good luck with that."

It took another twenty minutes before Ron finally disappeared as well. After locking up, I quickly walked around the front of the restaurant, putting the chairs up and wiping down the bar before returning to the back. Samuel was still busy with the dishes, no matter how many times we had pleaded for a dishwasher, Jane continued to ignore the need. I supposed she liked the fact that it took up so much of Samuel's lifetime to wash other people's dirty dishes and then polish them to a shine.

I stood next to him, dipped my hands in the sink and reached for the first plate.

"You don't have to do that, you know?" he started but stopped himself. Maybe because I shrugged, or maybe it was because we'd had this conversation every night since he started three quarters of a year ago.

"You should be home with your brother as soon as possible," was my reply, as it was every night.

Samuel and I were similar. I had been in the same position in the past. My younger sisters had been waiting for me. Waiting for me to come and feed them, tuck them in and read them a bedtime story. Samuel had a brother. And a mother who was never home.

"And your birthday's in twenty minutes."

"Just another day."

"What about your sisters? Not going to celebrate?"

I shrugged. They were both busy – with their husbands. Their children. Their jobs. Years ago, when we'd moved here together because our father had decided to move and I couldn't leave them alone with him, none of this had existed. Meanwhile, things had changed. It was just me still stuck in the same shithole as I was back then.

In silence, we worked side by side until there were no more dirty dishes and the kitchen was acceptable. Jane would make a mess again tomorrow, and we would clean it up in the evening.

Samuel dried his hands on his apron before going to the fridge and pulling out a foil-covered plate.

He handed it to me with the words, "Happy birthday, Nikau," before saying goodbye a few seconds later.

I peered under the foil, realized it was cheesecake, which I hated with passion, and let out a sigh.

"Happy birthday to me," I mumbled as I grabbed the plate and made my way home, so I could bury myself under the covers and sleep away as much of the coming day as was humanly possible.

Kaden

"But I tried, didn't I?" she asked, slightly annoyed, her red lips curling into a pout that made my insides tighten uncomfortably.

Unfortunately, sometimes effort wasn't enough, because it didn't automatically mean someone's heart was in something.

"Listen, Nancy," I began, pulling up my trousers to fasten the belt she had unbuckled five minutes ago. "I don't think it's going to work out between us."

"But you said I was perfect," she moaned. Her lower lip quivering didn't bode well. On the contrary, I would despair if she burst into tears while still on her knees. And only because I had withdrawn my cock and sent her off.

It had been perfect until I looked into her lifeless

eyes and realized this relationship was a one-way street. Whether it was about sex or something more. Her idea of me and what I wanted was so far from reality that the blood drained from my cock in a split second.

And I didn't even find it embarrassing, because it was the best indication that Nancy and I weren't compatible. I wasn't looking for a weak-willed woman to do whatever I wanted.

"Get up," I ordered, increasingly annoyed that she didn't seem to be able to process what was happening. "Get dressed, get your things and get out of here, will you?"

"Are you going to call me?"

I snorted. "Of course not. We've had a bit of fun together, but it's over now. So get out of here."

I had a hard time stopping myself from rolling my eyes, so I turned away and went to my desk to grab my phone. Kaia answered after a few seconds.

"Brother, how can I help you?"

"I need a flight to Iowa."

"What the hell do you want there?" she asked skeptically, although I could already hear her tapping away at the keyboard in the background, trying to make my wish come true.

Everyone had advised me against hiring my sister as an assistant, but it was the best decision I could have made. *The Haoa siblings are set to rise.* Or so the local newspaper had put it in their crappy article about us.

"Kaden? My question?"

I shook my head, looked over my shoulder and realized Nancy had already left. And without making a fuss. I was impressed.

"I need to visit someone there."

"And does this woman have a name?"

A sigh escaped me. Kaia was so damn curious. "Nik. It's Nik."

My sister was silent for a second. Then she really got going. "Why didn't you say so before? How long since you've seen each other? Does she have any idea you're on your way? I thought you said you hadn't spoken since she left Hawaii?"

"She doesn't have a clue," I muttered. Besides, it was an idea I had on a whim. Her birthday was in a few hours, Nancy was annoying me, and I had found the stupid reminder in my calendar. *One year from tomorrow – marry Nika.*

That in itself had been a rash idea then, a stupid idea in youthful fervor. But at that very moment, it seemed so much more tempting to make Nikau my wife than to waste one more day trying to find another woman who would make me feel something.

"Then she's probably going to rip your head off tomorrow."

"I want the first available flight, Kaia," I continued, not responding to her comment.

Wherever this sudden restlessness was coming from, I couldn't wait to get on that plane to Iowa and remind her of the deal we made.

Sometimes I would lie awake at night, tasting her blood on my tongue, feeling the warmth of the red liquid on my lips. I wondered how I had let nine fucking years go by before trying my luck with her.

It was probably because I had known full well that my former self would not have been the right one for her. Or maybe it had been the result of countless disappointments before the realization that Nikau had been right that night.

Or maybe it was just that I was an idiot occasionally, who didn't seem to be able to have a grip at the right moment.

What I should have done that night was to kiss her. To find out what she tasted like. How she'd react. And if I was able to enchant her. Because just as I had not forgotten the blood, I had not forgotten how her pulse had first quickened under the pressure of my fingers and then calmed down, as if her body was naturally capable of withstanding me and accepting what I had to give. Even if somewhat awkwardly at the time…

"Do you have a present? Please tell me you won't show up at her door without a gift."

Without further ado, I closed my eyes and took a deep breath. "I'm the gift, okay?"

"Wow. When did your ego get so obnoxiously big, huh?"

I decided I owed her no answer. She would not get it. In fact, it wasn't my intention for her to understand.

"So what about the flight?"

"Booked. And it leaves in less than an hour. So you better hurry."

"Thanks."

"When are you coming back?"

A question I had no answer to. "The best thing you can do is cancel all appointments for tomorrow. I'll be back the day after."

I heard her tapping away at her keyboard again. "You know what? I'll book the flight back when you tell me. And Kaden? Behave yourself. I don't want to read any headlines in some village paper in Iowa."

"Why not? *'Owner of Hawaiian luxury resort embarrassed in redneck state'* reads pretty interesting, don't you think?"

"I'd much rather read about a million-dollar deal."

I mimicked her words with a low growl before shaking my head and hanging up. Kaia was a kind soul, but sometimes she felt the need to be both my boss and a mother. I didn't hold it against her, but I wasn't going to let it get to me, either.

As I rushed from my office to my bedroom to throw the essentials into a bag, I informed my driver we were making an evening trip to the airport. I usually only used him for resort business, but I preferred not to leave my car parked at the airport.

Ten minutes later I was in the back seat, and shortly after that, I arrived at the terminal in time for the flight.

I had exactly eight hours to decide how to sell my

idea to Nikau in a way that would get her to agree with me. I doubted very much that she would still be susceptible to well-placed puppy dog eyes after all these years. Not to mention that I had learned other ways of convincing a woman to do my bidding. But I didn't want to be too hasty either, and after all the time we hadn't spoken it might be better to proceed with caution. Treading carefully into the unknown. To find out if she was still crazy enough to keep a promise from ten years ago.

I was still crazy enough, otherwise I would not be on a plane heading for the mainland, venturing into a state whose very location made me completely uncomfortable. No sea nearby. No palm trees. No balmy summer nights. And above all, people who weren't anywhere near as open and friendly as those who lived on the islands.

I loved my home. My origins. Which made it all the more incomprehensible to me that Nikau had decided to leave O'ahu and trade paradise on earth for something that could hardly make her happy.

I hated to admit it, and I would certainly hide it from her, but over the past few years I had kept an eye on what she shared in the online world. Her Instagram account, for example, was designed to convince everyone that she was happy in Cedar Rapids. Of course, I had also stalked the restaurant she worked at and noticed it didn't even compare to the one she had worked at in high school. I knew Nikau. Her dreams. The idea she had had for her life back then. No one changed so drastically in ten years that they would forget all that and happily settle for something much worse than their dreams.

At least that was my hope, because it would make things a lot easier for me. Starting with reminding her of our old agreement.

With my arms crossed, I looked out the small window as the plane climbed higher and higher, and the chain of islands grew smaller and smaller, until I could no longer make out the lights, and everything around us was just a dark night.

Over the past few years I had worked my way up. I had built an empire and found a passion that kept me busy and interested. I was used to getting what I wanted. At least when it came to business. Today, however, Nancy had demonstrated just how badly that worked in other areas.

A lovely woman. But not much more than an accessory. A decorative element to be taken out to make an impression on others. Or a woman to spend time with if you liked to surround yourself with "yes" and "amen" people who had no opinions and would let you do whatever other people wanted.

None of this appealed to me. But the idea of a ten-year-old deal and a woman I hadn't seen for almost as long did.

Whatever fucked-up part of my brain was at fault, I hoped it was also aware that nothing was going to be the way it had imagined.

Because after everything I thought I knew about

Nikau, I was damn sure nothing was going to be as easy as I wanted it to be.

Nikau

Blinking, I forced my eyes open, only to find it was the rain that had woken me up. A cool breeze blew through my bedroom as thick raindrops pelted the thin window pane. Iowa was terrible. It was not the first time I had noticed this in recent years. On O'ahu, I used to love the rain, especially when it was accompanied by a balmy summer thunderstorm. When lightning struck on the sand or over the water. Those were natural spectacles to watch. It made you feel good. In Iowa, though, I couldn't appreciate a rainstorm because the end result always seemed to be the same: you got wet. And it made you feel like crap.

I wrinkled my nose and looked out the window. Most of the sky was still dark grey, which probably meant I hadn't been asleep long. So without further ado I grabbed my phone, which only confirmed that assumption, and thundered it back onto the bedside table, burying myself deeper into my bed. I pulled the blanket up to my chin, wrapped myself in the cozy warmth and closed my eyes again. Even though I wasn't outside and not a single drop of rain had fallen on me, I still felt like crap. And it wasn't because of the few hours I'd slept.

Just as I was about to command my mind to rest to spend a few more hours in the world of dreams, I heard the sound that must have woken me up in the first place. A loud knock. On my bloody front door. In the dead of night.

I didn't even move. I had seen enough movies about serial killers to know this was the perfect setup. And I wasn't stupid. I wouldn't willingly surrender to Chucky, Ted or whatever the idiot's name was. No. Not ever.

But there was no lessening of the knocking, quite the opposite, it became more insistent. More desperate. It was still pouring outside, and the area outside my front door was not covered. Reluctantly, I dragged myself out of bed, wrapped the blanket around my body so not to give the nocturnal visitor any false hope – shorts and a top were so *inviting*, if the media were to be believed – and trudged down the hallway toward the front door. Once again, someone banged on it with their fists, which by now made me feel a little angry.

As I approached the front door, a growl rose in my throat. But instead of doing the idiotic thing and just yanking the door open, I pushed back the curtain that covered the glass next to the door and stared out. For a few seconds. Because my brain was incapable of processing what my eyes were seeing. Not a serial killer. Far from it.

Standing outside my front door, in the pouring rain, was none other than Kaden Haoa, who in recent years had become the owner of a luxury resort worth millions – on the island where we had grown up. And he stared at me as if I had lost my mind. Me, of all people!

He raised a hand in question. In the other he held a small box and a damned travel bag. What the hell was going on?

Nervousness washed over me, and it felt like hundreds of little bugs were crawling up my legs, only to settle in my stomach. Nevertheless, I reached for the door and yanked it open, panting a little.

"What are you doing here?" I shouted over the roar of thunder. The storm seemed to be hovering directly over our heads.

Kaden smiled wryly, small laugh lines forming around his eyes. Then he wiggled the box as if to tell me the reason for his unannounced visit. Years after we had last seen each other.

"Aren't you going to invite me in?" he asked instead of answering. Thick raindrops were running down his face. His hair was wet. His clothes had also turned dark and clung tightly to his body, leaving little to my imagination. I cleared my throat, remembered my good manners and stepped aside to let him in.

Kaden came in – only to immediately fill the house with his presence. He dropped the bag next to the door, closed it with a well-aimed kick and stood in front of me, soaking wet and dripping, still with that wry grin on his face.

He had hardly changed. Or he had. He had changed. He had grown up. The proportions of his body fit him better. He no longer looked like an awkward giant, but like someone who was comfortable in his own body, and who knew exactly what effect he had on the opposite sex. Kaden didn't fit into this town. Hawaii was written across his forehead. He carried the sun in him, even though there was another of these storms here that made it clear how far away from home we really were.

"Aren't you going to say anything, Nika?" he finally asked, amused, while I was still busy looking at him and absorbing his presence.

He looked so outrageously handsome, dripping wet, that I was almost ashamed to be in the same room.

"I... um," I moaned. "I don't know what to say. Really, I don't."

"How about: *It is good to see you, Kaden*. Or: *Nice to see you, Kaden*. That would be a good start, wouldn't it?"

My mouth opened, but no sound escaped my throat. I was too stunned to say anything.

So Kaden took the matter in hand. It was enough to make me freeze into a pillar of salt briefly. He put the box down on my dresser, came toward me with heavy steps and then wrapped his arms around me – together with the blanket, which slid to the floor.

Suddenly, he was not the only one wet. The warmth of his body slowly sank into mine. "I'm glad to see you, Nika. I know it's stupid to just show up like this, but…"

I had no choice but to wrap my arms around him as well. "But…" I groaned, barely able to catch my breath as he held me so tightly.

"But it's your birthday, and I wanted to make you happy."

Kaden. I hadn't seen him in years. I had not spoken to him for so long. The only time I ever saw him was when there was a gossip magazine article about him. Or about the many stories about women that had followed him since he was a young man. He hadn't got rid of them, and ever since he had been in the public eye, people loved to report that he had changed his girlfriends like his underwear.

And now he was standing right in front of me. I felt so much joy, because his status as my best friend had probably not changed, no matter how many miles and time had separated us since then.

As if by itself, a grin spread across my face. Was this what they called fate? Showing up on my birthday when I was miserable?

As if joy had been his cue, he loosened his

embrace and reached for the soaked cardboard box, pulling off the lid with wet hands. Several thick, round balls of pastry emerged, all dusted with sugar and fried in fat. *Malasadas*. From the little bakery right on our favorite beach, if I had to bet.

I felt tears well up in my eyes, even though it was unnecessary. What Kaden had done was more than just a nice gesture. It felt like he'd kicked open a door that hadn't been closed.

Not a cheesecake I didn't like. It was not a half-hearted birthday greeting, because that was expected but my favorite pastry straight from O'ahu. An eight hour flight. He had waited in the rain while I debated whether he was a serial killer.

I wiped my treacherously runny nose with the back of my hand, then pulled him into another hug. A real hug. One that didn't make me feel stiff.

"Thanks," I murmured softly against his shoulder, because I wasn't tall enough to reach his ear. "And now you should get out of your wet clothes."

He pushed me away, one eyebrow raised.

"Because if you don't, you'll get sick, Kaden. Not because I plan to thank you with sex."

"Sure," he replied with a smug grin. "Was too good to be true."

I shook my head and tapped him on the shoulder. "I'm sure I've got some shirts lying around somewhere."

"Whose?"

"From my ex. They should fit you just fine."

"No."

"You don't know what he looked like."

He tilted his head. "No," Kaden repeated more vehemently. "I'm not walking around in your ex-boyfriend's clothes."

"But you would naked?"

"If I have to."

His expression made it clear he would make good on that threat – if it was a threat at all.

Fuck.

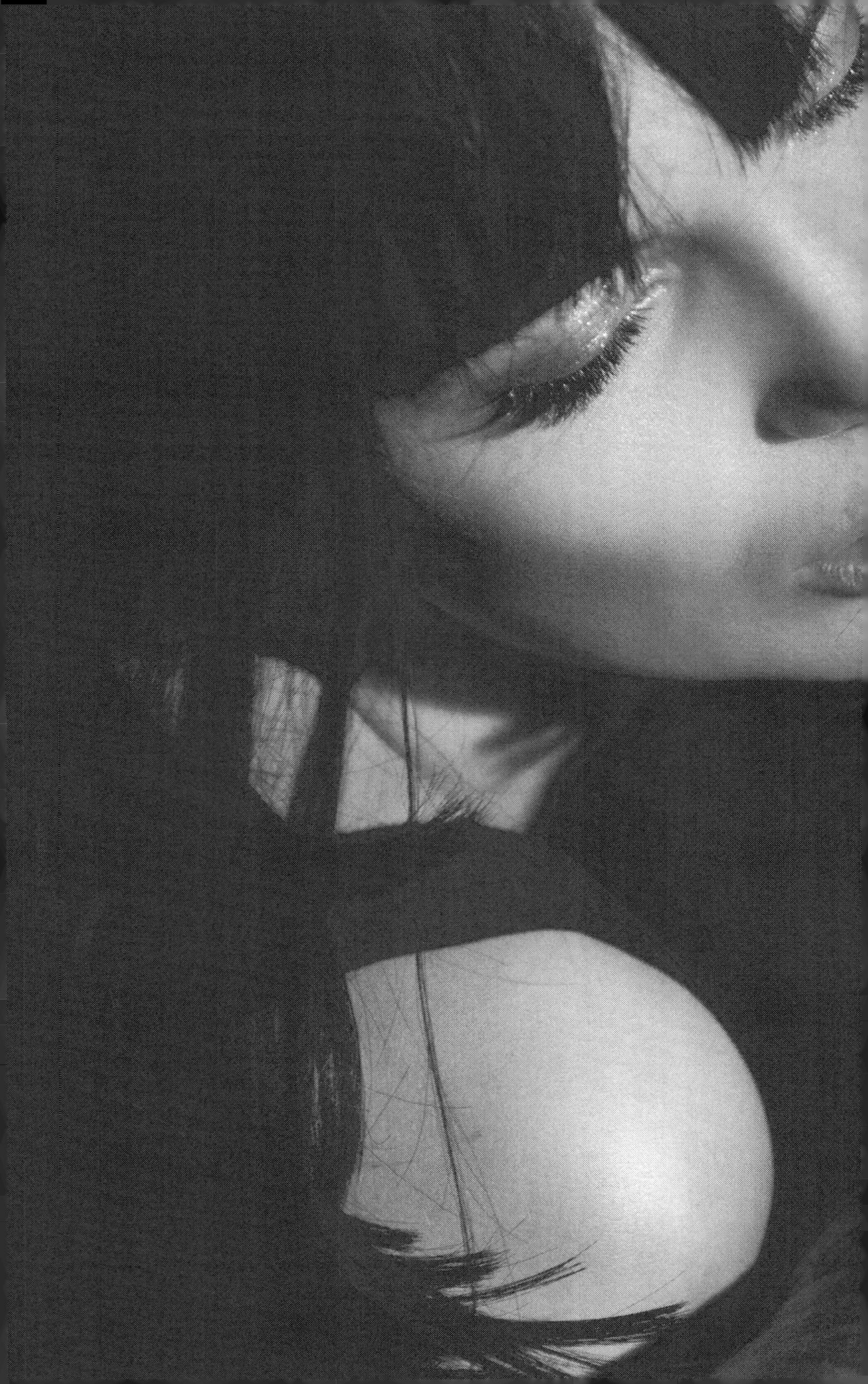

Kaden

Even as I registered her shock and saw her emotional side moments later, I realized I was in the right place at the right time. The flight to Iowa hadn't been such a bad idea after all.

I had decided to go in with no expectations, but as soon as my eyes settled on her, I realised how much I had expected from this reunion. And how glad I was about how it turned out. No discussion. No argument. Not even a slap in the face. It all seemed strange for a few seconds, and then it just felt like the good old days. How effortlessly we'd slipped back into the casual roles we'd occupied back then. How good it felt just to be around her, especially as she still delighted in the smallest things as if they meant everything. At the time, I hadn't realized it was true. Now I knew better. She wasn't the only one who had spoken wise words that night we had made the deal.

Before I left the bathroom, I wrapped the towel Nikau had thrown at me a few minutes earlier around my hips for lack of a better alternative. The hot shower had been necessary as the cold rain had soaked me. It was not the first thing that bothered me about Iowa.

I walked into her living room. I leaned against the doorframe with my arms crossed when I noticed she was sitting on the couch with the soggy package on her lap, and half the pastries were gone. There was powdered sugar not only on her fingers but also on her lips.

It was a sight that reminded me of the past. We had pulled all-nighters at weekends, only to wait outside the bakery early in the morning for one of the employees to sell us *malasadas* long before the shop even opened.

Nikau realized I was watching her, turned her head toward me, her long dark brown hair slipped over her shoulder and pulled down her top's strap. Her lips were parted slightly as she looked at me, forgetting to chew for a second. I could have sworn her mouth was watering, but before I could make a sarcastic comment, the expression was gone.

Instead, she shook her head. "You're so stubborn. Has anyone ever told you that?"

"You. And my sister once or twice, but you're still the front runner. Why am I so stubborn this time?"

"Because you'd rather stand half-naked in my doorway than borrow clothes."

"From your ex-boyfriend, mind you. I'm not walking around in another man's clothes."

"Just until your clothes come out of the dryer."

I shrugged indifferently. "I'll wait. Thanks."

She exhaled with effort before resigning herself to her fate and concentrating on the pastry in her hand. Other women would have called me crazy if I had shown up at their house with *malasadas* as a birthday present. Nikau, on the other hand, looked as if she had never been happier.

I dislodged myself from the doorway, and sat opposite her. Hesitantly, she held out the box. "Do you want some, or will it ruin your steely six-pack?"

"You make it sound like I waste hours a day trying to achieve that result," I said indignantly, leaning forward and grabbing one before she could take them away.

The muscles were just a nice by-product of my time on the surfboard.

We ate in silence. For a few minutes at least, until the silence became too heavy and Nikau looked at me curiously. "You can just up and leave your resort?"

"Kaia takes care of everything."

"For how long?"

"One day." I could hardly tell her that I planned to take her back to O'ahu at the end of the day.

She nodded. "So you wanted to take a short trip… to Iowa?"

The skepticism in her voice amused me as much as it impressed me. Nikau knew me well enough to know I didn't just do anything. She just hadn't figured out what I was doing yet. I wondered if she succeeded in putting it all together. If she remembered our agreement. If she realized I'd come a year early because I couldn't stand wasting my time with women who saw me as money and expensive gifts and who would never sit in front of me in old, short, partly wet pajamas and eat *malasadas* without a care in the world.

"I wanted to see you," I finally said.

"And how long before the paparazzi are outside my house? Will I read about you and me in the papers tomorrow?"

I pursed my lips. Even in a place like this, the gossip from Hawaii did not go unnoticed. "Only if you want to," I replied, my eyes narrowing slightly.

"I'm sure they're all dying to know why you flew to Iowa to visit a woman."

"I can already imagine the headlines. And how disappointed everyone will be because it's not the usual story." They'd probably get that from Nancy, who certainly had no qualms about selling her experience with me to the highest bidding gossip rag.

"So what kind of story is it, Kaden?"

I slowly leaned forward and held out my hand, motioning with my fingers for her to extend hers. Hesitantly, she leaned forward before giving me her hand.

Satisfied, I nodded, letting my eyes slide over the

powdered sugar on her fingers and brought her hand to my mouth as I looked her straight in the eye.

She held her breath. My tongue flicked forward until I tasted the sweetness of the sugar. Nikau did not remove her hand. Nor did she make any verbal protest at the sudden invasion of her privacy.

Instead, a delicate blush rose to her cheeks. Finally, I planted a soft kiss on her fingertips. "Do you remember?" I asked, my voice too harsh to let pass what had just happened without a trace.

Nikau, however, looked at me as if I were the wicked witch who had come to steal her firstborn child because she had foolishly made a deal with the devil in ancient times.

Still holding her hand, I tugged gently until she rose and followed my movement until she stood directly in front of me. I looked up at her, ignoring the seductive effect of her body, and with another movement of my hand forced her to climb astride my lap. Not for the first time.

But never before had it taken on the sexual note as it did at that moment.

"Is that really why you're here, Kaden?" she breathed.

I recognized the nervousness in her eyes. She clung to my arm with one hand.

"Honestly, I don't know. We're not thirty yet, but if I have to spend one more second with someone who thinks she's Mrs. Kaden Haoa, who's owned my empire, for years – without even knowing me, mind you – I'm going to kill myself."

She snorted. "You won't." It sounded partly like a threat. "You could just stop dating."

Less enthusiastically, I grimaced. "Or I'll get you out of this awful place and do us both a favor."

"You think I don't like being here?"

I shook my head. "We're talking about Iowa, Nik. Iowa. There's nothing here. No ocean. No sun. No beaches. This town looks like an industrial hellhole. I understand that you left so your sisters weren't alone. But for you to stay, even though they've long since grown up? Are you truly happy here?"

Her fingers dug deeper into my arm without her consciously noticing. That was the answer, but I wanted to hear the words from her mouth.

"I'm not marrying you, Kaden. I'm aware of everything your ex-girlfriends ever said about you. That's not my world."

To stifle an annoyed sound, I bit my tongue. Maybe it was a stupid instinct I was following, but I slid my free hand up her arm until I placed it on her neck to make the distance between us disappear.

There wasn't much pressure needed to pull her toward me and close the gap. Again, she didn't resist, relying on me to do the right thing. Yet I was the worst person to make such decisions – because I made them based on what would give us the most pleasure, not what was reasonable or had the least consequences.

I did not rush to her mouth but started with her jaw, using the hand on her neck to position her head. My lips slid over her soft skin. I felt goosebumps forming on her arms and she shivered barely noticeably, as the unexpected assault turned out to be not bad, but rather pleasant.

Only when her hand pressed against my chest, nails digging lightly into my skin, did I move further until I could finally look into her wide-open eyes. I didn't need a translator for the invitation I found in them.

I felt the heat emanating from her core, throbbing against my bare legs, and finally closed the distance between us completely without removing my hand from her throat. Instead, I used it to guide Nikau, to give her the support and reassurance that this was not a mistake but a fucking revelation.

The way her body nestled against mine, the way she let herself fall into the kiss, even opening her lips to me to deepen it, made my pulse race with excitement. But the kiss, as it quickly changed from hesitant and cautious to something far wilder and more passionate, also stirred another need in me.

Kissing Nikau was not enough to convince her she was doing the right thing by getting involved with me. Honoring the deal we had made with each other. She needed more. I had to ignite that unmistakable spark in her that made her curious. Curiosity about the world she had so vehemently closed her eyes to, a world in which, in her mind, she had no business being.

But she was wrong. So very, very wrong. But there was no way I could prove to her the potential I felt in her, even by kissing her unexpectedly.

I slid my tongue over hers, savoring the sweetness of the *malasadas* while fighting the urge to take off her top and shorts and explore her body before laying something at her feet that she wouldn't understand at the moment.

It was only when a soft moan escaped directly into my mouth that she seemed to realize what was happening. She tore herself away as if she had been burned. But she only got as far away from me as I let her.

I looked at her in amusement. I wasn't ashamed of the kiss – and Nika shouldn't be either.

"We shouldn't be doing this," she groaned. A telltale blush rose to her cheeks, but that wasn't the only way her body betrayed her.

"So you didn't like it?" I asked, convinced of the opposite. "Won't I find evidence that you'd be willing to do much more than kiss me if I let my hand slide from your neck inbetween your legs?"

Hissing, she drew in the air. I saw a little anger in Nikau's eyes that she was cleverly trying to hide from me.

"You can't come here and say things like that, Kaden."

"Why not? Because you liked it, and me coming

here gives you an out that you're willing to accept, even though your rational mind tells you it's stupid?" I was sure I had put my finger on the sore spot, and as she continued to rebel against my hand on her throat until I finally released it, I knew I was right about that too.

In some ominous way, I had managed to catch the right moment – and all she needed was a nudge in the direction that would finally convince her.

Annoyed, she threw her hands up in the air as she paced in front of me. "You can't come here and ask me to do this. We were children! Life is not so simple that you can ask me to jump and I do it without thinking."

"So you need time to think, right?" I leaned forward, a triumphant look in my eyes.

"I need..." Nikau sighed. Shaking her head, she turned away for a second before turning back to me. "The magic number was thirty, right? You still have a year to find a woman who's right for you. Why don't you give me a chance to find someone for you?"

A grin spread across my lips. So now she was trying to bargain with me? Well, she probably wouldn't come out on top. "You don't even know what I'm looking for."

"Then explain it to me."

"And you don't even have a presence in the scene I'm in. No one will take you seriously."

"If they hear you're behind it, they will."

A point that probably went to Nikau. I leaned

back. "One year. If you haven't found a wife for me by then…"

"The original deal stands," she replied, rolling her eyes. Nevertheless, she extended her hand to me, but I was not yet ready to accept this new arrangement.

"You're coming home with me. Iowa is history."

"You know I have a job here, don't you?"

I shrugged. "If that's the only thing keeping you here, I'll make sure you find a much better place on O'ahu. What other objections do you have?"

Gritting her teeth, she looked at me. "None, I suppose."

"Wonderful." I held my hand out to her but pulled it back before she could reach for it, hastily sealing the deal. "There's something else, Nika."

"What?" she growled.

"In the meantime, you are available to me."

"I'm… what?!"

Amused, I held out my hand again. "You are mine. No other men. No affairs. You commit to me. I'll show you what I'm looking for. Make it easier for you to find the right woman." Or, even better, she'd finally realize how much she had missed out on over the last few years by only getting involved with simple men. Or boring. Depending on your point of view.

"Never mind, Kaden. I won't be involved in your weird sex games."

"Don't pass judgment on me until you know what

you're talking about, Nika," I warned her with a raised eyebrow.

A muscle under her eye twitched, but she didn't answer. So I tilted my head, already armed with a solution to the problem.

"My counter-proposal is this: You accompany me to dinner and allow me to give you an insight. No sex – only at your express request. If you still think you're not interested in my weird sex games, we'll skip that part." This time, it wasn't the fact that I always got what I wanted that made me think I'd succeeded.

It was much more about the physical reaction I had witnessed a few minutes ago. The way her breath had caught and she had leaned against my hand, seeking protection. How her body had responded to the gentle dominance – not with rejection, but with a very natural welcome.

"You're still as annoying as you were then. Do you realize that?"

"Am I succeeding?"

Nikau laughed. "I hate to admit it, but yes. You're succeeding, idiot."

Perhaps I would get close to exorcising her overuse of affectionate insults, and instead get her to use names I much preferred to hear. "All right, dinner it is. You should pack so we can catch the next flight."

"There are plenty of restaurants here."

"We'll eat on O'ahu or nowhere."

She clicked her tongue before shaking her head.

Apparently, she realized she didn't stand a chance against me. I'd rather cook a five-course meal myself than go to a mediocre restaurant in Cedar Rapids.

Freestyle.

"Hawaii it is," she finally relented, and I nodded in satisfaction.

Then she pointed to my lap. "Now make sure your erection is no longer pointing in my direction. Got that, K?"

I had ignored this detail for the last few minutes, but now that she was drawing my attention to it... "But you're the reason. Why would I hide that?"

I still had the towel around my waist. Nikau couldn't see anything – except that my body had taken a general liking to having her on my lap while she was pressed against me and my tongue was in her mouth.

"Can't you just do as you're told for once?"

I pursed my lips. Perhaps one day she would realize the irony of that statement. So instead of complying with her request, I crossed my arms and leaned back in her chair.

"Shouldn't you be packing? Do some business? Quit your lousy job?" That wasn't usually my choice of words, and I would never have used them if I hadn't been absolutely certain that Nikau knew deep down that I was right. She probably even agreed with me – why else would she make it so easy for me to convince her to return home?

A woman who didn't want to would always find a

reason not to do what was asked of her. But with Nikau, all I had to do was present her with all the right stimuli to convince her she didn't want anything other than what I proposed. It wasn't manipulation – it was just deep-seated instinct whispering in my ear what she needed.

Empathy.

That was what it was called, when you could read other people's feelings and sensations without being consciously aware of their expressions. With Nika it was always easy for me. Sometimes it happened so subconsciously that I couldn't even pin it down to specific details.

Maybe I should have followed my instincts instead of waiting for the woman who was the last straw and made me want Nika back in my life. On the same island. Preferably in the same place. In my immediate vicinity. So I could get the one thing that had made me so happy before and make sure she finally opened her eyes and saw what had been right in front of her the whole time.

"I should kick your butt, Kaden. That's what I should do." And in truth, she was excited about returning to the islands, away from this place she hadn't even chosen. Maybe she was using that part as motivation. An excuse to forget about the rest of our deal for the time being.

But I was not going to let that happen.

Grinning, I held my hand out again and told her with a look that I insisted. Reluctantly, but without too much hesitation, she took my hand. "No blood this time?"

No. But the alternative, between her legs, was still too forbidden for me to commit a faux pas for which she probably wouldn't forgive me.

"The kiss is enough as a promise. For now."

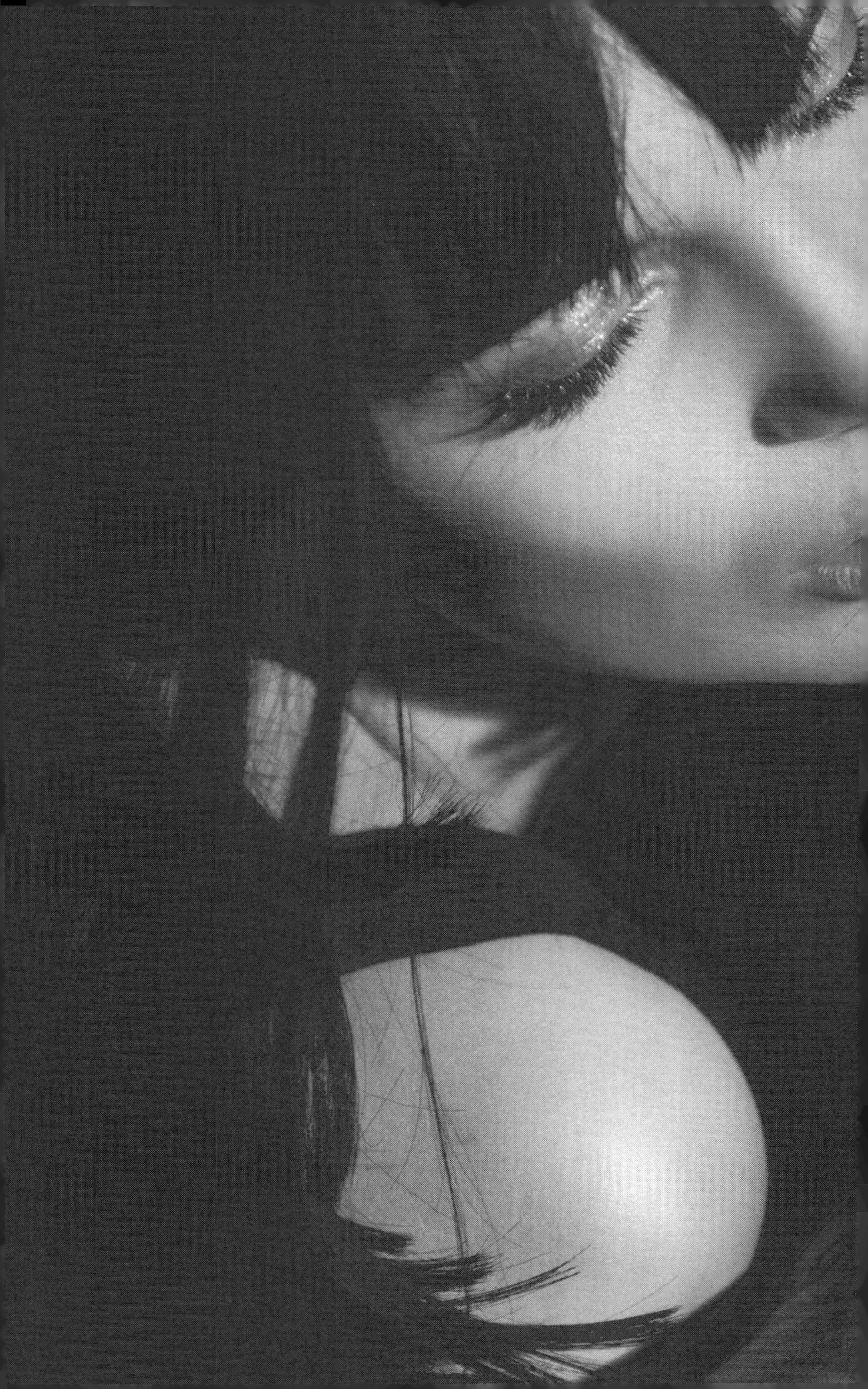

Nikau

My deep-seated aversion to airplanes, heights, and small spaces with lots of people made me take my headphones out of my pocket, pull the hood of my hoodie over my head and sink into my tablet shortly after boarding the plane. At the same time, Kaden stared down at his laptop next to me, absorbed in his work.

Staring was an excellent cue here, because I wasn't doing anything else. I stared at the search bar in the browser, wondering if it wouldn't be a better idea to distract myself with a film or series. Even music was a better choice than typing something into the search engine that would pull me down a rabbit hole I wouldn't be able to get out of any time soon. Besides, Kaden was sitting right next to me. If he found out that I was searching the internet for all the words I had read about in the articles about him, he would make fun of me again – and probably point out that I could just ask him about it if I was so interested.

But it wasn't like that.

I wanted to make up my own mind, far away from what he told me. A view uninfluenced by him, because he had spent years doing all these things, while in my bedroom the most dangerous thing was that it was lit. The more research I did, the more I was actually anticipating what would be happening. Namely, the fact that in a split second I had agreed to leave my life in Iowa behind and return to Hawaii. Even if only for a short time, because I didn't want to host the search for the perfect woman in his immediate vicinity – or be available to him, as he had so strangely called it.

Admittedly, the kiss had been good. And it had reminded me of that night ten years ago when he had wrapped his hand around my neck to show me there were people who were not afraid. That wasn't the only thing I remembered, but how it felt. What it had done to me. The nervousness followed by an intense tingling sensation that shot through my whole body. It should have triggered me afterward. Caused panic. But the opposite had happened, and I had felt a similar sensation earlier when he had pressed his hand against my throat.

I straightened a little more in my seat instead of hanging over my tablet like the Hunchback of Notre Dame. Kaden didn't look in my direction, but I kept thinking someone might recognize him and take a picture. I didn't want to look like a country bumpkin next to him.

I gritted my teeth and typed on the tablet. *Choking.* After a few seconds I realized that these were not the search results I had hoped for. The average person probably didn't associate "choking" with sex but with actually choking. That's why information about the Heimlich maneuver and other first aid measures popped up. I bit my tongue and made minimal changes to the search query, although it did take some effort to type the four letters. *Choking BDSM.*

Well, at least the search engine no longer disappointed me with its results, even if I was a little shocked. *Dangerous. Potentially fatal. Not for beginners. Not a safe kind of power play.*

But it didn't stop there, of course. Apparently, it was not uncommon for people to have themselves choked for their own pleasure. Oxygen was restricted, which automatically led to increased sexual arousal and more intense orgasms. I skimmed the paragraph listing the potential risks, just to absorb the physiological explanation. Hormones. Serotonin, dopamine, endorphins – all released at different times and then... well, basically you felt high.

The more I read, the bigger my eyes got. Anatomy. A guide to choking another person in a relatively safe manner. Consent. Rules. *Aftercare.* And when I finally got to the part about the so-called power play, my head was buzzing with hundreds of thoughts, questions and more words to type into the search engine.

A small voice in my head told me that choking was probably not the first thing an absolute beginner would look up. However, with no other clues to go on, and at least knowing that I was having a bit of fun with *that*... I dismissed the thought and tried the search engine again. This time I typed in *Power Play* and learned it was better to formulate the search term directly with the addition of *BDSM*, otherwise it would spit out everything but what I wanted to know.

My eyes were glued to the screen and the article, which told me that these power dynamics exist in every relationship – consciously or unconsciously. While, dominance and submissiveness were part of a sexual practice that could be played out in many ways and required a foundation of trust, communication, and safety that few people experienced with each other.

Other terms jumped out at me. *Role-playing. Edging. Spanking. Kinks.* Although it felt like just a few minutes of staring at the screen, it was actually several hours of flicking from one term to the next, finding more and more subjects I had absolutely no idea about and certainly wouldn't be reading up on in that plane.

I felt like I was being watched, like I had a red dot on my forehead that told everyone what I was looking up, so I didn't want to plunge full speed into a theoretical world about sex that was far off from what I had experienced so far.

Besides, a knot had formed in my stomach. Kaden had an idea about all these things. He had probably tried them himself. He was interested in taking control of his partners, making decisions for them and... doing other things that I didn't even want to think about because I didn't know what to make of the fact that my best friend didn't just have this one side that I knew and loved, but also a much darker side. I was aware, but hadn't the faintest idea about it.

And now he wanted to prove that I could find myself in these practices if only I got involved. Shit, wasn't he afraid of destroying our friendship? Or was it, after all this time, already more than friendship? Was that why he kissed me without thinking about it? Was he suddenly so open about all of his sexuality, not just chosen parts, and his attractive side because he knew he had to break out of the friend zone before anything else could happen?

Wonderful.

My brain was spinning with questions, even though a few hours ago I had refused to make another deal with him.

But it had always been like that, hadn't it?

I didn't want to marry Kaden. So there was another deal.

I didn't want to go to Hawaii, so he reminded me how much I hated living in Iowa.

I didn't want to be available to him, so he wanted to show me what that entailed.

I didn't want sex, so he promised it would only happen if I asked for.

Why did I feel like I was losing badly? I couldn't even do anything about it because my subconscious was standing on the sidelines cheering with pom-poms, happy that I was breaking out of my boring life for a brief adventure.

That was how Samuel had described it when I had said goodbye to him. Jane, of course, had been less than thrilled that I'd quit, and the regulars didn't seem too keen on having someone else serve them in the future, but in the end, no one had stopped me from leaving.

And since neither my father nor my sisters had called or even sent a quick note to wish me a happy birthday, I found it surprisingly easy to pack my things into a suitcase and get on a plane to Hawaii. I had made many decisions in my life, but this was probably the first one that was likely to lead to anything. However one wanted to interpret that now.

I took a deep breath before turning off the tablet and stepping out of my safe online world to quickly look around. In front of me was a bottle of water and a plate of covered food. Now that both had appeared, I felt somehow grateful. My grumbling stomach made sure I pounced on both and destroyed them within minutes.

Due to the time difference, we would probably

land on O'ahu sometime late in the evening. I was afraid that by then food options would be minimal. And before I starved miserably to death…

Out of the corner of my eye I noticed Kaden looking at me with interest. I pointed to my mouth to show I would have liked to say something about his staring, but my full mouth prevented me from doing so.

"Isn't there enough food in Iowa?" he asked. His lips were only slightly parted, but it was clear he was struggling to hold back a grin. Making the dimple on his right cheek stand out.

I felt like a raccoon caught rummaging in the rubbish bin. Two seconds later I stopped thinking about that and shook my head.

"You're impossible. Just because I'm hungry doesn't mean…"

"That you didn't have someone to make sure you ate something proper every day? Your fridge had some interesting contents…"

I let out a snort of indignation. It might be that my fridge was more a testimony to the fact that I did no cooking at all, but I was still not a bad eater. Maybe a nutritionist would have laughed about that.

His statement was a reminder of who had been primarily responsible for my proper eating during our school days. I probably owed Kaden for the fact that I did not suffer from an eating disorder.

"Let me guess…"

He raised an eyebrow.

"You'll make sure that I'm not neglecting myself."

Kaden shrugged. "You won't have a choice if you join me for dinner."

"You don't cook for yourself anymore?"

He gestured to his laptop as if that would answer my question. "The resort doesn't run itself. And I can't expect Kaia to do everything."

"But you have employees, don't you?"

"Who shouldn't think I'm only resting in their presence, yes. I built this resort, so I'm the one working on the front line. Where else would my employees gain the motivation to always give their best?"

The words Kaden chose were so different from the ones that had been spread about him in the media. Not that I'd ever believed the claims of a money-grubbing bachelor, I simply knew him too well for that, but hearing it from his mouth now soothed my conscience in a way I hadn't even known I needed.

"Am I not an unwelcome distraction for you?"

His expression told me he could not believe what he had just heard from my mouth. I thought he would grab my chin and force me to look directly at him.

Instead, he clenched his hand into a fist and leaned back in his seat.

"An unwelcome distraction," he repeated, letting out the breath he had been holding. "Nika, if I hear anything like that from you again…"

"So you have time to cook with me, right?" I replied, barely able to hide my grin.

Kaden's eyes narrowed as he realized I had just maneuvered him into a trap without him seeing it coming.

Still, he gave me no answer.

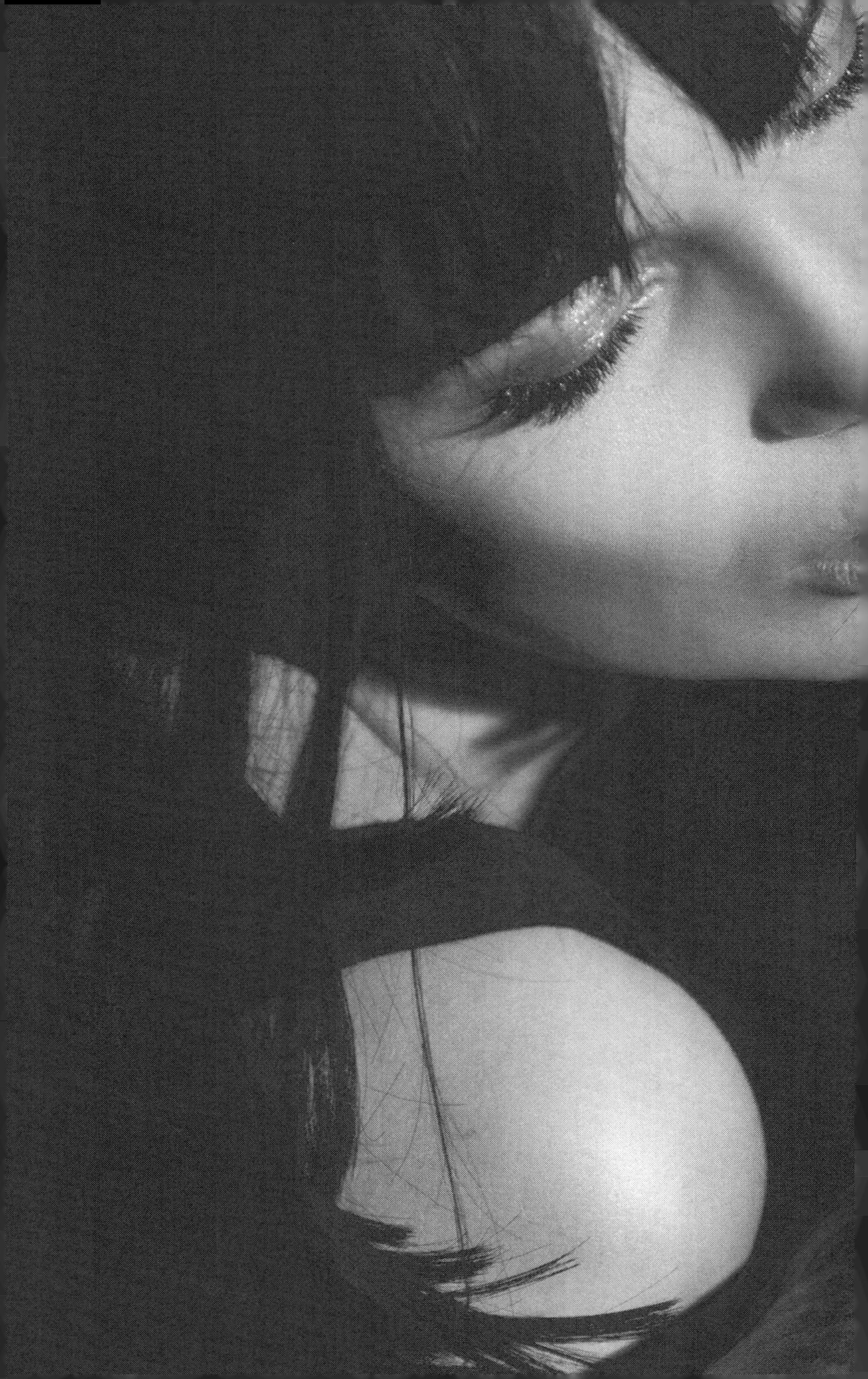

Kaden

I had always seen more advantages than disadvantages to living in an apartment within the resort. However, as soon as we arrived on O'ahu, I realized I could not come up with a reasonable excuse for having Nikau stay with me. The only sensible thing to do was to give her one of the other vacant apartments and hope to see her enough to carry on with my plans.

She had agreed to have dinner together at the restaurant, but by the time we reached the resort it was already late. Both of us were tired from the eight-hour flight, which I did twice in one day, and after a quick tour of the apartment and an explanation of how the resort works, I sent her to bed.

However, this was not the point at which I fell into a sleep coma. I noticed Kaia's missed calls as soon as we landed. Even though she was a grown woman and quite capable of making her own decisions, I knew she would not call me several times in a row for no good reason.

So I took my phone out of my pocket and dialed her number. It didn't even take her five seconds to pick up the phone.

"So two tickets back to Hawaii, huh? How did you convince her so quickly?"

And I hadn't told Kaia about my plan. So either she knew me damn well... or she had done the math in the hours I had been gone.

"And that's why you called me five times in a row?"

"I don't want to miss something important happening in my brother's life."

"You mean apart from the things that have happened in the last few years?" The opening of a luxury resort and all my other achievements in the business.

"Well, maybe next there will be a story about Kaden Haoa falling head over heels in love and finally finding the one."

I shook my head. "That's not what this is about," I replied emphatically.

"It isn't? Then enlighten me."

Perhaps this was where I should tell her about the arrangement between Nikau and myself that had been in place for ten years, and which had undergone a significant change today. But I preferred to keep this little secret to myself. Firstly, it was none of Kaia's business, and secondly, I didn't want to hear her make fun of me. Her brother needed a hell of a deal to convince a woman to stay by his side for more than a few weeks.

"There's nothing to sort out," I finally said. "Nikau's here; if everything goes as I think it will, she'll stay here."

And while she found me a wife, I showed her what she had been missing with her boring sex life. A win-win situation for both of us, wasn't it?

"Is that how it is? But you didn't force her to be here, did you?"

"Of course not!"

"I just wanted to make sure. You never know what's going on in that clever head of yours," she murmured.

I ignored her comment. "By the way, I'd like you to find her a job. And one that makes her happy."

Kaia would make of that whatever she wanted. After seeing the restaurant where Nikau had worked for the past few years and meeting the people who also staffed it, I wondered even more how she had survived in Iowa.

Her supervisor seemed to be an insufferable monster – with a name you'd only expect from a prostitute – and a couple of underage waiters and dishwashers didn't exactly mean less work for Nikau. All this had come to my attention in the two minutes I had waited by the door while Nikau handed in her notice and said her goodbyes.

She may have made a life for herself there, but it was a far cry from anything the young woman who had left Hawaii had once dreamed of.

But that made it easier for me to show her that this island was where she belonged. It wasn't hard to remind her how comfortable she felt here, and that life was so much easier. Happier. More pleasurable.

And once she fell in love with O'ahu again, the rest would only get easier. Because even if she found a woman who lasted longer than Nancy and all the other women whose names I couldn't even remember, I didn't want her to disappear and the contact between us to fade again.

It was only on the plane back to Hawaii that I realized how much I missed her. Somewhere along the line, my brain must have realized that as long as Nikau was with me, I'd be fine – and that's precisely how I'd felt on the plane.

The emails and meeting summaries had stressed me out, but a glance to the left and they hadn't been so relevant anymore. Even though Nika had done nothing but sit in her seat staring intently at her tablet.

She had not noticed me. Not heard me. Not seen. None of that. She was just there. That alone had made everything better.

But also made me wonder if I'd really managed to get royally fucked within twenty-four hours.

"Sure. Job for Nikau. Consider it done." Kaia snapped me out of my thoughts so abruptly that the sound of her voice confused me for a moment. I liked it even less when she hung up and left me alone with my thoughts.

I watched with satisfaction as Nikau joined me on the terrace, wearing a dress that competed in vibrant colors with the sun and made her complexion – pale for someone of Hawaiian descent – seem a little more vibrant.

Relaxed, she sank into the chair opposite me and crossed her legs. "You really can't leave this alone, can you, Kaden?"

I pretended not to know what she was talking about. Only when she rolled her eyes did I answer, "You hate going shopping. So I thought…"

But before I could finish the sentence, Nikau cut me off. "Thank you," she said, catching me off guard. "That's what I was going to say."

"Your first sentence didn't sound like a thank you," I replied, a little irritated.

"Because I wasn't sure if this was some weird dominance thing where you were trying to tell me what to wear or… well. Anyway, thanks."

A weird dominance thing where I told her what to wear… where the hell did Nikau get such ideas? I stopped eating, put the phone down and gave her my full attention.

"Would you like to tell me where you got the idea

that I would want to decide such things for you?" I had simply wanted to relieve her from something that I knew she hated. A nice gesture so she wouldn't have to spend half the day running around the island in a jumper looking for clothes that would suit the local temperatures.

Under my questioning gaze, Nikau made a face and leaned back, automatically mimicking my position. I could sense she didn't want to answer the question because of that telltale blush on her cheeks, but I wasn't going to let her off the hook that easily.

"So?"

She rolled her eyes. "When you talked about me being available to you, you didn't mean a 24/7 dynamic where you control everything in my life – right down to when I'm allowed to go to the toilet, did you?"

Horror was written all over her face; to be fair, I had to admit I understood. I had little interest in people who could not think for themselves. I also didn't want to rule over others in that way. I had a high regard for normal relationships – which on a sexual level were influenced by penchants.

"No. I also have no interest in feeding someone from a dog bowl, having my shoes licked, or bringing unusual bodily fluids into the game. Not that I condemned these preferences. Everyone should and could act out what they like, as long as no one is harmed." But these were just not the kinds of things I was interested in.

With each point I listed, Nikau opened her mouth a little wider. "There are people who actually do this and enjoy it?"

She sounded so shocked. But I would soon show her that sometimes there are things you think you can never have fun with... until you are proven absolutely wrong.

"I know a few people who do, yes," I replied. "But we don't judge other people's kinks."

Nikau had never done that to me, so I hoped she would show the same reasonableness to others. Even if she didn't know what it was that attracted me so much.

She shook her head. "I'm not judging, K. I'm trying to understand what I've gotten myself into."

"And you couldn't wait for me to show you?"

"I wanted to be prepared."

"For what? The internet doesn't know everything. It can neither tell you what I like nor what you like. Besides, I would take the information with a pinch of salt."

"Like what?"

It didn't take me more than a second to find an example, but I took a moment to think about it. This was not the way I had wanted to introduce Nikau to the concept. But it seemed too late for caution now that she had stuck her nose so deeply into the internet that she had stumbled upon the existence of extreme dynamics.

"On the net you can find countless instructions on

how to tie someone up. Not just hands to a bedpost, but more aesthetic. Shibari, if you want to know the technical term. But just because you've read the instructions on the internet doesn't mean you should put it into practice. The anatomy of the human body is unique. Some parts of the body can be very fragile, and there are places that you should never bind. Too much pressure can also cause damage. Or the wrong weight distribution. You can learn a lot of theory on the net, Nika. But it never prepares you for reality."

"Do you know how…"

"No. But an acquaintance is very accomplished," I replied before she could finish her sentence.

And yet none of this would give her any real insight, because bondage techniques like this weren't necessarily about sex – but how was I supposed to explain that to her when there were so many other things she hadn't even begun to understand?

"Your interest is piqued, isn't it?" I asked after a few seconds. I was curious to see if she would deny it or dare to admit that she was, at least in theory, interested in what I had been practicing for years.

Instead of giving me an immediate answer, she spent a few seconds playing with the breakfast on her plate. Only then did she raise her eyes in my direction. "I'm trying to understand and approach this with an open mind. That's all."

Of course. If she were more comfortable with that attitude, I would let her keep the illusion for a while longer. But once you stuck your big toe in those waters, I knew exactly what it did to you. It seemed so innocent and calm, but as soon as you broke the surface, there was a pull you couldn't escape, no matter how hard you tried.

You wandered from one experience to another. You started with the light fare before it lost its appeal and then tried something else, something more exciting. Only to find that you liked it even more. And in the end, you licked the wound you had just inflicted on your best friend's finger, realizing that while playing with blood and pain had its appeal, it might have been a step too far when it came to the sexual component.

"Then it's only fitting that we have dinner tonight," I said.

"I'm still not sure what dinner has to do with anything, but…. all right."

Nikau would make the connection soon enough. That much I was sure of.

ACTUALLY, DINNER WAS JUST AN EXCUSE. A WAY TO TAKE her somewhere she felt comfortable. Somewhere she wouldn't have to worry all the time that something might happen.

I had chosen a restaurant right on the beach, with an excellent selection of local dishes, and I had arranged for the table to be a bit away from the others so we would have a good view of the sea and the sunset. However, we were not unduly disturbed by any of the other people present.

There was nothing that should have surprised me that night – until Nikau looked at me intently before raising an eyebrow. "I'm not sure I've ever seen you in a suit before, K."

She hadn't. That was something that had come about after the resort opened, because most investors simply took you more seriously if you looked and acted the part.

"And that's why you can't take me seriously now, or why are you grinning so stupidly?"

She shrugged nonchalantly. "Seems to be just the right packaging for what's underneath," she said, surprising me.

Since when did Nikau have an interest in what was underneath my clothes?

"That's an odd way to put it, but I'll take the compliment anyway," I murmured. I also took it upon myself to have a closer look at her dress.

Whether it was a summer dress, a short black one or something more festive, she had always looked good in dresses that clung tightly to her body and she knew it.

My attention made her nervous, as I could feel her foot bobbing up and down under the table.

"Excited?" I asked, amused.

She narrowed her eyes, preparing to protest, until I reached under the table for her leg, closed my hand around her calf and ran my thumb over the soft, warm skin. In a split second, the movement stopped. Instead, she seemed frozen.

"Don't worry, I won't embarrass you in the middle of the restaurant," I said, watching closely as her eyes fell on the table – as if my hand underneath it was enough to embarrass her.

"We've done this many times, Nika – eaten together. There's no need to get nervous."

"But it's different now," she sighed, almost breathlessly.

"In what way?"

"I know something will happen. But I don't know when. Or what. That's what worries me."

All the while, I kept running my thumb over her calf, even when the touch gave her shivers.

"We used to talk about the people we went out with. I'd like to do that again," I said, knowing my statement irritated her. "I want to know if your last relationship fulfilled you."

"As much as yours did, I suppose," she replied, sarcastically.

I could overlook that – because I would probably have reacted similarly if she had asked me a question about Nancy.

"What did you miss?"

"I don't know. A bit of everything, I guess. The sex wasn't bad, but... his skills were limited. I tried to show him how I would like it better, but he was not interested. He didn't want to learn anything new."

This was an answer I had not expected – so

closely related to sex, even though I had not explicitly asked about it.

"And apart from that?"

"Well, at least he showed me what I don't want to get involved with in the future."

I nodded. Nancy had the same effect on me.

"And now I'm sitting in a restaurant with my best friend who's trying his best to seduce me – and I'm mentally debating how smart I am for getting involved in all this."

"Nothing has happened yet," I reminded her, gripping her calf tighter. She couldn't possibly be alluding to that. Could she? Besides, I wasn't trying to seduce Nikau, at least not at that moment. The kiss in Iowa had already proven how easily that could happen. But taking advantage of her was far from my mind. I wanted her to approach me of her own volition. I wanted the tension to become so unbearable that she couldn't help but ask if we'd ever stop playing around and make something real of it.

The moment would come. I was certain. I just wasn't sure when and under what circumstances it would be, which my impatient side wasn't really in favor of.

"It could ruin it all," she finally replied.

"Everything? Just because you get a glimpse of another side of me, your world view changes? You think that just because we might find ourselves incompatible on other levels, you can no longer look me in the eye and display the same carefree demeanor?"

A sigh escaped her. "I think ten years have passed and we're on thin ice anyway. The only question is what lies underneath."

The question of what lay beneath this ice was on the tip of my tongue. However, I was sure I was about to cross an invisible boundary that I would be better off ignoring at this moment.

"So... what exactly are you trying to say?"

"That I'm unsure and maybe a little confused. And that guy over there keeps staring in our direction." Her eyes glanced over my shoulder, probably at one of the guests.

I didn't turn around – too conspicuous. Instead, I signaled it didn't matter. No one could see what was going on under the table. And even if they did – it was a gesture to make Nikau feel safe. No more, no less. Hardly anyone could argue with that.

"Let's finish the meal and see what happens." I motioned for the waiter to take our order so she wouldn't have a chance to object.

I GLANCED SUSPICIOUSLY IN THE DIRECTION WHERE Nikau had disappeared a good ten minutes ago. Just a quick trip to the toilet, but the small voice in my head whispered that something was wrong.

My first thought was that she had a change of

heart and had run away from me. Then I remembered Nikau was old enough to speak her mind. She would not abandon me. However, I was even less comfortable with the other options, so after another two minutes I got up and took large strides toward the separated area.

I heard their furious voices from a several feet away, adding to the anger that was already boiling inside of me. Nikau wasn't alone. She was being harassed. By a man. Probably the one she had mentioned earlier.

I didn't know if it would have been easier for me if it had been the classic harassment – then I would have been justified in punching the guy in the face. But since I had clearly heard his last question to Nikau, there was no question as to what he actually wanted from her. Namely, information for his rubbish newspaper, which wanted a piece of the action and the big headline before anyone else. It was disgusting that he felt the need to verbally attack and physically harass an innocent woman.

Pissed off, I cleared my throat because he hadn't noticed my presence in the last few seconds. As his head snapped in my direction, I clearly saw the blood drain from his face.

Obviously his balls retreated too, because suddenly it wasn't so hard for him to take a step away from Nikau.

"You're interested in my private life?" I asked, the provocative undertone already in my voice.

He opened his mouth before narrowing his eyes. Not sure what to answer, because anything would be the wrong answer. "I just wanted to know if she was your new girlfriend."

"I don't think that's any of your business, is it?" I held out my hand to Nikau. Without hesitating, she took it, allowing me to lead her out of the other man's immediate vicinity. My hand moved from hers up the length of her arm until it came to rest on the nape of her neck.

Although he began to speak, I did not let him dictate the course of the conversation. I usually just ignored journalists, paparazzi, and all those pesky members of the tabloid press because I didn't care what they said about me and the women I had little interest in. But Nikau... she didn't deserve to be lumped in with influencer celebs and have things attributed to her just because she was in direct contact with me.

"Here's what's going to happen. You are going to apologize to her and then you are going to leave the restaurant. If I see you near us again, you'll be in trouble. If I read speculation about who she is and what our relationship is in a sleazy tabloid tomorrow, you'll be in trouble too. She is off limits. You can tell that to all your little friends too." Somehow I managed to say the words to him in a calm and civilized manner, instead of shouting at him and really scaring him.

For a moment, I thought he would laugh and

continue his behavior until he held out his hand. Nikau didn't take it, so he withdrew it embarrassed. "My behavior was wrong and I didn't realize it was more than a fling this time," he said to her before turning his eyes in my direction. "If you want to do an exclusive interview…"

"Get out," I growled, nodding toward the door. He had better get out of my sight before I lost control and clarified everything I had said to him in another way.

He vanished, although it must've annoyed him to go home without a story.

Nikau slowly turned in my direction. "Is it always like this?"

"When we attract the attention of these idiots, it is." I didn't want to tell her that all these people were jerks. That there was no quiet place outside the resort for me, because she would find out soon enough now that she had been seen with me for the first time.

"Why all this exaggerated interest in you?" Apparently she wasn't interested in returning to the table just yet. Which was fine with me, as I didn't want to know how many other curious people were waiting for us to return.

I was surprised that it was only now that she had asked the question. It was obvious, and after all her comments about my status as the paparazzi's favorite, I had expected to hear it much sooner.

"There was an incident a few years ago…"

"Before or after the resort opened?"

"Before. The media attention did me a favor, if you'd like to put it that way." And ensured that, years later, people would still be interested in what I did in private.

"And what was this incident?"

I had paid a lot of money and gone to court to keep this story out of the public domain. But I didn't mind telling her. "My partner at the time wanted to swap roles for an evening. I went along with it, knowing full well that I did not enjoy it. I was doing it for her – so she could gain the security she had been lacking. In the middle of the session, however, she decided to leave. And because I could not get out of the situation she had put me in, she called and sent one of her friends. He was a well-known paparazzi. He took some pictures, had a good laugh about it, and by the next morning the story was in the local paper. I only discovered it after Kaia found me and freed me. They've been after all my partners ever since, in search of the next big viral story."

Even as I spoke, Nikau's face was contorted in disgust. Probably because of the people who had taken advantage of my situation. Not because I had been willing to give up control only to regret it bitterly afterward.

"That's disgusting, K. Taking advantage of someone because they're in a vulnerable position …" She shook herself. "No wonder you have bad luck with all these women. They only see the picture the media paints of you. And not the real you."

Slowly I let my gaze sweep over her face. The thick lashes, the dark eyes, the curve of her lips and nose made her look like a real person, not a perfect supermodel. She didn't know the business or the media cadence. And it was probably better to keep it that way, because I certainly didn't want her to see me differently just because outsiders suggested she should.

Nikau

Kaden's story seemed to have switched something in my head. The anxiety I had felt all along had magically vanished. He had put himself in a situation where he was totally vulnerable and had been mercilessly exploited. He had trusted and been disappointed.

I followed this line of thought, even though it was a stupid one. Kaden and I had known each other forever. Probably long before we were even aware of it. Even in my earliest memories he played a role. Kaden was always there somehow. In preschool, in high school, when I graduated. We had always been friends, no matter what stage of life we were at. We had fought, had fun together, and finally made a deal, before the seriousness of life struck and tore us from that perfect world. We trusted each other. It had always been that way, and I couldn't imagine for the life of me that it would change. It was just an irrational fear that plagued me, trying to keep me away from possible danger.

In the end, however, I felt I owed him something – the willingness to really commit to what we had agreed. I didn't want to be another disappointment. I couldn't be.

So I needed a plan for the coming year. First, I had to make sure I didn't fall back in love with my homeland. That would only make my departure harder. I also had to find a woman who would be able to give Kaden everything he wanted and needed. Someone who could get to know him for real. And last but not least, I had to try to enter the other part of our agreement unprejudicedly. Most importantly, without losing myself. It sounded like an impossible task, but I had twelve months. I was going to do it. Wouldn't I?

Kaden pulled me out of my thoughts by telling me to follow him to his apartment. In no time at all, I had the chance to prove that everything I had in my head was a perfectly realistic plan.

But Kaden wasn't going to let me slide slowly into the freezing cold water. Less than a second after the door had closed, his voice filled the entire room. It made the fine hairs on my arms and neck stand on end.

"Stand in the center of the room, Nika, and wait for further instructions. I'd like to see what we're going to work with." Suddenly my mouth rivaled the Sahara.

I had never heard him speak like this before. Serious. Dominant. With an undertone that made the order in his words clear without making him sound like a sergeant. Instead, it had a seductive effect on me, as if he was appealing to a subconscious part of me that wanted to respond to his words immediately in a well-behaved way. It seemed so unnaturally normal to do just that

Irritated, I narrowed my eyes. But I moved, even though my body was suddenly very tense. Up to this point, I had not even been fully aware of the meaning of his words, but now it was sinking in.

And I didn't know what I was more disturbed about: that I was so eager to find out what the meaning of his words was, or that the slightest change in his demeanor had effectively separated Kaden's two sides. Best friend? Goodbye. Kaden, the... I had no idea what to call him, but *hello*.

My legs carried me to the center of the room and I crossed my arms. Promptly, I heard a chiding sound. "That's not one of the positions I would like to see you in."

"But..."

"And you only speak when I ask or allow you to, or when there's a serious problem to be dealt with."

Ready to turn his statement into a discussion, I opened my mouth. But I also remembered what I had read on the internet. So I decided to play along, at least for now.

"Got it?"

"I think I do."

"Try yes or no."

It was interesting to see how his words could have such an effect on me. One moment they fascinated me. The next, I felt irritated. This was not the way we usually communicated.

"Yes."

I heard his approach from behind and resisted the urge to turn toward him.

"Normally, you wouldn't just answer with a simple yes, you'd end the sentence with a title. Honorifics, if you want to look it up later. I'm not going to ask for it, though, because it has to be earned."

So he was just assuming I would later open the search engine and look up all the stuff he was about to throw at me?

"Hands behind your back. Keep your shoulders straight and your chin up."

As he spoke I corrected my position and immediately felt it would be exhausting to stay this way for a while.

"Well done, Nika," he praised after a moment. The words felt like getting hit by a freight train. Though there was no sensible reason for it, a tingling sensation began to creep up my spine.

I swallowed. Unable to grasp what exactly was happening. Was it intentional? Or was it the adrenaline coursing through my veins, making me feel high? As if my normal feelings were separated from what had just happened.

"Later on, I'm going to ask you to take off your shoes and your dress. Your underwear... but you can always say no. There is no obligation on your part to do anything. I just want you to be clear with me about the reasons why you don't want to do it," he went on. He was standing right behind me and I felt his hot breath on the nape of my neck. A delightful shiver ran down my spine, reminding me that my mouth could still compete with the Sahara. I couldn't even swallow.

Somehow, and I didn't know if I was comfortable with this, the moisture in my body seemed to gather in other places. I should have been really worried that Kaden could influence me like that with just a few sentences. But right now, I was enjoying it too much to raise my voice in protest.

"Let's see... I will ask you a series of questions and you will answer them as honestly as possible, okay?"

"Yes," I groaned. Ordinarily I would have thought about what he might ask me so I was prepared. But my brain was blank. A blank page waiting for him to write upon.

"How many relationships have you had in the last few years?"

This was an easy one. "Four."

"And how many of them have been happy?"

"I'm not with them anymore, am I? So they couldn't have been happy."

"Touché," he murmured, a little amused. "Then let me put it another way: how many of those men were capable of putting you in the state you're in now?"

So he knew... I took a sharp breath. The next moment I felt his hand on the small of my back. Warm. Supporting me. As if I had no reason to be ashamed.

I gritted my teeth. "Not one."

"Did they make you feel appreciated? Seduced you without thinking about getting laid?"

So Kaden had also become a relationship coach and psychologist in the last few years. Wonderful. My mouth was agape, and again I had a hard time with the depth of this question.

"I can't be the judge of their ulterior motives, can I?"

"But you are aware of your feelings in their presence."

"Not in that way," I muttered.

"What was that?"

Of course, he'd made me say it loud and clear. "I've never felt the way I feel right now."

"Are you going to describe it to me?"

Taking a deep breath, and clenching my toes so he wouldn't notice the tension in the rest of my body. Even though it was pointless, because if there was one thing I noticed, it was that Kaden didn't miss a thing. Whatever I was trying to hide from him, he already knew.

"I'm nervous. But not in a bad way. I am thrilled in a positive way. I can't focus. It makes me want to follow your voice and forget everything else. That's ridiculous, right? You haven't even done a thing."

"None of your feelings are ridiculous, Nika." There it was again, the admonishing tone telling me not to be so hard on myself. "I like that you can express what you're feeling so clearly. Verbally as well as physically."

It was a strange compliment and yet it made me feel better. All of a sudden, I didn't feel quite so bad about being able to express what was going on inside of me.

"I have another question. Your ex-boyfriends did they prefer your ass or your breasts?"

Slowly I opened my mouth to speak. An indiscreet question. I knew the answer. But why did he want to know? Would he get jealous?

"Just give me the answer, Nika. I'm not judging."

"Ass, I guess." How people could reduce a person's appearance to this one question and two body parts was still a mystery to me.

Kaden mumbled something I couldn't quite make out. Until his hand moved up my back, I took it as an agreement.

"What is the first thing that catches your eye when you look at me?"

His touch distracted me, but the answer came to

me immediately. I'd been looking at him a lot since he showed up at my door. "Your presence. The way you move. Little details. Your expression, for example. Or that you still don't care about taming those curls."

"And how is it that these guys reduce everything to your ass?"

"Because they're men?"

"No," he replied sternly, "because they don't know. They don't have an eye for the important details."

Instinctively I knew he would not stop there. He ran his fingers over my bare shoulder and down my back. "This, for example. Your back. I could spend half an eternity on that alone... Take off your shoes, Nika."

With his hand on the small of my back, I had no problem taking off one shoe and then the other. His hand slid to my waist.

"The curve here... also perfect."

He took a step around me, only to lean forward just a little. Suddenly, the subtle scent of his aftershave surrounded me. It tickled my nose and almost forced me to close my eyes so I wouldn't react to it. Or to the warmth that seemed to radiate from his body. All of this made me want to stand on my tiptoes to be on the same level as him.

I tilted of my head slightly which Kaden took as an invitation to lean closer to my ear. Even so, there was still a distance between our bodies. Apart from his hand on my waist and the warmth he emanated, I could not feel him.

And yet, somehow, I felt everything.

His hot breath brushed against my ear, causing me to shiver. "The color of your skin. The shape of your fingers. Your stomach. The curve of your ribs. That you're comfortable with who you are. The way your brain works. The way your eyes light up and your lips curl up in smiles, even though you're fighting them. And the flush of color that slowly rises up your neck. When it reaches your cheeks, do you know how it brings out your freckles? Don't get me wrong, your ass is sexy and your breasts look incredibly seductive in that dress. But those aren't the attributes that make me think about how I'd like to have you naked in front of me."

I swallowed. I had been aware that I had a certain reaction to voices – but Kaden couldn't possibly be aware of it. He couldn't know that it drove me crazy when the right man pressed his mouth to my ear, whispered things that found their way between my legs and threw my brain into absolute chaos. And yet... yet he just used his voice and effortlessly wrapped me around his little finger. One compliment and a blush rose on my face. Even so, I didn't want him to stop. On the contrary, I wanted him to go on until I had an idea of where this was going and whether there would ever be an end to it. I suddenly didn't care anymore that he was playing with me and was turning me into a willing participant. What mattered was that he kept whispering things to me in that damned attractive voice that I hadn't expected. Just for my ears, and no one else's.

"I know you're thinking about what to say about this. But I don't want you to say anything. You will leave everything as I have said and you will accept it."

There was no question. So there was no answer. I quickly understood the principle. Even though it was difficult to bite my tongue and keep silent.

Kaden was merciless in using this advantage he had over me right now. If I had been able to protest and tell him all the reasons why I couldn't believe him, he wouldn't have told me any of this. Or had any desire to. After all, he had sounded sincere. To be honest, I didn't want to doubt that he was sincere, but I was too eager to find reasons not to let all those words touch me.

"Are you ready for me to undress you, Nika?"

I nodded, much to my own surprise. What was the big deal? In our youth, we had gone skinny dipping more than once. He knew my body. And I knew his. Still, I wasn't prepared for the feel of his warm, rough hand on my bare skin. Piece by piece he exposed it.

First, he unzipped my dress, then he pulled it down over my arms until it slid down my body to the floor. But he never let go, his fingers gliding almost unnoticeably over all the places he had just listed. All the while, he didn't break eye contact. That made it even harder for me to keep control of my body.

I stood in front of Kaden in my underwear, feeling more breathless in his presence than ever before. I didn't even know what he was trying to achieve with this. Was it about dominance? Was it about building up a sense of expectation? Something else entirely? Whatever it was, it seemed to be working. When he slid two fingers under the strap of my bra and pulled it down slowly, my pulse raced.

Who would have expected that? I suddenly craved for Kaden to undress me. To see me naked. And give me more of what he was doing to me right now.

"Just remember you can always tell me if you don't want to do something," he reminded me. But I thought there was not even the slightest need for me to do that.

Kaden took a step back and bent down to remove my panties after my bra had joined my dress on the floor. Without further ado, he lifted my leg and removed the thin material from my body.

I felt the warm breeze coming from the open patio door, but even more I felt Kaden's intense gaze on my naked body. Nothing was hidden from him, I realized as his gaze lingered on my core for a second longer than I had expected.

But it was not hunger I read in his face. It was admiration. Awe, if I wanted to be more specific.

And yet he made no comment about how wet I was for him that I could already feel it on the inside of my thighs. The heat pulsating inside me was fed solely by the undivided attention he was giving me, without giving the impression that his primary goal was to get me into bed.

Briefly, the thought crossed my mind that I would have given it to him voluntarily by now. But then I remembered I didn't have to do that. That wasn't the point. And he wouldn't take it without my explicit consent.

"Do you remember what this was about?"

"You wanted to see what you had to work with."

"Right. And you don't seem to be struggling to follow the simple commands. That's a good thing. Now get down on your knees."

Another surge of adrenaline coursed through my veins. Still, without a second thought, I sank to my knees and looked up at him. Questioningly.

Kaden possessed that power. It was the first time I was really aware of it. He said something and I blindly followed him. Without noticing, I had slipped into the role of the submissive. And that there would be no end to it, he demonstrated impressively when he squatted down and pushed my knees apart, only to place my hands loosely on my thighs.

"I'm not really interested in making you kneel anywhere, but your expression…" I saw him swallow. Then he bit the inside of his cheek.

His jacket came off, the sleeves unbuttoned and pulled up over his well-muscled forearms. My breath caught as I watched, transfixed by this simple gesture. In everyday life, it would only have attracted my attention for a brief moment. It was sexy, but not enough to watch in fascination while my body reacted with full force. It was a different story right now.

The air around us now felt as if it were electrified. As if it was loaded with tension. The only question was what would be the outcome when the point of overload was reached.

"Tell me where to touch you." His voice was suddenly so dark. Rough. Aroused.

I was tempted to clench my hands into fists. Instead, I let them rest loosely on my thighs. The whole position was designed for submission. To show it, to feel it. But there was something else... something I couldn't quite grasp.

"Wherever your heart desires, Kaden." Without thinking about its scope or meaning, the phrase slipped out. I simply said what I wanted to say. I wanted more of everything. Of his words, which did not sound sinful at all, but which had exactly the same effect on me. His hands on my body. I secretly wanted him to show me why all these women always bored him. Why he threw them to the wind. Why they couldn't hold his interest when he spent so much on this situation – and without him even knowing about the possibility that I would actually ask him for more?

"Are you sure?" His nostrils quivered. Had he not expected me to give him this honor?

Fuck. Honor. As if I ever have had that kind of

thought in my head before. After a few hours in his presence, sex was suddenly no longer just sex, but a privilege that I alone could grant – with everything that came with it.

"Yes. I am, Kaden."

And just like that, he moved his fingers down my thigh, past my hands and to my middle. "Don't move," he commanded, just before his fingers slid through my sex, over my entrance and lightly across my already irritated clit.

But he did not pause, instead he pulled his hand back again, only to lift it between our bodies. At the level of my face, so I – and he – could see my wetness on his fingers.

"And I haven't even touched you properly, Nika," he said, slightly surprised. "That's how damn wet you got from a few words and the fact that I took your hand to bring you into my world."

Kaden made my head spin in every possible direction. His statement had the same effect on me as dizziness. And yet it felt good. I had managed to astonish him. To put him under my spell. To satisfy him. Even though I had no idea what I was doing.

His fingers came to my lips and I automatically opened them for him. I tasted myself. First on the tip of my tongue, then further back and finally on the roof of my mouth as I closed my lips around his fingers and pressed against them from below. Instinctively. Not because anyone had ever dared to put their fingers in my mouth before. Not because I thought I would find some strange pleasure in tasting myself against his skin.

Something flashed in Kaden's eyes.

"So you see. You thought there was nothing but an angel in you. But angels don't suck my fingers in a way that makes me wonder what it would feel like if it was my cock instead. Such a good little whore."

My right arm twitched with the need to punch him in the face for this humiliation. But my brain just shut down. Because he wasn't saying it to be a serious insult to me.

"Yeah, right," he murmured. "I can simultaneously praise and degrade you, *and* say it in a way that means I admire you."

Fuck. Together with the tone in which all this was directed at me... I suddenly felt the need to squeeze my legs together to control my desire.

This thought didn't seem to escape Kaden's attention either, for he barely shook his head. "Don't," he warned. "Otherwise I'll have to make sure you hold the position, and that would be a shame."

Images immediately flashed through my mind. Pictures I had seen on the internet. Of women tied to the bed. Or to a device on the wall. The result was always the same: they were forced to stay in that position. Helpless, at the mercy of someone else's will. Helpless – if you ignore that they had voluntarily put themselves in that position and actually enjoyed being in it.

But the thought frightened me. To be tied up by

Kaden so he could do whatever he wanted... that was beyond my current confidence – and especially beyond my ability to deal with these new scenarios.

So I had no choice but to keep my legs slightly apart. Heat rose in my core and made me breathe faster.

"You're doing so well, Nika. I'm impressed," he said promptly as if he had understood my inner conflict. Kaden put his hand to my chin, ran his thumb over my skin, searched my gaze to make sure everything was still okay. That we were on the same page.

My body responded automatically, signaling that I was still comfortable. Safe.

"No sex, that was the deal, right?" he asked, and I nodded. "Do you still feel that way?"

I bit my lower lip. If we went one step further now, if we took the last step that separated us, if we got too close, it would mean we had thrown everything we had talked about to the wind. Just like that. Because our bodies had spoken the same language.

Kaden interpreted my hesitation as an uncertain no – and I was grateful for that. Especially since my opinion had changed so often during the time we'd been in his apartment that I couldn't keep up. I would need time to mentally process everything and come back to the here and now but after he declared the session to be over.

"No sex. No harder games. But I won't leave you like this. It wouldn't be fair." He didn't ask permission this time. He didn't need to, because I could have stopped him at any time. If I had wanted to.

Kaden stood without taking his hand off my chin, so I automatically had to follow him with my gaze. He stepped around me, only to crouch until my back rested against his chest. He put his arms around me, resting his hands on mine for a moment.

I frowned. Why did this feel so familiar? Why was everything we had done so far so much more intense than mere sex had ever been? Every nerve ending in my body was alive and active, constantly sending electric impulses through me.

"May I... may I ask a question?" I had asked the question before I could even think about the consequences of speaking without being asked.

It reassured me that there wasn't any tension or negative reaction on his part. Instead, his deep voice was right next to my ear. "Of course," he replied.

"Do you do this with your usual dates?"

"In some form, yes. But it's always individual. It depends on how they take it."

"So why doesn't it work with them?"

I heard him laugh softly. "That is... complicated. Most of them have experience playing this way. But it doesn't feel right. It loses its appeal pretty quickly when their reactions could just as easily be from porn, or when it's clear they're not in it for the long haul."

"Do you think I'm faking it?"

All of a sudden, Kaden's hand slipped between

my legs and covered my sex in a warm embrace without touching me. Still, I felt the throbbing. The telltale tug. Instinctively, I sucked in air and held it.

"No," Kaden murmured directly into my ear. "You're not faking. You're not pretending just because you think I like it. I know it's hard for you. But you're doing it anyway. And part of you is enjoying it, while the other part is probably wondering how that's possible. But that's okay. I can dispel your doubts bit by bit."

He took his hand away from my sex and let it slide down the inside of my thighs and back up again, right past my folds and over my mons veneris to my hip bone, only to come back agonizingly slowly and continue exploring my skin, not even making contact with the place where I really wanted to feel his fingers.

What he did to me was torture. Kaden was playing with me. Making me want what only he could give me. He teased me with lust until the muscles in my legs tightened and every breath I took was strained.

Kaden teased me until I had no choice but to give free rein to the moans stuck in my throat all this time.

"That took a long time, Nika. I don't want you to hide anything from me or hold back. Nothing. I need to hear your voice. Do you want to know why?" That was a rhetorical question, wasn't it? "Because it tells me how much you enjoy it. It is also an indication of what you want. My fingers on your clit, for example?

And it would drive you even crazier if I slid them inside you very slowly afterward. Wouldn't it? I could press them against that sensitive spot inside you as I teased you with my thumb. Now that you have had to wait so long, how quickly do you think you would come? You're so wet it's clinging to your thighs. *Impressive*. But that's not the only thing going through your mind at the moment, is it? You have ideas about what it would be like if it wasn't my fingers inside you, but something else. What it would feel like to come on my cock instead of on my hand." He snarled. A growl escaped him as he made everything he said come true, and by now my muscles couldn't help but twitch uncontrollably. Over and over again, even though I still hadn't come. Each time he delayed it, paused for a moment. Took a break. And then he would start the ordeal all over again, making me tremble, moan, sweat and lean against him with all my weight, barely able to hold the position he wanted me in.

A curse escaped him. "Do you realize what you're doing to me, Nika? Your muscles are contracting so tightly around my fingers that I can barely move them. They're screaming for more. You'd like it so much better to be wrapped around my cock. To be stretched by me because my fingers are no longer sufficient. To feel the warmth. The twitch. I could fuck you until you let go of all control. Because you could no longer think, let alone want to, you would let me use you. You'd be happy if I took all the decisions away from you and you could just concentrate on being *good* for me," he said.

With that, it was finally over for me. My whole body suddenly tensed as the orgasm raced through me. I couldn't help but moan his name as he held me down and made sure I didn't shake his hand away, but instead rode out my climax, coming so hard that I felt myself getting even wetter.

Goading me and my body's reaction even further, he whispered in my ear in a raspy voice.

"Fuck, Nika, how hard you come for me. When you moan my name like that, it sounds so fucking sexy. And how good it feels when your muscles twitch helplessly around me."

The more he said, the more I responded to him. My orgasm seemed to go on forever until I couldn't take it anymore. What I'd just felt made me want to burst out laughing, almost crying.

"You have to stop or I'm going to pass out because it's so much," I moaned.

Kaden stopped – just to turn me around to face him, one hand on my throat. I felt a rush of adrenaline as he forced me to look straight into his eyes.

With a jerk, he pulled me onto his body, still controlling my neck. Without warning, he kissed me, I didn't push him away and stop it. Instead, I let myself go, enjoying the feeling that I had just come, that he was now restricting my air supply and kissing me in a way that once again doused the fire in my abdomen with gasoline

What I had said had not been a lie. I could feel all that had just happened and was still happening threatening to overwhelm me.

With a powerful bite on my lower lip, Kaden finally let go of me, but not without verbally telling me to run into a steel-hard concrete wall one last time. He just pulled the rug out from under me. And I couldn't get enough of it.

"You've been so fucking good for me." The admiration. The praise. As if he had found an instruction manual for my body and decided to follow it step by step – because the result was satisfying for both of us.

In spite of this, he broke away from me, stood up, and bent down to pick me up. Not just onto my legs, but into his arms.

"I can manage…"

He raised an eyebrow and I fell silent.

"This part is not optional," he explained. He carried me into his bedroom. "As you come down from this experience and your body slowly returns to normal, I want you to feel safe. So you'll let me take care of you."

Something told me there was no point in discussing this. So I left it at that. "And what about you? Who is going to take care of you? According to this principle, it shouldn't just be me," I replied instead of my real protest.

"What makes you think that?" Kaden sat me down on the bed with a raised eyebrow.

"It just seems logical to me. You were in a different

role, and... it must have had a similar physical effect on you."

"Have you read about it?"

This time I was the one who raised an eyebrow. "No. Should I?"

He shook his head. "You'd better tell me what you have in mind."

"Melons, National Geographic, a trip to the hot tub, which you obviously didn't tell me about, and this bed. Not necessarily in that order." Some of this was part of the Friday night routine we had followed in our youth.

Kaden's satisfied expression told me this was also on his mind.

"And by the way," he asked after he fell onto the bed next to me, "are we going to talk about how this is all going to work out?"

I rolled onto my stomach, pulled his pillow close to me and buried my face in it. I wanted to scream, because I could only think of one possible response to his words, and it was probably in his best interest.

After another deep breath, I emerged from the soft pillow, only to find Kaden staring at me curiously. "What does that mean?"

"I don't know, K. Maybe this is all insanely overwhelming and yet I would be more than willing to sign anything you put in front of me right now. Because that's what you'll do next if I agree, isn't it?"

"You remember my penchant for contracts well." He clicked his tongue before slipping his hands under his head and staring at the ceiling. Kaden was so damn confident in everything he did that I almost felt a little jealous. "I'll give you time to think about it. This is not the state to make such decisions."

"But you wanted to talk about it?"

"Especially about how you liked certain elements."

"Oh, you mean because my reactions weren't answer enough," I replied with a snort, which he returned not a second later.

"Or because I would like it if it was normal to talk about it."

I shook my head in disbelief. "Then give me some time, K. Or my brain will implode."

And as if agreeing with me wasn't enough, he slid further toward me and casually let an arm slide across my back. As if it was perfectly normal. As if we hadn't just turned a hundred and eighty degrees in the blink of an eye, which had recently led to my best friend giving me orgasms and fucking my head in a way that had left me completely helpless.

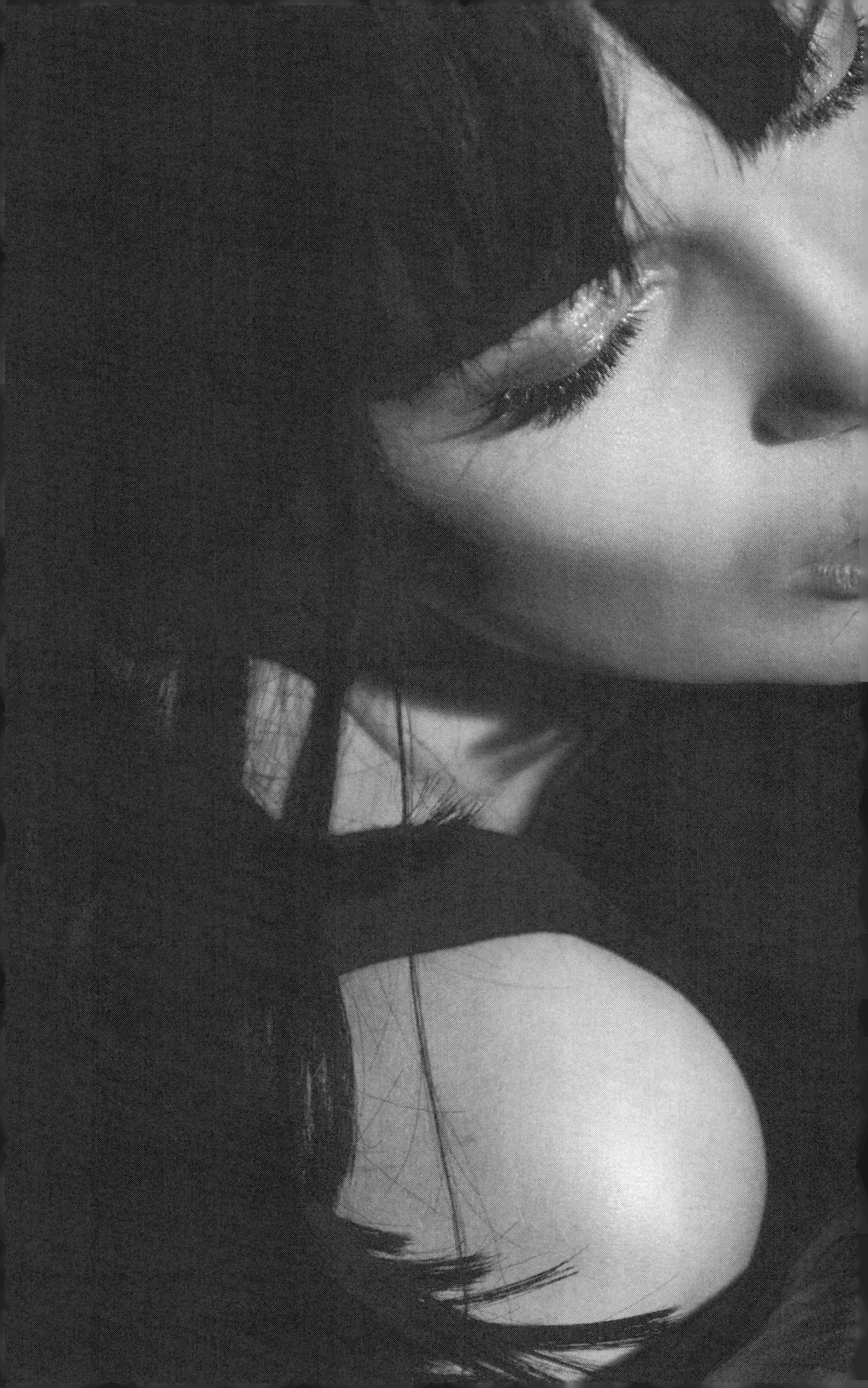

Kaden

Honolulu Sun. That was the name I had given to the luxury resort that covered about 30 acres and offered guests everything a Hawaiian holidaymaker could wish for. We were close to the beach – which was the hotel's private beach – and we had a huge elevated pool area so you could see the sea and the neighboring islands from the infinity pool. On clear, sunny days you could see for miles, and the sunsets, when you lay by the pool looking up at the sky between the yards of green palms, were awe-inspiring.

All of this was done because we didn't want to make Hawaii look like it does in the media.

In addition to the classic hotel rooms, there were some separate apartments and small cottages right on the beach. Hundreds of staff made sure everything ran smoothly.

So it was no surprise to hear loud summer music coming from the neighboring apartments early in the morning – and to find Kaia working on my terrace as soon as I rose to take stock of the previous night.

Well, so much for that.

My eyes fell on Nikau, who was still fast asleep. She was lying on her stomach, the blanket wrapped around her waist just enough to keep her from giving Kaia an impressive show. Normally this would be the point where I would wake the woman in my bed and send her home, but I had no desire to get rid of Nika, nor did I intend to lie to my sister about what had happened. Especially as it was too late for that anyway.

She was sitting on my patio. It was likely she had a very clear idea of what had happened here.

I got up, grabbed a pair of boxers, pulled them on and decided not to ignore Kaia's presence. Instead, I joined her, eager to hear what she had to say.

"Do you realize what time it is?" I started the conversation.

She looked at me with slightly narrowed eyes. "It's noon, yes. That means you missed two meetings already. And, believe it or not, all your nice business partners are insanely reluctant to talk numbers with a woman."

But that didn't stop Kaia from putting her feet on the table and pretending she had more balls than all my business partners combined.

"I was otherwise occupied," I replied, not a bit

sorry I had missed anything.

Kaia tipped her head back and stared directly into my bedroom for a few seconds, then straightened up to look at me. "Yeah, I noticed. I didn't realize you and Nikau were in this kind of relationship."

It was clear from her words that she was teasing. Still, I did not like it.

"Is that why you want her to work here?"

"I want her to work here because I don't want her to feel the need to go back to Iowa."

Kaia wrinkled her nose. "Who would volunteer to live there?"

Well, that was a question she'd better discuss with Nikau, because I hadn't found an explanation for it yet.

"Speaking of work," Kaia changed the subject a few seconds later. "I can put her in the kitchen. They always need help and I remember her doing it before?"

Confirming, I nodded.

"And what if she doesn't want you to be her boss?"

I couldn't help but grin. I only wanted to give Nikau orders in one respect, and that had very little to do with the resort. But I wouldn't tell Kaia. Even if she could figure it out for herself, I certainly wouldn't be having a conversation with my sister about what had happened if she hadn't commandeered my terrace and ambushed me there. "I think that would be my problem, not yours."

"Sure," she murmured, "and you do know what you're doing here, don't you? Or are you planning on missing any more important meetings in the future? If so, I'd like to know about it in advance."

"Don't worry. Everything will be fine from now on," I assured her. In fact, I hadn't missed a meeting in the last few years, for any reason, but that didn't mean Nikau was going to make sure I missed any more critical appointments.

"And are you going to show her the grounds, or do you want me to organize someone to do that?"

I made a face. "Just forget everything I said before about any woman. Or any rules that existed. This is Nikau we're talking about."

And I couldn't think of a single good reason to shove her into the hands of some employee to get her out of the way.

"Is the magic between her legs that strong?"

The question came so abruptly that it almost made me cough. I caught myself just in time to avoid making a fool of myself. "I don't know. I haven't been there yet."

She raised an eyebrow.

"And now you should leave with your nosy questions. You'll find out soon enough through the media or your stalking skills."

"So there were problems again, were there?" she asked as she rose.

"When are there no problems?" I asked the crucial counter-question. Because basically not a day went by that we didn't have to deal with some kind of attention we didn't really need.

Even though the whole facility offered enough reasons to look around and discover something new, Nikau was constantly looking in my direction – and I in hers, otherwise I would not have noticed this little detail. Even now, as she sat down at the edge of the pool and slid her feet into the water, she chose to look at me rather than look around.

My work over the past few years, and Nikau made it seem like it didn't matter anyway. And not in a negative way, not at all. Quite casually, she made it clear that this place was far less interesting than I was, and that was strange and refreshing at the same time.

"I only have one question about this place," she finally said, propping herself up on her hands and leaning back a little. "And you can probably guess what it is."

I had a vague idea, but I wasn't going to make any wild guesses until I heard the words come out of her mouth.

I tilted my head to indicate she should continue.

"Why this place? O'ahu has many beautiful areas, and Honolulu is big. So why this beach? This property?"

Ah. So my premonition had been right. And

Nikau had taken a good look at the place, although her attention was on me the whole time, even when I was explaining or showing her something. The question caught me off guard, although I shouldn't have been surprised that she had noticed.

"I never got the impression that you were particularly sentimental, K. But still, that's the beach we sat on ten years ago."

I shoved my hands into my trouser pockets. "Maybe there just weren't any other properties that appealed to me."

"This place wasn't one then. And it wasn't for sale."

Good. It had just taken some money to bribe an official at the planning department. But that didn't mean I... "I liked the view. And the guests like it too."

"So it has no further significance?"

"Not for the time being," I replied, because anything else would have been an admission of things I wasn't ready to admit.

Nikau looked at me skeptically, but ended up letting it go. "It's a beautiful place. And I like what you've done with it. Although I never expected to see you in a suit juggling hundreds of guests."

"What would have been the alternative?"

She shrugged. "Surfing school, maybe?"

"Yeah. Preferably on Waikiki Beach, everyone wearing leis and dance the hula." Inwardly I shuddered at the thought. "When was the last time you stood on a board?"

"When you made me do it. Iowa doesn't exactly have a reputation for big waves. Or oceans, for that matter."

"If you decide to stay, we could..." I deliberately left the sentence unfinished because only the first part was relevant. I was very interested in her answer, even though I didn't want to pressure her.

After her reaction to everything last night, I found it harder and harder to believe she had no interest in the scene. Besides, she had pulled the rug out from under me with her behavior. I could not remember ever feeling so intense during a session. She had absolutely no idea, even if she had read up on the internet and had some idea of what might be possible.

I had found it surprisingly difficult to restrain myself – although I had no problems with making Nika the center of attention. In any case, I wanted to prevent her from falling too far too fast. Even so, it had been a revelation to me in a way I'd had no idea was possible. It was even harder for me and my uncontrollable erection to keep my composure when her body was clearly screaming for more. I was good at pretending otherwise, but with every hour I spent in her presence, it became harder and harder not to imagine what it would be like if... Well, if she decided that none of this was for her...

Better not to imagine it.

"Just put the damn contract in front of me, K.

Then I'll do us both a favour, sign it, and whatever happens after that is between *Lono* and us, I guess."

"I'm not sure I'm comfortable with a fertility god having anything to do with this," I replied dryly, before laughing at myself.

"You should put in the contract that you have to go on all the dates I set up for you," she continued, tempting me to put my hand on the back of her neck.

"I'll draw up the contract."

"And if I don't sign it, it means nothing to you. So you should consider taking my wishes into account."

Of course. Nikau seemed to have already internalized that she was only at my mercy in certain scenarios and that she would continue to be a person who could think and act for herself in all other respects. Something that made me smile. And made her different from other women like Nancy.

"And there are things I will never do."

If she mentioned sex, I would probably die on the spot.

"I didn't know you'd recently become an expert on all the possibilities."

"At least I'm able to use a search engine for that."

"You can make me a list as soon as you sign the contract. And while you're at it, read mine now, so you know what you're getting yourself into."

She turned her head to look at me. "Is there anything in it that might surprise me?"

I wouldn't anticipate that for her. "Just wait and see. You'll find out soon enough."

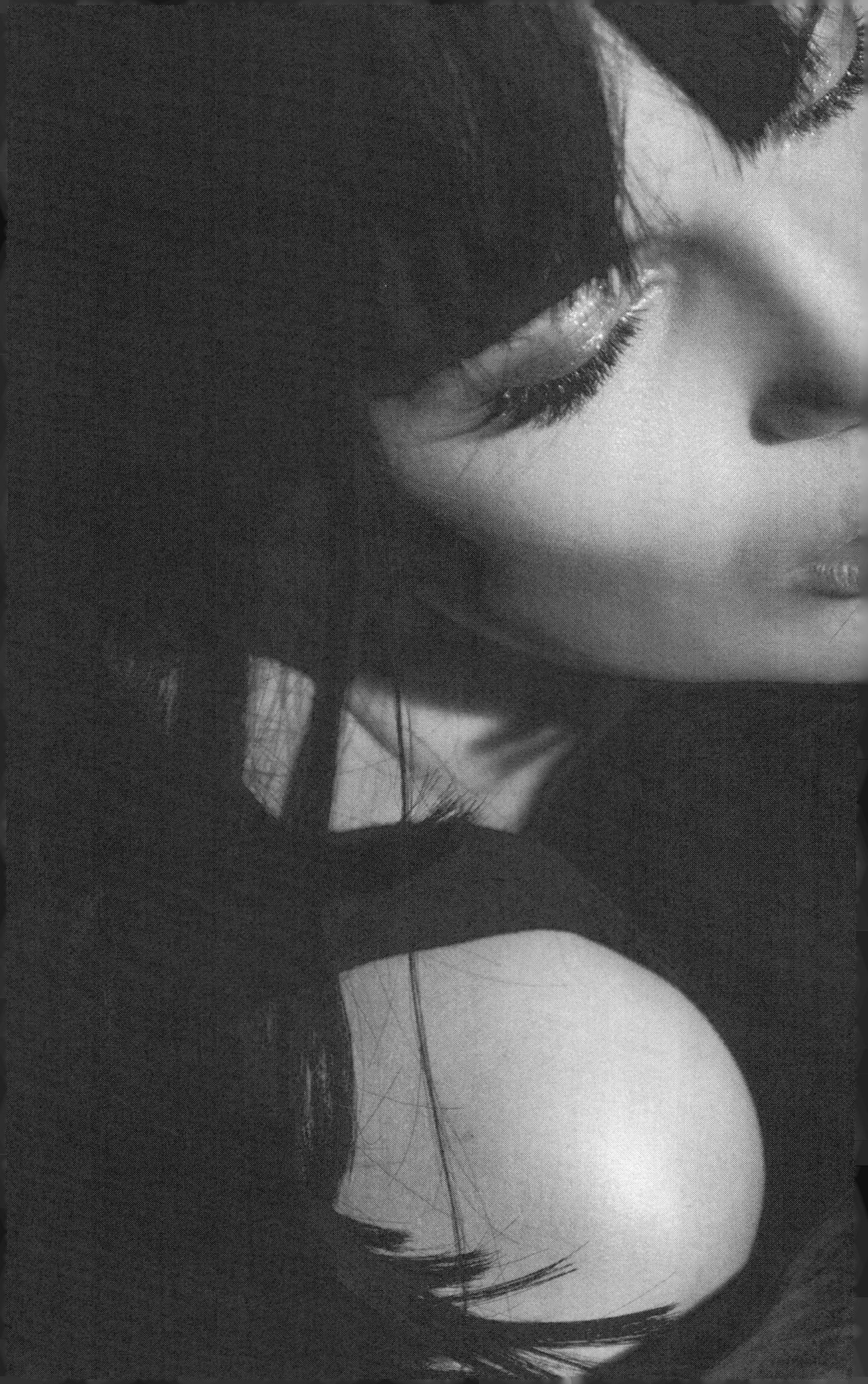

Nikau

It was fair to say I had not found my way back to Hawaii in the usual way. Even though Kaden and I seemed to be on the same wavelength, there were some things we hadn't even talked about, even though this stupid contract had been in the air for a long time.

I still had no idea what it was about, because when it came to things like exclusivity, Kaden didn't have to worry. I had no intention of going out with any men. My one and only goal was to find him a damn good woman and to make sure this man was happy. Even though I had not yet been able to fathom the real problem behind his eternal search, he was not very forthcoming about it.

It was probably not lost on Kaden that I had been sitting on the shore for some time, watching him ponderously as, with the sunset behind him, he shot through the waves, impressively demonstrating his control over the board, his body, and the water. I was not the only one with my not so discreet, or even surreptitious, observation. There were other people on the beach watching Kaden. Sometimes unabashedly, sometimes out of the corner of their eye, but all with the same fascination. And Kaden? When he looked at the shore, it was always in my direction.

That didn't make it any easier to stay on track and think about what was wrong with this man, that he needed me to find him a woman. He was charming. He definitely had a good sense of humour and intelligence behind his actions. Kaden looked forbiddingly handsome, basically like a younger version of Aquaman. An apt comparison as he broke through the waves and looked like he was one with the water.

Or maybe I was seeing him through a pair of transfigured glasses, because we had already been insanely close then, and now it continued seamlessly, as if our connection had never stopped.

I didn't get to finish my thought because Kaden rose from the sea and came straight at me, his wetsuit already pulled down to his hips. I could hear the other women catch their breath. Well. Apparently I was enjoying the attention of a man they were all miles away from. The difference was that I hadn't asked for it. I didn't even want it.

As long as you broke it down to the essentials and didn't just focus on the fact that he had selflessly given me an orgasm, a gesture a lot of other men had probably only heard of in legends.

Without commenting, he settled down next to me and I decided musing aloud on what I'd said earlier. Kaden was beside me, so I might as well talk to him about it then try to find the answers to all my questions on my own.

"Why weren't you angry with me, Kaden?"

"Angry?" he asked irritably, unable to understand what I wanted to say.

"When I left and said that I didn't want to hear from you."

He made a knowing sound, as if he had found the thread. "You didn't want your nostalgia for Hawaii to be so strong – or you wouldn't have remained in Iowa."

"And yet I went away and left you on your own. You could have been mad and upset."

"But you didn't just decide to leave. And at some point, I just kind of blocked it out."

"Until you did an eight-hour flight to remind me of the deal."

"Until I realized I couldn't do it if I was dealing with women like… Nancy."

"Your ex-girlfriend?"

"My last playmate. I dumped her before I got on the plane."

I narrowed my eyes. Not because I wanted to pass judgment on Kaden's numerous playmates. But because I suddenly wondered how long he could stand this arrangement with me. Someone who didn't know better was bound to slip up sooner or later.

"If I am no longer able to entertain you, will you do the same to me? Please don't get me wrong. I'm glad we've picked up where we left off with our friendship – but I wonder how long that's going to last when... well..."

He tilted his head. "I told you, Nika. We can leave it out if it doesn't fit."

"But you've never done it that way with any other woman, have you? Until now it always ended with you dumping her sooner or later."

Kaden remained silent. For a long, agonizing moment he remained absolutely silent. "Do you remember the fight we had when we were thirteen?"

"When we found ourselves outside the headmaster's office?"

"Exactly."

"You never told me why you ended up there."

"That's what I'm getting at. Up until that school year, I thought my family was fine. That there were no problems and that everyone was content and happy. I was as far off as I could be – the night before I saw my mum hit my dad. He was in A&E, claiming it was a bar fight. To make a long story short, until that night, I always thought I would have a relationship like theirs one day. After that night, I decided to cut out the one component that made it possible in the first place."

"Kaden..." I began.

"No. I'm not done yet," he replied promptly. "I hate all of this. Not the resort or what I've achieved. It's the loneliness. I can't share any of it with anyone except my sister. And just before I decided to go to Iowa, I remembered what it was like with us. How you made sure everything was all right. And I wanted that back. Rather selfish, don't you think? Ripping you out of your life and finding an excuse just so I wouldn't feel lonely anymore."

I opened my mouth. I raised an eyebrow. And yet I didn't know what to say.

"It doesn't stop there. When I ambushed you with that deal... It was clear to me that I would never be in love because of my mother and her actions. So it seemed right to eventually marry my best friend and hope for the best. Because all I want is sex. You as my best friend and damn good sex. Nothing more."

At his words, one realization followed the other. And where others might have felt betrayed, I realized that the next twelve months with Kaden would not just be about what he wanted. No, it would be an intense therapy because if Kaden thought he was immune to feelings and love simply because he was afraid of becoming like his mother, or of meeting a woman like his mother, then there were probably more serious problems than just being alone. But I wouldn't hand it to him on a silver platter.

"I have no idea how this is going to work, K, but I hope for your sake you've thought about the contract."

"That's an abrupt change of subject," he remarked skeptically.

"What am I supposed to say? There are so many people who come from broken homes. You're not the only one."

"Of course not. Then tell me how it's worked out for you." My parents' separation had been ugly, and even before my father took us to Iowa, it had often been up to me to take care of my sisters.

"That's a very unfair statement, and you know it," I replied, shaking my head. "You can't use the information from those sessions against me like that. If I make myself vulnerable in front of you, I want you to handle it accordingly. I'm not going to judge you for anything you choose to confide in me."

Out of the corner of my eye I saw him clench his hand into a fist before he let out a loud gasp and finally relented. "Okay. That wasn't fair. I just expected you to get angry and storm off."

"Why? Because you're human?" I snorted. Kaden and I had been through so many different things that a selfish act on his part didn't tip the scales in one direction. Somehow I had been aware that he had not flown to Iowa out of selflessness. Everyone acted for a reason; in Kaden's case it had been a mixture of desperation, loneliness, and perhaps destiny. Maybe his subconscious knew the answer. Maybe Kaden was just in need of someone to set him on the right path and make sure he found happiness.

So, while I would use Kaden to get to know

myself a little better, I would also make sure that Kaden would recognize one fact.

"You didn't betray me. You weren't an asshole. You gave me good reasons. You don't force me to do anything. Even if I sometimes tell myself I'm not, I do everything of my own free will. So why should I run away when I can just as easily talk to you about it?"

"There's always the accusation that I'm just taking advantage of you," he interjected.

"Oh, come on, K. We both know that's not true. At least not in the negative way you have in mind with that word."

"So no problems between us?"

"No. You'll only get them if we continue to deal with each other on that level. You still talk to your sister the way you used to."

"And you expect me to limit it to more than just my sister?"

"I expect you not to treat me like a business partner."

"I don't usually make my business partners scream with delight," he replied nonchalantly.

The comment made the heat rise in my face, but it was exactly what I had meant. So I grinned at him. "Maybe that's the corruption you keep hearing about. Other resort owners…"

"I'd rather go bankrupt than touch a seventy-year-old white investor who needs blue pills to feel anything, Nika," he replied, far too seriously, until the telltale glint appeared in his eyes. The idea still amused him.

Without warning, he stood up and wrapped his arms around my waist. Within a second I was in the air – upside down. The sea moved faster and faster toward us until I felt the spray on my face. The next thing I knew, Kaden let go of me, and I hit the water screaming, coming up like a soaked poodle.

Breathing heavily, I straightened up and stared at him. Furious. "What was that for?"

"You needed to cool off."

I tilted my head before jumping in his direction, pulling him into the waves with me, though it took far too much strength to even move him. Only when we were both soaking wet did I let go. But I knew he would not leave it there.

So on the way back to the apartment I ended up in the pool not once, but three times. Only on the fourth time did I manage to grab his arm and pull him in too.

We emerged splashing, his hands wrapped tightly around my waist. He carried me like a wet punching bag out of the pool and toward the apartments.

"You're coming with me, you know that, right?"

I made a sound of feigned fear. "Ohhh, are you going to give me a spanking now because you got wet as well?"

But as soon as I had said the words, I realized I was not afraid of the idea. But it did make me feel heat spreading through my stomach. Which could only mean the end for me.

Sitting on the beach at dawn, the sound of the waves as a backdrop to one's thoughts as the first fiery streaks appeared on the horizon, was something I had missed. Without realizing it, because once you'd been away from something for a while, it became easier to forget the details and how it made you feel. The memory was still there, but never strong enough to match the feeling that spread through my chest at that moment.

This island was my home. O'ahu would always be where I was rooted. And even though I had resolved not to fall in love with it again, I already suspected that it would be a difficult undertaking when it continued to show its best side and wrap me around its finger so easily.

In fact, I was glad for the soft sand because Kaden had made my thoughts come true – even if this time there was no end in sight for him or me. Not that I wanted to complain about the imprint of his teeth on my ass and the constant throbbing between my legs. I couldn't remember the last time I'd felt such anticipation of sex.

My heart was pounding all the more when I finally turned the paper in my hand over and looked at it. A post-it caught my eye, so I started with it.

Nika, this is the unofficial version. The one I'd really like to present to you because it's so much more personal and expresses what I'm actually about. But if you want to sign the official version, that's perfectly fine, too. You're not selling your soul to me in any way, shape or form – it's just that I can't do without the recording.

I ran my thumb over the handwritten note. Then I turned it aside and looked at the next post-it.

Even the first one made me feel something I couldn't begin to describe. But it tightened my chest and for a moment breathing was damn near impossible.

1. *Your body and with it your pleasure, desire, passion, and orgasms are now owned by me.*

Kaden's property. The mere mention of these words made me tingle. How far had I come from what I'd originally said about his funny sex games?

I swallowed and let my eyes slide down to the next point on the list.

2. *It is my duty to do my best to introduce you to the scene and make you feel at ease. Even though I am in control, your well-being will always be my first priority.*

Something he didn't have to mention explicitly. I knew he would take care of me. Kaden had proven that more than once. He made it clear with almost every action he took toward me, especially when his hand casually ran down my neck or pressed against my lower back, giving me the support I didn't know I needed.

I continued to read.

3. *You agree to obey my orders and demands. Even if it means venturing into new, unfamiliar territory.*

I didn't mind doing that. Because it made it easy for me to forget what was happening and that I didn't really want to be interested in any of it. Sure, there would be times when I disagreed, but Kaden had already shown that I needn't worry and could talk to him. And who knew if it wouldn't be interesting to rebel against his orders at some point? After last night, I wondered how creative he could get when it came to punishing me... and how much I could enjoy it.

I had to smile at the next point.

4. *After all the sessions you are to sleep in the same bed as me. There will be no exceptions.*

In his mind he had added to this rule that I was to wear absolutely nothing during this time – because Kaden was just Kaden, and after our first session he had laid his head on my thigh and let me run my fingers through his hair. It was just like before. Only without the cloth between us.

And then there was one last point that almost made me refuse to read the real contract at all.

5. *I will not force you to do anything, but I will honor everything you give me with the utmost respect.*

Kaden claimed to have no interest in feelings or even love, but when I skimmed over these words, I noticed nothing but that. Appreciation, on a level you only experienced with people you cared about for a long time. And our friendship seemed to be just that, significant.

Still, I tore the post-its off the actual sheet and stuck them to my thigh instead, so I could also read what he called the official contract. It did look a bit more formal. Typed on a computer and printed out. There was no personal touch and no indication that Kaden had been the one to do the drafting. I read the first few lines cautiously.

The following contract shall be subject to a period of one year. Within this period of time the submissive will have enough time to find a suitable sub for her Dominant. If she fails to do so, the contract ends with the original agreement to marry each other when they turn thirty. The following contract is only intended to outline the twelve months between now and then and to lay down clear rules for the way they deal with each other in terms of sexual encounters. These rules are only valid during this period and have no bearing on the actual relationship between the two parties.

Kaden had already explained that these contracts were not meant to stand up in a court of law. It was not about being on the safe side legally, but about personal security and the gesture behind it. Some couples seemed to go as far as having the dominant part of the relationship own all the submissive part's possessions – something I didn't want to imagine.

No matter what kind of relationship you were in, platonic or romantic, outside of the bedroom you should always be on equal terms, at least in my opinion. When it came to sex, I was happy – I could see this now – for Kaden to take the lead. But outside of that, he was never going to be allowed to interfere or decide what I wanted to happen. I was a grown woman. The moment he stopped seeing me as such, or tried to change me into something else, our sexual relationship would come to an abrupt end. Kaden was not inclined to do this by nature, but even I understood that the boundaries could be blurred far too easily if care was not taken to make them clear and unambiguous.

Dependence was always poisonous. That was why it had no place in this kind of relationship. So I was surprised to find myself thinking about these issues for the first time. And all of this because I was supposed to sign a contract with Kaden that was supposed to regulate the way we would play with each other.

Even though I was alone, I shook my head a little. I just couldn't believe how much I needed to evolve to keep up with Kaden's lifestyle.

Nevertheless, I looked at the first paragraph.

1. The submissive has the right to refuse an order at any time, with an explanation of the reasons. In principle, however, the submissive has to comply with all requests without asking any questions. No order may cause serious physical injury, permanent damage or trauma.

The fact that we were not Kaden and Nikau in this contract bothered me enormously. It was as if we were two other people who could only be seen from the outside, and who could be called submissive and Dominant without making any difference. But for me, it was there – because I didn't want to turn into a different person when I discovered that side of myself. For other people, this demarcation may have been necessary to keep in touch with reality and to maintain a clear boundary, but for me it just felt wrong. I felt uncomfortable even reading about it.

2. Accordingly, the welfare and safety of the submissive is paramount. The Dominant undertakes to ensure that these criteria are met at all times.

The second rule sounded much more uncharitable than what I had read in his handwritten rules. The contract seemed to have taken all emotion and feeling out of the equation and reduced everything to a sterile level. But I didn't want that. Kaden was not a stranger. He was my best friend. And if I didn't find him in the words of the contract, it would be very difficult for me to sign it in the end.

Did he think this was what I needed? Or was it really just a matter of him having a soft spot for it? What did he think I was going to choose? Which of the two contracts would I end up signing?

3. Possible penalties are not up for discussion and are to be accepted – under the aspects already mentioned. Hard limits also apply. None of the sanctions can be based on actual abuse.

Abuse. Fuck. This was not a point I wanted to read or discuss at all. We were adults, after all, and both his opinion and mine carried weight, whether we were in a dynamic like this or not. Did he really think we were in danger of what had happened to his parents?

I closed my eyes for a moment. Why hadn't he told me before? At the time when it happened, or in the years since? I had to force myself to read on.

4. *The Dominant agrees to attend all dates arranged by the submissive. In the case of a successful date, the contract will be considered to be null and void. The submissive is not allowed to go on dates with other men (or women) for the duration of the contract, unless she has the explicit order or consent of the Dominant.*

At least one point that made me smile. Kaden promised to go on all the dates I arranged for him – as if he'd toyed with the idea of avoiding them because he didn't believe in my success.

But again, I read something I had not expected from Kaden. Was he really afraid that I would cheat on him? Had that happened to him in other relationships? Did that play a part in his distancing himself from any feelings? So many questions, and yet I wasn't quite sure if Kaden would ever volunteer an answer.

I had expected the next point, but it still brought new questions. And insights.

5. *All points in this relationship remain secret.*

Of course, he didn't want me to talk to the press. Not that I had ever intended to, certainly not since that unpleasant encounter in the restaurant. But until then I had firmly believed he was relatively indifferent to how he was portrayed in the media. All his other relationships, however, had been scrutinized by the press. His former playmates had given interviews, gushed about him and painted a picture that almost made him out to be a sex-crazed bachelor, scaring off women by the dozen with his quirky tastes.

Maybe it was time to get rid of that image for good and to show him in the media as the man that he really was. Even if it meant putting myself in the spotlight. Changing an entrenched image required credible sources.

Although there was still much to be considered in this regard, I read on.

6. Verbal agreements about rules or wishes are valid as long as the other party has verbally agreed to them.

Like that evening after the restaurant, a simple rule carried a lot of weight when you looked at it more closely.

7. All meetings are immediately interrupted if the word red or coconut is mentioned.

I had read about this too. When things got rough or certain types of play were being practiced, the word stop was not enough to interrupt the current action, because it could just as well be part of the game. So other words were needed. Words that could be clearly separated from the game and the action.

I would probably no longer think of coconuts as being as harmless as they were before. But I would put up with that if it meant I was always on the safe side.

The next rule made me raise an eyebrow.

8. The relationship, which is the subject of this contract, does not affect the other life, including the profession and work of either party.

The rule referred to what I had noticed earlier. That there were play relationships in which the Dominant determined everything. Whether the submissive was allowed to work, what happened to their money, how they had to dress. When they would work out, what they would eat... all these things that you would normally be able to decide freely were in these cases decided by another person.

I think this is a responsibility nobody should refuse. But that was just my personal feeling. Just because I couldn't imagine it didn't mean it might not be the right thing for another person. A kind of help. Or fulfillment. Who could know for sure?

9. The enclosed lists of taboos and practices are to be filled in and adhered to.

The mention of this made me look at the following papers, which were arranged in a table and contained innumerable terms. I would probably have to deal with them in a moment. But first I turned to the very last point of the contract.

10. If at any time the friendship between Kaden and Nikau is in danger of being damaged, this contract is also null and void. An immediate return to normal is a prerequisite.

I knew exactly why he had included this point. What had moved him to include our friendship in a contract about a BDSM play relationship. And here Kaden proved again that he was not left cold by what I wanted to say. He gave it a lot more thought than I would have expected from him or than I was used to from other men.

And even if I would respect all these rules, this would not be the contract I would sign in the end. I already knew.

So I turned the page – and found nine pages of a complex table. The first field was the interaction, followed by a column in which you could indicate how open you were to this kind of play. There also seemed to be space for additional comments, and the list was not limited to the submissive role, but also offered space for the Dominant to note their preferences.

Suddenly I remembered why I had always called it Kaden's weird sex stories. Because there were things on that list that I didn't even want to imagine. *Nappies. Feces. Permanent scars. Plastic surgery.* Toys that weren't really toys: *Electric cattle prods*, for example.

I knew the list was from the internet, and that much of it probably wouldn't work for Kaden either, but I couldn't help frowning and wondering how it had come about that people had discovered all these ideas for themselves. People out there liked it when their partner peed on them or engaged in incestuous role-playing. When you were treated like an animal, made to behave like one, or literally played with fire.

My first impulse was to go back to Kaden's apartment. I wanted to discuss with him, point by point, whether the practice was an option for me or an absolute hard limit. At the same time, I wanted to know what his preferences were, what he absolutely disliked, and how he felt about some things on the list.

Was this an attempt to shock me? Was it an attempt to make me realize once again what it was I was really in for? I swallowed and tried to remind myself that none of this was a commitment. This was just about exploring the possibilities. I could always find out later during the session if I really liked it. If it happened at all. Neither of us would do something we didn't really want to do.

Nevertheless, I went through the list, from A to Z.

Abrasion, Age Play, Anal Sex (giving and taking), Anal Plugs (small, large, in public), Animal Roles, Arm/Leg Sleeves (Armbinders), Aromas, Asphyxiation, Auctioned for charity, Ball stretching, Bathroom use control, Beastiality-Fantasy, Beating (soft and hard), Blindfolds, Being serviced (sexual), Being bitten, Boot worship, Bondage (light, heavy, all day, in public, e.g. under clothing), Branding, Breast/Chest Bondage, Breast whipping, Breath Control, Brown Showers (scat), Bruises, Cages (being enclosed), Caning, Castration fantasy, Catheterization, Cattle Prod (electricity), Cells/Closets (being enclosed), Chains, Champer-Pot use, Chastity belts,

Chauffeuring, Choking, Chores (domestic help), Clothespins, Cock Rings/Straps, Cock worship, Collars (private, public), Competition (with other subs), Corsets (normal, for waist training), Cross-dressing, Cuffs (leather, metal), Cutting, Diapers (to put on, to use), Dilation, Dildoes, Double Penetration, Electricity, Enemas (to clean, as punishment), Enforced chastity, Erotic dance (with spectators), Examination (physical), Exercise (forced, as duty), Exhibitionism (with acquaintances, with strangers), Eye Contact Restrictions, Face Slapping, Fantasy Abandonment, Fantasy Breeding, Fantasy Rape, Fantasy Gang-Rape, Fantasy Necrophilia, Fear (being scared), Fire Play, Fisting (anal, vaginal), Following orders, Food Play, Foot worship, Forced bedwetting...

Three pages and my head was already spinning. If I had thought at the beginning that BDSM was a huge field with a myriad of practices, I would have been bursting at the seams. It was worse than I expected – and some of the things listed I couldn't even relate to. I felt lost. Even so, I forced myself to read on and on.

Forced dressing, Forced eating, Forced homosexuality, Forced heterosexuality, Forced masturbation, Forced nudity (private, public), Forced servitude, Forced smoking, Full head hoods, Gags (various options), Gas masks, Gates of Hell (m), Genital sex, Given away to another Dom (temporary, permanent), Golden showers, Gun Play-Fantasy, Hairbrush spankings, Hair pulling, Hand jobs (give, take), Harems (serving with other subs), Harnessing (leather, rope), Having food chosen for you, Having clothing chosen for you, Head (give, take), High heel wearing, High heel worship, Homage with tongue (non-sexual), Hoods, Hot oils (intimate), Hot waxing, Housework (performing), Human puppy dog, Humiliation (private, public), Hypnotism, Ice cubes, Immobilization, Incestual Roleplay-Fantasy, Infantilism, Initiation rites, Injections, Intricate (Japanese) Rope bondage, Interrogations, Kidnapping, Kneeling, Knife play, Leather clothing, Leather restraints, Lectures for misbehavior, Licking (non-sexual), Lingerie (wearing), Manacles & Irons, Manicures (give), Massage (give, take), Medical scenes, Modeling for erotic photos, Mouth bits, Mummification, Name change (for one scene, permanent), Nipple clamps, Nipple rings (piercings), Nipple play/torture, Nipple weights, Oral/anal play, Over-the-knee spanking, Orgasm denial, Orgasm control, Outdoor Scenes, Pain (soft, medium, hard), Persona training, Personality modification, Phone Sex (for the Dom, friends, commercial), Piercings (temporary, permanent), Plastic Surgery, Poison Tolerance-Fantasy, Prison Scenes, Prostitution (public)...

Now I was at my wit's end. But there were still three pages waiting for me to read. I had not yet made up my mind. I had no idea what had been written at the beginning. Once again, I had to force myself to the end of the list.

Prostitution-Fantasy, Pony slave, Public exposure, Punishment scene (private), Cock whipping, Pussy worship, Riding crops, Riding the "horse", Rituals, Religious scenes, Restrictive rules on behavior, Rubber/latex clothing, Rope body harness, Saran wrapping, Scarification, Scratching (give, take), Sensory deprivation,

Serving (various options), Sexual deprivation (short term, long term), Shaving (body, private parts, head), Skinny-dipping, Sleep deprivation, Sleepsacks, Slutty clothing (private, public), Spandex clothing, Spanking, Speech restrictions (when, what), Speculums (anal), Spitting, Spreader bars, Standing in corner, Stocks, Straight jackets, Strap-on dildos (give, take), Strapping, Suspension, Supplying partners for Dom, Swallowing (feces, semen, urine), Swapping (with other couple), Swinging (multiple couples), Tampon training (anal), Tattooing, Teasing, TENS unit (electricity), Thumbcuffs (metal), Tickling, Triple penetration, Urethral sounds, Uniforms, Including others, Verbal Humiliation, Vibrator on genitals, Vampire Scenes, Violet wand (electricity), Voyeurism, Video (watching others, recording oneself), Water torture, Waxing (hair removal), Wax play, Wearing symbolic jewelry, Weight gain (compulsion), Weight loss (compulsion), Whipping, Wooden paddles, Wrestling.

The list ended, but my mind continued to spin. Some of these terms I'd never heard before, others frightened me without even knowing what they were, and some made me think of what Kaden had already done to me. And how I hadn't felt bad about it, but rather the opposite.

But the longer I thought about it, the more I realized how lost I was in this sea of concepts. So many possibilities, so many choices. Not all of them were designed for pleasure, and the overload increased as soon as I thought about which of them Kaden would like, and whether we might disagree so much about them that the project would fail before it began.

If I told him that I thought my sleep was necessary and that there was nothing attractive about being forced to stay awake by him, would he see it the same way? Or did he secretly enjoy depriving someone of sleep? Probably not even in a good way, but for some strange punitive purpose, the implications of which were still a mystery to me.

I felt a dull throbbing in my left temple. This was too much. I couldn't possibly become the mistress of this chaos that all these words were causing in me. What if I just told him to have a go at what he liked and then I would let him know if that was an option for me in the future?

As soon as the idea came to me, I knew instinctively that he would not go for it. I had to give him at least an approximate direction. Tell him what I couldn't even imagine, what points I wasn't averse to, and what I might like. Or had liked, if it counted among the things I had already experienced in the last few days.

So I took the pen and read the list a second time. This time I ticked off what I liked and crossed out what I couldn't imagine – after googling. At the same time, my preferences seemed pretty clear: I didn't want him to be in charge of my life or my body. I didn't want him to cause me permanent harm or put me in situations I would be ashamed of for the rest of my life. I also didn't want him to degrade me to an object or play with bodily fluids other than those naturally present during sex. I didn't want to be pushed, manipulated or forced into anything. I didn't want to live out any strange fantasies, although I didn't mind if he took away all my defenses for a session.

Basically, I wanted nothing more than pleasure and excitement. These experiences broadened my horizons and perhaps helped Kaden and me with our problems. Nothing would break the trust between us or permanently changed us into different people.

However, I could just imagine where the general opinion about Kaden came from with all this new information. Some of these practices were not socially acceptable, and he had never spoken out against the accusations made against him. When one of the women claimed that he liked to use electricity, Kaden had never said anything to the contrary, he had simply let the statement stand on its own merits. It might not have been his preference, but his partner's.

No matter how you looked at it, in the end, Kaden was always called a freak and the woman became a victim because she had to put up with a horrible man like him. The thought almost made me laugh. Kaden was anything but how they made him appear. No one had the right to treat him like this and there was no way I was talking to the press. No matter how close they got to me or what they wanted from me. They would get nothing from me. Even if they saw us together somewhere or published some strange allegations.

It took me quite a while to get back to the last page, and I had written my opinion everywhere. Sometimes I had also noted a comment – for example, that I was not averse to the whole breath control thing, but that Kaden had my complete trust in this case and should not overdo it if he was still interested in playing such games with me.

It was also this comment that made me realize that, in this whole relationship, it was not really Kaden who was the one in control. At least not as far as he was concerned with the dynamics and the rules. At the end of the day, it was always me who decided what he could and couldn't do with me. The loss of my trust was the loss of his privilege in our relationship.

Even though he was ascribed the attribute of dominant and I automatically slipped into the role of submissive, it did not mean he was in control. Or that I was at the mercy of his power.

Kaden was just the one I trusted enough to let it all go, to let myself be drawn into seeing him in that position. Maybe it was even an advantage that we had known each other for so long and were such good friends. He didn't have to earn that trust. After all, he had made sure that I felt it and could rely on him all those years. I hadn't realized how easily that could be extended to other areas. Still, it couldn't get any clearer than in those moments when I filled out nine pages about BDSM practices and signed a contract on a post-it that would make him my master.

I did not feel a trace of anxiety when I walked into Kaden's office later that morning. There was no doubt that I might have made the wrong decision or had to back out. Only absolute certainty that I was doing something that felt right and would take us both forward.

Still, Kaden seemed surprised to see me. Maybe because I had walked right past his secretary and into his office.

He looked at me with a raised eyebrow before ending the phone call without comment and leaning back in his chair with his hands clasped behind his head.

The glass front at his back offered a view of the resort and the sea beyond, but I was busy studying his face, trying to fathom the question I could read on it.

With a little effort, I walked over to his desk and stuck the post-its on the glass in front of him. I tapped my finger on the signature I had placed underneath.

"I recognize the rules from the other contract, but I'm not going to sign it," I explained, sliding the list under his nose. "This confused me for the most part, to be honest. So I ignored the actual scale and instead crossed out what I didn't like, marked what I do like, and noted where I could imagine something but wasn't sure. A few things I had to comment on. And a few things to research."

Again he raised an eyebrow.

"If you want me to eat out of a bowl, that's an immediate deal breaker," I explained.

"Sure. This afternoon we'll go to the nearest pet store so you can pick out your collar and leash," he replied dryly, shaking his head. "Believe me, I'm not interested in making you my lapdog."

An invisible weight fell from my shoulders, but I didn't let it show. A part of me had feared there would be discrepancies and that we would not agree in the end.

Kaden glanced at the list but didn't let on what was going through his mind. There was not the slightest hint of it on his face. No muscle twitch, no reaction in his eyes, not even a grin.

His finger just glided across the paper. Meanwhile he went through the points. "Don't worry. I don't want faeces in my bed," he muttered at one point.

I bounced up and down on my feet, a little unsure. "Why use the list at all when there are so many things that don't even apply?"

He raised his eyes for a moment. "Because I wouldn't present you with a list that has already been filtered through my views. That would mean influencing you. And that's not something I'm in favor of either."

I opened my mouth then closed it again because I wasn't sure what to say, Kaden continued to study the list. I had a strange feeling in my chest, just standing there with my arms crossed in front of his desk, watching him hunch over my most intimate preferences.

I had made myself vulnerable, opened myself up to him in a way that I had never done before, and yet Kaden didn't make me feel like I should regret it.

"I like how honest you were with that list," he said at one point, still not at the end.

Kaden had no idea how overwhelmed I felt. My head was still buzzing, and another concept kept popping up in my mind, bothering me. He had no way of knowing what a monumental effect all this new knowledge had on me – and would have if things continued to develop in this direction. What if there was no more normal sex for me after Kaden? What if he had dragged me into his personal hell and I could no longer live without him because I had become a part of it, just as he had become a part of me?

Had it been the same with him? Had he just wanted to dip his toe in the water and then sunk hopelessly, looking for a needle in a haystack because he hadn't found a woman who could fulfill all his needs?

In spite of everything, his praise gave me a feeling of security. Once again he showed me how responsible he was. How attentive he was to me.

"Thank you," I mumbled after a while, bouncing up and down because I couldn't help but be distracted.

"Your comments could have been a little less sarcastic, but otherwise..." He raised his eyes again and looked at me so intensely that I immediately stopped moving. "I'm very pleased with what I read here, Nika."

"And when will the time come when you strip your soul bare, too and show me the same trust?"

He tilted his head, a little amused by my insistence. "So you can spend the rest of the day turning the internet upside down?"

"I would never..."

"No, you won't. I have a list for you, but I want you to leave everything as it is. No research. When and how I bring any of it to you is my decision."

I pressed my lips together. "That's like showing me a trailer and telling me the film will be released in parts at unknown times."

Kaden raised his hands and shrugged. "But that's the way it is. In easily digestible chunks and whenever I feel like it."

"That's torture."

"And therefore exactly my specialty," he replied with amusement. I saw his expression change in a split second. "Which is why you'll lock the door and do me one more favor."

Immediately, I felt a tingling sensation in my stomach, which spread to my spine and to the rest of my body. I involuntarily held my breath and went to the door to lock it.

When I turned back, Kaden had moved back a foot in his chair and with a simple gesture motioned for me to join him.

My body obeyed without questioning what was happening. My logical mind immediately ceased to function, giving way to a more primitive part that was wired to do exactly what was ordered.

As I rounded Kaden's desk, he gestured with his chin for me to get on my knees in front of him.

I sank to my knees, automatically falling into the position he had taught me. The look on his face made my heart beat even faster.

"You're quick to learn, I like that," he said, with a rough undertone that sent shivers up my arms. "I'm about to finish my conversation from earlier. You'll be under my desk and why don't you try to rattle me? So I have an idea of what that pretty mouth of yours is capable of."

My eyebrow raised. This was a challenge, wasn't it? Not only did Kaden spur me on, no. He made me want to work him so hard that by the end of the conversation he had no idea what it had been all about.

"You can open my belt with your hands. But as soon as your lips are on my cock, your hands are on your thighs. Or your back. I don't want to feel them," he continued. "That's always the case, by the way, Nika. No hands during oral sex."

I suppressed the impulse to nod and waited for him to move closer. As soon as he was sat directly in front of me and I knelt between his strong thighs, I unbuckled his belt and zip, pulled the fabric aside, and leaned back to take a look at what was presented to me.

I had never been interested in Kaden's body in this way before. Now it made me swallow hard to think that his massive erection would be between my lips at any moment, and I had permission to do anything I wanted to him.

I had seen a few cocks in the last few years, but none had this effect on me. I usually avoided looking at them, but in Kaden's case... From his belly button, a dark line stretched downwards, running straight down the middle between the strands of muscle, forming a pronounced V. At the end was what could only be described as God's gift to womankind. Beautiful to look at, enough to make anyone happy, and so hard it would probably catapult me into other spheres when his erection found its way between my legs for the first time, penetrating me inch by inch.

I could feel myself getting wetter – and Kaden's waiting look brought me back to his orders. As much as I would have liked to let my thoughts run wild, I kept them to myself and put my hands on my thighs.

How difficult everything became when you could suddenly only use your mouth. Kaden concentrated on his phone and I had to move closer to reach him.

It was a challenge. But after a few seconds I was

confident enough to slide my tongue along his erection. Warm, slow and wet. I trailed over the places I knew were sensitive and noted with satisfaction how he twitched.

It was only in passing that I realized he was already in the middle of the conversation, which meant I had to hurry – I wanted him to make a mistake. I would give him such a good blowjob that he would lose the plot, not be able to suppress a sound of pleasure or end the call to take control. Depending on the result and Kaden's mood, it wouldn't end with him coming. He would probably punish me for succeeding in making him aroused.

A performance that not only motivated me, but also made me feel another wave of excitement shooting through me and settling between my legs.

I had always loved spoiling a man like that. Although I was in the submissive role, at least in terms of position, this was one of those moments when I felt particularly powerful. It was my doing, what he felt. Caused by my tongue and my skill. I was able to drive him mad. To make him feel dependent because what I was doing was so damn good that he could not just have it only once.

At least, that was my goal. I would soon find out if Kaden felt the same way.

I lowered my eyes as I let his cock slide between my lips for the first time, sucking it lightly before letting it penetrate me even deeper, my mouth closing tightly around it. I pressed my tongue against his erection from below, moving it slightly against him. At first I only worked on his glans, not taking it in all the way, but after a few seconds that was not enough anymore.

Feeling Kaden's erection deeper in my mouth, in my throat, became a necessity. Even though a mixture of spit and precum were already running from my lips, I couldn't help it.

He pressed against my throat, sliding down, making it impossible for me to breathe, but I pushed him deeper into me before I began to find a rhythm. One where he inhaled sharply as soon as I got it just right – and then I kept it up until his chair made a protesting noise and his hand gripped my hair far too tightly.

I continued. Even though I missed the sound of his voice in my ear. All the words he could be whispering to me right now, and he was busy having boring conversations with a business partner…

It wasn't lost on me that there was an attempt on his part to pull away from me. The muscles in his abdomen tightened as he tried unsuccessfully to pull my head back. I teased and stimulated him more and more, lost in the sound of his breathing. By now his grip on my hair was even tighter. His hips jerked toward me, making it clear how close he was to coming.

No reason to stop, was there?

In fact, I should try harder. I let out a sound of amusement. It made his cock twitch so violently I couldn't help humming softly. The throbbing that spread through his erection a second later made me smile.

For the first time since I had started working him with my mouth, I looked up at Kaden. I grinned as I saw the emotion dancing across his face.

He was probably on the verge of killing me at that moment. He hadn't expected me to spoil him like this. Or that it would affect him like that, I guess. It took a lot of strength for him to keep his voice calm and continue the conversation as if he hadn't had the best blowjob in a long time. Kaden looked like he was trying to decide whether to wrap his hands around my neck or grab my head to hold it in place as he used my mouth for his own purposes.

Whatever he decided, the throbbing between my legs would gratefully return the favor. I dug my fingers deeper into my thighs. How perfect would it be if I could touch myself now? Pamper him while I raced toward an orgasm myself?

But his rules were clear. Without his instructions, I wouldn't satisfy myself. So far his punishments had been fun – I didn't really need to know how things would turn out when it got serious. Although it was almost physically painful to feel this arousal and not be able to do anything about it except squeezing my thighs together to feel at least a little friction.

Unexpectedly, the magic words I was looking for reached my ear. "Sorry, but something's come up. I'll call you back later."

Kaden almost growled the words into his phone before carelessly tossing it on his desk.

The next thing I knew, his hands were on my head, pushing it down until my nose brushed against his skin, and for a brief moment I felt truly helpless.

My hands were on my thighs. His erection filled every inch of my mouth, down to my throat. I couldn't breathe and tears gathered in my eyes as drool dripped down my chin.

"I'd fuck you on my desk right now if it wasn't our first time. Or up against the window so all the guests at the resort could see how fucking hot it makes you to enjoy my cock like that. I really do wonder where the hell you learned that."

His last words were accompanied by a guttural sound. It turned into a moan. Kaden liked having control over my mouth. But that didn't stop me from creating a slight vacuum, which made everything so much more intense for him.

He pulled me back a little to give me some air, which I immediately sucked greedily into my lungs. It was only three seconds later, though, that he was back in control of my head. Kaden slid forward on the chair, toward me, before pushing me down and pulling me up again, finding a rhythm that suited him.

With every downward movement of my head, he spoke to me.

"That feels so damn good to me. Do you realize how good?"

I slid upwards.

"Your mouth is so warm and wet. I wonder how much better it will feel when it's your pussy that wraps around me instead of your mouth."

As if my body was forced to respond, the muscles in my pelvis contracted, holding onto nothing... an annoying sensation as I grew to want the feel of him inside me. Even if it was just two fingers teasing me.

"You've done this before, haven't you? You have experience and you like it. The only question is: is it the blowjob itself, your position or my control?" he continued.

He moved my head, accompanied by a deep moan that went right through my bones.

"Show me what you're made of. Show me how much of a good girl you can be. I want you to swallow, Nika. All of it. Every drop. If you don't, you're going to have to clean it all up. From you. My cock. If you spill it, maybe even the floor..." In a reassuring gesture, he ran a finger along my jaw. "And we don't want that now, do we?"

My brain automatically stopped, surrendered and resigned. The mixture of praise and humiliation, command and appreciation, caused some synapses to malfunction. It was as if Kaden knew exactly what words to use to knock me out. As if he had trained to use words to drive me to the brink of madness, to make me forget myself.

I allowed him to continue directing my head and mouth, taking every inch of him. He had not spoken his warning too soon, for seconds later I felt his muscles tense and he finally lost control. He jerked inside me, pulsating as the hot fluid shot into my mouth. I continued to suck on him until the last drop had collected on my tongue and he let me go, breathing heavily as he did so.

With a smug grin on my lips, I leaned back, looked at him triumphantly and opened my mouth to present his seed before swallowing demonstratively, running my tongue over my lips and watching something absolutely wild flash across his face.

Not the reaction I had prepared myself for. Part of me thought he would scoff. Shake his head. Gave any sign that he was disgusted by the gesture. But the opposite was true. A muscle in his cheek twitched, he leaned forward, grabbed my hair and pulled me effortlessly onto his lap so my core was pressed against his hard as steel thigh, creating a friction that almost made me roll my eyes in pleasure.

Kaden grabbed my chin, forcing me to look into his smoldering eyes. "Proud enough to show me your reward like that, too? Fuck. Do you have any idea how hot that was?"

As if that wasn't surprising enough, he pulled me closer. One hand was on my hip, applying pressure so I was forced to rub against him with every movement. The other continued to rest on my chin, guiding me so he could kiss me. His tongue slid into my mouth and for the first time since this little session had begun, I couldn't help but use my hands.

I buried them in his hair, pulled his head back and moaned into the kiss.

It was the fact that he had no objection to me kissing him after I had his dick in my mouth. After coming on my tongue. He didn't even mind tasting himself as he kissed me. It made me long for the next opportunity to get down on my knees and repeat what we had just done.

The kiss pulled me into an ever deepening abyss. Caught in a vortex that only intensified my desire for Kaden and what he dangled in front of me like a juicy steak.

I felt like I would scream if he didn't let me feel his cock inside me soon. But the way things were going, I knew that wasn't going to happen today – and that was on purpose. Not only because he didn't want to fuck me on his desk, but for other reasons that came to me gradually.

Kaden was training me. Making me wait. Increased my lust. He would make me beg for his cock and sex, because he'd made it clear that it wouldn't happen unless I asked for it. This was a game – and whoever gave in first would be the loser. Even if neither of us would lose anything, we'd both get what we wanted.

While Kaden deepened the kiss, I let him feel my teeth and did something that surprised me. I caught his tongue and sucked on it just like I had on his cock. And with the deep rumbling in his chest, his cock rising up between us and pressing against my stomach, I knew he enjoyed it.

He grabbed my hair, pulled my head back and looked me in the eyes. My body was on fire – and not just because of that intense look. But I couldn't name it. I wanted him and what he was doing to me so badly that it almost hurt physically.

"And you've always been convinced you wouldn't like my weird sexual games," he said. "Something tells me you've never felt as good as you do now. Is it the fact that I can feel your wetness through our clothes? The way you look at me? Or that I know how much you're enjoying every second of it? That's even though I haven't even begun, Nika."

All that was just the prelude. Foreplay for what was to come when Kaden really got started. By the time we had taken the next step, there was no longer any barrier stopping him from doing whatever he wanted. He hadn't found a boundary yet, but I was sure he would – because what we'd done so far was just the beginning. Quite normal, though as hot and intense as I had ever known.

How long would it take him to make me burn without anything there to extinguish it?

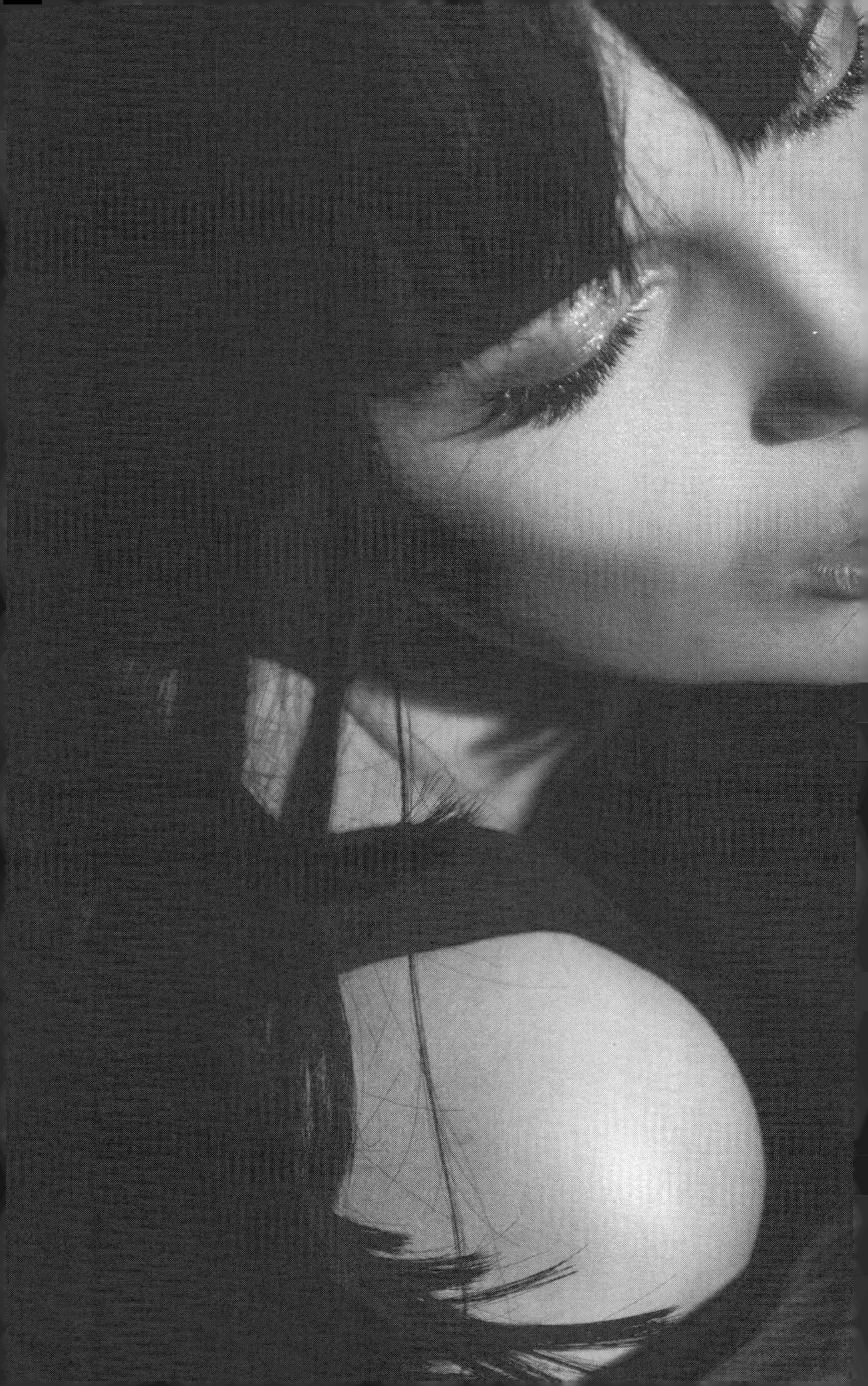

Kaden

It had taken Nikau exactly two weeks to find a woman for me to go out with. Two weeks was far too little time for my taste. It meant she was really trying and following the plan we had discussed. I hated to admit it, but I would have been better off not dating for a while. At least not someone who wasn't Nikau.

Yet here I was in the *Honolulu Sun* restaurant, sitting opposite a woman who wasn't bad-looking, boredly picking at her salad. Either she didn't like it – which made me wonder why she'd even ordered it – or some other explanation had to be found. Was she nervous? Excited?

Actually, she shouldn't have been, because the conversation was like any other I've had on a first date. I asked questions that were relevant to the way things were going. Some people might have found them uncomfortable. But in the end, they made things easier for me. Not that I could say that I have had a great deal of success so far. After all, asking hadn't prevented me from ending up disappointed.

"How many relationships of this kind have you had?" I asked, looking directly at my food so she wouldn't feel I was pressuring her for a quick answer.

"None," she replied after a few seconds, making me raise my eyebrows.

"None? Then what is it that attracts you to the idea?"

"You."

Me? God, that was a rare and stupid reason to get involved in the world of kinks and fetishes.

Since I couldn't help it, I put her to the test. Maybe she just wasn't very good at expressing herself. Or didn't know exactly what she wanted, but had the potential to get better.

As I formulated my question, I looked her straight in the eye. "What would your reaction be if I hit you in the face with my dick during a blowjob?"

And there it was. As reliable as ever. She wrinkled her nose in a fit of disgust and shock. It was minimal and barely noticeable unless you were looking for it. But the reaction was there and sealed her doom in glorious fashion.

I tilted my head. "I don't think it's going to work out between us," I announced, dropping my napkin on the table.

After all, the memory of Nikau's reaction was still

there – enough to make my cock come alive. She didn't know it, but sometimes when I did certain things, this filthy smirk would creep across her lips, showing just how dirty she could be and how much she liked the situation we were in.

However, we had not ended up in bed in the last two weeks because I wanted to give her some time to get used to the new circumstances. To what I was showing her. To working in the kitchen. Coming to O'ahu was certainly an adjustment after almost ten years in Iowa.

But that reticence was finally over. And the failed date seemed like the perfect hook for what I had wanted to do to her for so long.

So, without further ado, I got up, waved to the waiter to settle the bill, and nonchalantly said goodbye to the lady sitting across from me, who didn't seem to have quite grasped what was going on.

She looked as if something had been stolen from her. Something she would never have got anyway. Because she just wasn't the right woman.

SOMEHOW I FAILED TO KNOCK ON THE DOOR OF NIKAU'S apartment in a self-effacing manner. I heard footsteps and seconds later she opened the door. She looked at me suspiciously.

"Aren't you supposed to have a date?" She

glanced over her shoulder at the clock on the wall, then back at me. Inquiringly.

"Where did you find her?"

"Trade secret."

"And she told you she had experience in doing what I'm looking for, right?"

"I wouldn't have chosen her otherwise."

"Do you know how she reacted when I asked her what she would do if I hit her in the face during a blowjob – with my cock?"

Nikau made a face. "No. I wasn't there, K."

"She wrinkled her nose. Like that was so weird. And disgusting."

"You can't expect everyone to be enthusiastic about that."

"Well, assuming it's still relatively normal compared to the rest... I'm afraid her and I are not going to see eye to eye."

"And you've come to me with a complaint that the first date wasn't the one?"

I heard the challenge in her voice. The way she looked at me, waiting to see what I would do next.

"What is it that upsets you so much, K?" she continued after a few seconds of me not giving her an answer.

Maybe it was the wasted time that upset me. Or maybe it was the way it had always happened in the past few years. Or maybe it was just because a part of me was relieved that the adventure with Nikau wasn't over yet, but would officially begin tonight.

"I'm just wondering what I'd like better. Spanking you for letting that woman lie to you. Or tying you to my bed and watching the *Hitachi* rip ten orgasms out of you in a row. Either way, before you feel me inside you, some part of your body will be sensitive as hell." Satisfied, I noticed her lips parting slightly. Was she shocked? Or did I sense anticipation in the air?

"It wasn't my fault she lied to me," she answered, too obstinate to notice I was already half way to tearing off her clothes and using her body against her. At least mentally. In reality, she wasn't even in my flat. She was still in her own.

"You should know these women would say anything to date me. So that's no plausible excuse."

"Excuse? God, K, it's like I send you on bad dates on purpose," she grumbled, shaking her head. "But fine. Punish me for her lies. If it makes you feel better about yourself."

We both knew this was just an act. A way to build the bridge that had only existed in theory up to that point.

For two weeks, I had denied myself the pleasure of putting my cock anywhere near her pussy. And every day it felt more and more like torture. Using her mouth and exploring the limits of her body was no longer enough. I wanted to be inside her, to torture her in new ways, and to make her come while being as close to her as possible.

"You know what to do," I finally announced in a

dark voice, stepping aside so she could leave her apartment and comply with my request.

With her head held high, Nikau walked past me and let herself into my apartment under my watchful eye. I pulled out my phone, took one look at the notifications and made sure I would have peace and quiet for the rest of the night. No interruptions. Just Nika and me. And what I wanted to do.

I walked into the open living room, letting the door fall into the lock behind me. For the past two weeks, I had been teaching her to kneel and wait for my attention – with her back to the door, looking out onto the open terrace. The reason for this was rather selfish: I liked to see the moon and the palm trees towering above her, the cool breeze blowing around our feet, and the soft light casting shadows on her skin, which had regained a sunny tan. Hawaii had done her good, even if she wouldn't admit it.

Although I couldn't wait to get started, I took my time. As I watched her, I rolled up the sleeves of my shirt, my eyes fixed on the curve of her back.

She was undressed and kneeling on the cold tiles, legs slightly apart, hands on her thighs. Her chin was raised, her back straight, and her shoulders relaxed.

Most people didn't realize how appealing it could be to see a person posed like that. Not only because of the body's appearance, but also because of its meaning. It would mean weakness to some. But it filled me with pride when I saw Nika like this.

And I wasn't the only one affected by the position.

Even from several feet away I could see goosebumps on her arms, slowly spreading down her back. She was tense. A feeling of anticipation. A little excitement because she never knew exactly what was going to happen. But that, too, was a point of appreciation on my part. She had enough trust in me to hold the position and not turn her head every few seconds for a peek.

I casually opened a dresser drawer, took out some items and placed them on the bed. I knew this would drive her more insane – knowing I was preparing something, but not able to guess what it was.

Finally, I approached her and placed a hand on the nape of her neck, circling my thumb until she tilted her head. She almost made me smile as her temple rested against my leg.

Every time I touched her in this way, there was a response. To every word. To every praise, even if it was accompanied by a rather harsh term of endearment. Maybe it was the support she needed, the reassurance that her actions and reactions would not be the subject of ridicule. Or maybe Nika just liked it, because every time I used my words against her, she just got all the wilder. And wetter.

To get her to that point I didn't really need my hands or toys. All it took was the right choice of words. Which in turn made me want her even more. It was a vicious circle I couldn't escape.

"You do realize I could spend all night looking at you kneeling in the moonlight, don't you?"

Of course she didn't react. Just as I had taught her. She had learned these rules quickly. And obviously Nika had no problem sticking to them, except for when she wanted to challenge me. These were the moments when she seemed to forget everything. So I learned what sort of reaction she expected from me and played along.

But that would not be the case tonight, so I let my fingers run through her hair until I finally decided it was time to move on to the fun part.

So I grabbed her by the hair, wrapped it around my fist, and in one fluid motion pulled her to her feet, dragging her behind me as I headed for the bedroom.

There was no need to force her into any position. As soon as I led her to the bed, she automatically got down on all fours before lowering her upper body so only her bare ass was facing me. My eyes slid over the flawless skin and between her legs. Her pussy gleamed.

Words and gestures. Nothing more.

For I had not yet touched her in any place that could be described as an erogenous zone.

Without me being able to stop it, I made a satisfied, almost appreciative sound. Whenever I had Nika wet in front of me, I wanted nothing more than to bury my face between her legs and taste her until I could no longer breathe. But this was a small detail I would rather keep to myself.

"The plans have changed. I want to see how long it takes for your arousal to run down your thighs while I spank you. If you're good... we'll see if it's enough to make you come." I loved playing with this idea. To make her think this was not going to end with her coming. It had recently become one of my favorites, watching her come uncontrollably after torturing her for a while by denying it.

In an inviting gesture, she stretched her ass toward me again. As if she couldn't wait for me to start torturing her. Smirking, I slid my hand down her back before moving over her hips and finally to her ass, which nestled perfectly and roundly in the palm of my hand.

At first it was just a light slap, warming her skin and testing how sensitive she was today. It was not our first time in this position, so I was not surprised how quietly she accepted the first smack.

I increased the intensity of the slaps as Nika's skin began to redden.

"If you could see what I see..." I murmured. There was no hiding the excitement in my voice.

Her hips swayed from side to side. Back and forth, always waiting for the next blow to come down. It was certainly unintentional, which made it all the more seductive.

But it was equally attractive to see the marks of my hand and fingernails on her ass. The light scratches, the red discoloration, the way she moaned when I switched sides, without the slightest hint of pain in her moans... It was moments like these that made me wonder who was controlling whom, who was twisting whom around their finger.

I was the one who dominated Nika. But she had at least as intense an effect on me. I was into manipulating her body and getting the reactions I liked – only most of the time it was the same things she liked. Which made it even better...

I struck again, enjoying the way she drew in the air sharply, and then let my fingers slide through her folds, only to bring them to my lips and taste her. A soft moan escaped my lips before I slid my fingers through her core again. This time I spread her wetness all over her ass.

"Do you feel that? You are soaking wet. It's from my spanking, isn't it? Do you think other women get so wet when you spank them, whispering *good girl* into their ears? Or is it the thought of calling you *my dirty little whore* again?" I tried a different combination of words each time we played. Sometimes I would just praise her and tell her how much fun I had playing with her. But other times I would use much harsher language. In a normal context, the statements were in no way perceived as nice or flattering. Nika accepted them all. A little voice in my head kept whispering that it wouldn't be long before it became a fixed term of endearment. I would no longer be able to hold myself back when she accidentally used one for me.

Feeling her pussy throbbing, I trailed my fingertip over her clit, letting her soar in the pleasure this simple touch brought, before sliding back down to her reddened ass to continue what I'd done before. But not without giving her what I had hinted at earlier.

With a smug grin, I reached for the vibrator and turned it on at the lowest level. It was only then that I reached out for the tape. Without commenting, I pressed it against her thigh and taped it down. The head of the vibrator rested just below her pussy. She felt the vibrations but had no direct contact.

What was sure to become torture sooner or later, because to have her own orgasm just out of reach again and again, without making it over the edge, would soon be more painful than any spanking I could give her. Regardless of whether I used my hand or the paddle I had prepared.

I watched in amusement as her leg muscles tensed and she moved her hips, this time looking for a position that would allow her to press her pussy against the vibrations and give herself the release she desperately needed.

I stroked her hip with a reproving sound before giving her another slap. Once again the imprint of my hand appeared. There was no doubt that she would think of this moment over and over again tomorrow whenever she sat down. And I liked the idea of her walking around for a few hours with my handprint on her ass, even though we both agreed there would be no permanent traces of our games with each other. Maybe later I would add the marks of my teeth…

Her frustrated moans encouraged me, so I reached for the paddle. Sliding the smooth wood across the back of her thighs, I let her know what was coming next.

"I hope you are prepared," I mused. The combined pain and pleasure, the constant arousal, would bring her to her limits sooner than I preferred. I knew the addiction from finding pleasure in the combination of the two. As long as the pleasure was greater than the pain, the latter would always fade into the background, a mere side note that added to the overall mix and provided additional stimulation.

I let the paddle whiz across her bottom and watched as she jerked, followed by an uncontrolled sigh. Her hands dug into the mattress but her body made no attempt to escape me or the source of the blow. Instead, she tilted slightly, exposing her neck.

Whether it was an invitation or a natural movement of her body, I leaned forward. I let my tongue slide over her shoulders and continued upward until my erection pressed against her ass through my trousers. She let out a sharp hiss. The friction against her irritated skin must have given her an exceptional sensation...

Grinning, I moved to her neck. I kissed it and let her feel my teeth. I sucked the sensitive spot under her ear until she moaned in pleasure and bit her lower lip.

"I know what you're doing," I murmured. Leaning over her, I could almost feel the vibrations hitting her clit. "But it doesn't work like that. You'll get to the point where you'll find out how it works," I assured her as I pulled back to give her the next stroke. Nika jumped.

"What the hell could I possibly want from you, huh?" I asked, letting my hand glide over her ass for a change. I felt the heat of the skin, the swelling that appeared and especially where it was now most sensitive.

From the very first second, I had secretly waited for those words to come out of her mouth. I wanted her to beg me to fuck her. I wanted to hear her say she finally wanted to feel my cock inside her. That she needed me and was ready for anything I could give. Time and time again she had come close. Only to bite her tongue and remain silent.

Did she think I would abandon my principles because her pussy was too tempting to resist? Even if it caused me physical pain not to sink into her. I could wait. Waiting for her to swallow her pride, as she had already done several times, and finally do us both a favor.

Since the night I made her kneel for the first time, we both had been aware this would eventually lead to sex. Only one final step was needed.

I licked my lips and struck her again with the paddle. Then I put it down to let her feel my hand again.

Her moisture was now clinging to her thighs, just as I had predicted. It glimmered in the soft light of the bedside lamp, the only source of light in the otherwise darkened bedroom.

The vibrator was still vibrating just below her pussy and when I leaned down to let her feel my hot breath on her sensitive core, it was the first breach in the dam.

Nika cursed. "Please let me come," she whimpered. The mattress almost swallowed her plea.

"Is that all you desire? Just one orgasm? Pressing the vibrator against your pussy and making you come is enough for you?"

She shook her head.

"Be a good little slut for me and use your goddamn words," I growled, grabbing her hair and pulling her head back enough to force her to open her eyes and look at me.

I recognized her rapt gaze, the lust dancing in her dark pupils. The way her breath caught as she was trapped in this aroused state, with no way out... but secretly, she had. All she had to do was tell me what it was she wanted.

"Words, Nika," I admonished again, leaning toward her. Once again, my erection pressed against her ass and pussy. "This is what you want, isn't it? Why do you find it so hard to say it? Why don't you just say that you want my cock, huh? I've heard a lot of dirty things come out of your mouth in the last two weeks, but those words have never left your lips. I wonder why that is."

I let go, straightened up, and removed the tape.

Then I increased the vibrations. I grabbed her neck, pressed her torso into the mattress and her face into the sheet before sliding the vibrator over her pussy.

A gasp of surprise escaped her. It was a nice response, but it was not enough.

"Give me a few seconds and you'll be screaming for me all on your own," I continued before pressing the vibrator against her clit, applying extra pressure that caused her to automatically try to escape the thrilling sensation.

But no matter how hard she tried to pull away from me or break contact with the toy, there was no escaping.

"All along you've been so eager to rub your clit against it... now I'm giving you what you want, and you..." I stopped myself as her climax hit her so unexpectedly that I had trouble keeping her on her knees and the vibrator in the same place.

For a few seconds the muscles in her body twitched. Her pussy clenched, accompanied by her panting and moaning. Then the tension drained from her completely. But of course, the vibrator never stopped.

"What? Were you under the impression that it was over after that one orgasm?" Not two minutes passed before she came again, this time even more violently than before. My name left her mouth. I almost believed she wasn't going to give in this time either, but then she seemed to have finally reached the point where she was no longer afraid to say what she really wanted.

"Please," she began. The sound of her voice was a clear indication of how much she still had to overcome – and how much the two orgasms had already taken away from her. "Please fuck me already, Kaden, please. I need to feel you inside me. Orgasms are no longer enough... I want more."

I tossed the toy aside at the pleading undertone in her voice. I grabbed her by the ankles and with a jerk I flipped her onto her back.

Nika's hair was dishevelled and her cheeks flushed. There was a glassy glint in her eyes as her gaze followed my hands, which were pulling the belt out of the loops of my trousers. I let it fall to the floor, got out of my trousers and took off my shirt in record time. And still I did not lie down with her.

Instead, I reached for my cock, which had been almost painfully hard since the first minute, and pumped it into my fist a couple of times, my eyes fixed on her face as Nika stared at my erection.

I felt my cock throbbing in my hand, the head getting wetter... and saw her impatience growing.

"Legs, Nika," I growled, watching her spread her thighs.

She ran her tongue over her lips and as much as I loved watching my cock disappear into her mouth, that wasn't going to happen today. Today I would have the pleasure of watching my cock slide into her to the hilt.

I climbed onto the bed and lay down between her legs, which promptly closed around my hips, because it was no longer just torture for me. With one hand I took hold of her thigh and pushed her back down onto the bed, making her open up even more for me.

It was only then that I allowed the tip of my cock to slide through her pussy, spreading her moisture all over me, and when I finally pressed against her entrance, I did not feel the slightest resistance, but rather an invitation.

It took all my patience not to close my eyes and just let go.

I almost lost my mind as the first few inches slid into her. I felt something savage rise inside me. The need to just fuck her. Not considering that this was our first time together, but just to make sure all the pent-up excitement finally subsided.

I grabbed her chin and forced her to look me in the eye.

"You know how much I fucking care about you, don't you?" I asked, my voice barely under control.

She nodded, unable to do anything else.

I was only a few inches inside her and yet her pussy was already tightening around me. As if she was never going to let me go.

"Good, because I'm going to fuck you like I don't." That was all the warning I could give her before I released her head, grabbed the wall in front of us and hit home inside her with a well-aimed, long and powerful thrust.

She slid up on her own, but I followed her until I had a hand between the headboard and her skull to keep her from hurting herself.

But that didn't stop me from thrusting furiously into her. I forgot my plans, my intentions, my role. I just fucked her. It was the sounds of us, aroused and pleasured, that filled the room.

Nika's fingernails dug into my upper arms as her legs spread further apart, giving me more room to move. It almost hurt when our hips collided. But it wasn't enough.

This wasn't just sex. My world was in turmoil – and, from the look on her face, so was hers.

For a brief moment I had a smug grin. "What's wrong, huh?" I asked, almost provocatively. "Tell me what you need."

At the same time I knew what it was that she needed. More orgasms and me turning her brain to mush, so she would continue to be unable to use words.

The only thing that came out of her mouth was a moan – and my name, which now sounded more like a prayer.

Deeper and deeper I went, harder and harder. Faster and faster because I could no longer hold back. Or wanted to. Instead, there was only one goal: to bring us both to orgasm, to feel her pussy tighten around me as I came deep inside her, absorbing every last drop of my cum.

I did not expect it to feel so intense. Or that it

would make me want to go on like this all night. That I would make her mine in every position imaginable.

Perhaps later, when I put her on my cock and watched her ride me, it would catapult me into another dimension. But for now...

I leaned down and brought our lips together, pulling her lower lip between mine before releasing it. "I didn't know it would feel so good to be inside you. Do you know how ferocious it feels when you squeeze me? God, if I didn't want to experience your orgasm like this, I could come inside you right now."

Her answer was a moan, as if the words had put her in a completely different sphere and made everything even more intense. She probably had the same feeling as I did – sex with Nika was like everything I had ever had before was just a bad copy of what I really wanted all the time.

My imagination had never been in tune with reality, and at one point I really did think it was me, and I had just had too much imagination. Too much desire. But now... Now I knew it had not been.

There was someone who could claim my mind and make sure everything I had longed for would happen. Nikau was what I had never looked for, but somehow found. And if she was somehow able to present me with a woman who could do the same, I would persuade her to teach her how to have the same effect on me as she did. Only then would I release her from her duties.

Thoughts raced through my mind. But they

weren't enough to delay the inevitable. The way Nika's body pressed against mine, her muscles contracting around my cock, making it almost painful to thrust into her, made me see stars just seconds later.

I came inside her, fingers digging into her thigh so that I could at least find something to hold on to as the seconds dragged on, my cock twitching inside her.

When I finally pulled out of her and dropped onto the bed next to her, I would have liked to have just closed my eyes and stayed there. At least for a few minutes, so my body could come back into harmony with my mind, and it would no longer feel like I was in a beehive.

But Nika stopped me in my tracks as I caught a glimpse of her smirk out of the corner of my eye. I turned in her direction. There was that telltale twinkle in her eyes too, just before she shook her head and laughed.

"We're fucked, aren't we?" she asked. "Sex with your bestie. Everyone says there's no going back. I now have a feeling all those people were right."

I raised my eyebrows skeptically. But she continued. She turned in my direction, still seemingly amused by something I could not quite comprehend.

"I'll always have to compare it to tonight, no matter who I go to bed with in the future." There was a hint of uncertainty in her voice as to whether that was a good or a bad thing.

But I had a very clear opinion about it – and that was that I was only too happy to accept this compliment. And I was glad that for the next few months there would be no comparison between me and anyone else. It was not only in the contract. My ego also had a say in this.

And although I could have said something about it, I decided to keep my mouth shut and let this statement stand for itself. Nikau didn't like to admit it, but she was slowly being taken over by the dark side. In a horror movie, this would have been the part where you would have seen black tentacles approaching the main character, just to bore into her skin and claim her, down to the last fiber of her being. To possess her.

That's how it felt when you first started getting involved with kinks. In the beginning, you believed there was nothing out there that could in any way hold you captive. But the more you discovered and attempted, the worse it became.

So in the future, Nika would not be comparing just this one night. She would compare everything. Every moment we had spent together. Every gesture on my part that no other man had made toward her. With everything I did, with every action I took, I infiltrated her and her mind. Her needs.

Not that I didn't know that before. That's what an intense relationship of this kind entailed, but slowly thoughts began to creep in, pointing out what this could do to reality.

I pushed the thoughts away and instead reached for Nikau, forcing her to slide closer to me. Not only did she deserve the physical closeness, she needed it to properly process what had happened and gently come down from the high without falling into a deep hole.

So I made sure she felt comfortable, I forgot what I'd been thinking, and it all came to a fitting end, leaving nothing unresolved.

I was as happy about my rule that she had to sleep beside me on such nights as I was about the fact that she could grow from all these sessions. Finally taking that last step didn't feel like a mistake. In fact, it was opening up entirely new possibilities that had never occurred to us before.

If I wanted to fuck her on my desk while a boring meeting went on in the background, I could do that now. If I wanted to claim her in the pool in the middle of the night, nothing stood in the way – except maybe the one curious guest who wandered the grounds at midnight.

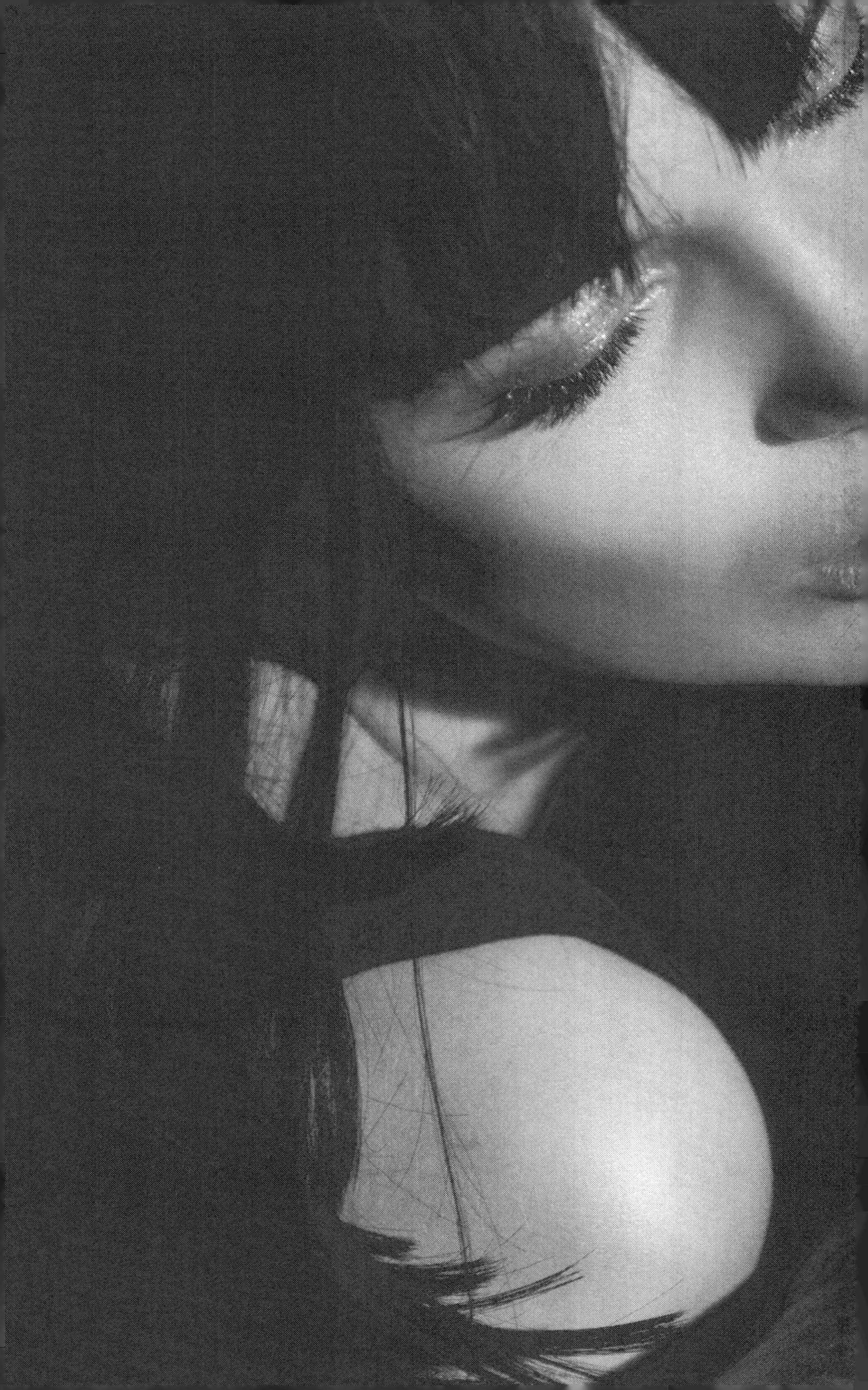

Nikau

Since I started working at the *Honolulu Sun* restaurant, I had never felt more comfortable going to work. Instead of a boss like Jane, I now had a team of people who loved their work. People who loved being available for all the guests every day. People who, even after eight hours, still had a real smile on their face. Maybe it was the place of work – or maybe it was just the fact that everyone had that kind of appreciation and no one felt like they were carrying the whole team on their shoulders.

The *Honolulu Sun* restaurant was top-notch. The kitchen was run by a star chef and his highly professional team. All the waitresses were given exclusive training. The interior was equally sophisticated. The huge glass front opened to the sea, while the walls were painted in dark colours. The almost black wood used for the furnishings made everything look even nobler when the sun's rays flooded the rooms, making you remember what a unique place you were in.

Not only did I appreciate my colleagues, but also the guests. They were a completely different experience to those I had served in Iowa. There was also a bar and people drinking – but for some reason everything seemed more friendly. Maybe that was the cultural difference. Maybe it was the fact that the bartender was also specially trained and knew exactly what he was doing when he pointed out that something wasn't going as it was supposed to go.

Working in the restaurant also showed me what kind of guests the resort catered for. It was one thing to run a luxury resort, but quite another to decide what kind of clientele it attracted. If Kaden had any say in the matter, he had probably chosen the best of both worlds. Most of the guests seemed to be well off. They had traveled from various countries to spend a few quiet and relaxing days here. The other guests were locals. They didn't come for the beauty of Hawaii, but because they appreciated what the *Honolulu Sun* had to offer.

The spa took up a considerable amount of space and made even those happy who didn't normally like to relax.

I had spent almost four weeks in Hawaii, and it didn't take more than two days for the island to captivate me again. Every day that I worked at the restaurant, the idea of going back to Iowa became less in my mind. To be honest, I didn't want to leave Hawaii. There was no place I felt more at home than O'ahu. It may have been a couple of years in the making, but now that I was clear about it... it was also obvious that I had already broken one of my intentions.

Because I had fallen in love with this island, this place, and had re-rooted. I tried to ignore it, but it was probably so deep that by the end of twelve months it would be impossible to leave. My heart would be broken – just as it was back then.

To wake up every morning and feel the sun on my face. To go outside and smell the unique scent of nature. To feel good all over. To the point where work didn't feel like work.

No matter how late I stayed up, I got up with renewed vigor the next day. Not once did the thought cross my mind to pull the blanket over my head and stay in bed.

Life in Hawaii seemed too good to miss a second of it. Secretly, it bothered me because it meant that Kaden's plan was coming to fruition. Only because I was here.

As if my thoughts had summoned the devil, I noticed someone entering the restaurant, though it was some time before the first customers arrived.

It was not Kaden, as I had suspected, but his sister. It was impossible to overlook the fact that the two of them were related. Kaia was also tall. Long, dark curls fell over her shoulders, covered with freckles. She grinned as she approached me.

Her eyes glanced around the room, but she didn't seem to dislike anything she saw. I had grown fond of the restaurant, and it was important to me that it always looked its best. Accordingly, I invested a lot of time in the realization of everything that was part of the resort.

"How's it going?" she asked, leaning against the bar next to me. The kitchen was busy, but it would be awhile before the service team arrived.

"I can't complain," I replied. She probably knew that was an understatement. So I just went on. "I thought it would be weird working for Kaden. We spend a lot of time together, and then he pays me... but to be honest, I wouldn't change it."

Kaia's face lit up. "That's what I wanted to hear. Jean told me how happy he is with you. He may not be the boss here, but his word carries weight. We'd be out of business without his cooking."

I felt a blush creep up my neck. Jean was one of those men who had seen most of the world. Who could have worked anywhere, but for some genuine reason had chosen a particular place. In everything he created, you could see how passionate he was about it – and whenever he needed me to help, I came to help. He could use every hand, even when it was hectic outside.

"That's why I want you to take over the position as our restaurant manager. Kelsi resigned this morning because she has to go back to her family on the mainland and the position has become vacant. I had considered giving it to Corey because he's been here the longest. But I think we should give promotions according to other criteria."

I slowly opened my mouth, then closed it again, not knowing what to say.

Kaia laughed. "You're entitled to be happy, Nika. This is a wonderful development."

"Does Kaden know?"

"Meaning is he behind this in secret?"

I nodded and she shook her head. "I haven't told him about the resignation or my decision. I didn't want you to think he was favoring you."

"And you don't either?"

"I value your work and what I've heard about it. But if you don't want to…"

"Yes, I do," I sighed quickly. Nervously. Take charge? Even though I had done it many times in Iowa, it had never come with the title. Nor had it come with the perks that went with it. I'd always felt the duties and punishments when things didn't go Jane's way… and now I was about to be officially promoted to restaurant manager of the *Honolulu Sun*?

Now a grin spread across my face.

"There you go. That's what I wanted to see," Kaia purred. "I'll email you the amended contract later. There's a party on the beach tomorrow night. You pick up where Kelsi left off with her planning. Oh, and I'll see you at Kaden's tonight – we're celebrating the promotion."

She backed away, waved, and disappeared from

the restaurant. I didn't wait a second, though, and ran to the back and burst through the swinging doors. Jean looked up from his pot just in time to intercept my fierce embrace.

Grinning, I planted a kiss on the older man's cheek.

"Promotion?" he asked in his French accent – a slight hint in his voice that he already knew.

I nodded. The next thing I knew, he was grabbing my hand, spinning me around, and doing a happy dance with me.

"Congratulations, girl. What I've seen of you in the last few weeks shows that you've got what it takes. Kelsi was good, but you're going to rock. Take two hours to familiarise yourself with everything and tonight you'll show everyone". The genuine joy on his face made me happy. It showed me that I had come to the right place. That I hadn't made a mistake in accepting Kaden's strange offer.

Hawaii was my home. O'ahu was my island. And I could finally explore the version of myself I had suppressed for so long in the *Honolulu Sun*. Because of my family. Iowa. Jane. All those things that had always mattered. Now they had absolutely no value.

I hugged Jean once more before heading into the office. It wasn't going to get any easier just because I got promoted.

Kaia handed me the champagne glass, a mint leaf and a raspberry floating in it, and toasted me. It was just before midnight, Kaden was still in the office and I had been back from the restaurant for less than an hour. But I wasn't tired, nor did I feel the need to send Kaia away.

We had got on well before, although we had never spent much time together. Sometimes we had just bumped into each other. At school. At her parents' house. In between, Kaden had dragged her along when he had to look after her.

Our glasses clinked and I took a sip. It tingled on my tongue. Kaia pointed to the table and the small cake on top.

"Jean made that. Nothing you can get in the supermarket."

I would have recognized the star chef's signature even without her mentioning it. He was always meticulous about what he cooked, trying to add that extra kick that ordinary food didn't provide. So whatever he had backed was bound to be a surprise in my mouth. He had probably been experimenting with unusual flavor combinations again and – just like that – had come up with something that could only be described as terrific.

"I still don't know what to say about this favor." Even though, strictly speaking, it hadn't been one. In fact, there was no doubt in my mind that Kaia's choice had been on the basis of the criteria she had mentioned, but not explained any further.

"How about I put a cherry on top?" she asked, emptying her glass and setting it down before looking at me urgently. "I'm glad you're here, Nika. Not just glad. Euphoric is more like it. For the past few weeks, Kaden has been... more Kaden than ever. I don't think anyone but me has noticed, but he'd lost himself in the last few years. Work was his priority. I don't know if I ever saw him relax. I can't remember if he ever laughed in all that time. But since you've been here... he's at peace again. I'd like to slap him for waiting so long to bring you here. After all, I've had to put up with his moods, and it's rarely been fun." Kaia winked. But she stood by her words. I knew that. None of what she said was meant to reflect poorly on Kaden. She used what she said to make a point.

And I understood that point, even though one of those statements made my chest tighten. We had been moving at cross-purposes for so long and had no problem finding each other again. It was as if we had never been apart. It was uncanny. A little dubious, if you like.

Still, I was happy about it. Especially for Kaden, but also for myself, because without him I wouldn't be here.

"It's not only good for him if we're honest," I replied. I mumbled because I didn't want to admit it in front of Kaia. "I still can't believe he screwed up the second date already."

Though Kaia didn't know the exact details, she

did know that Kaden and I were going to bed together – and that I was in the process of finding him a wife. She'd never asked me to elaborate, but I hadn't failed to notice the raised eyebrows whenever we talked about this.

"Maybe you need to practice dating with him. Who knows, maybe he acts like a total idiot," Kaia suggested, with the broad grin of a younger sister who loved nothing more than getting on her brother's nerves.

"You mean I should establish myself as his personal dating coach?"

"Exactly. He doesn't need coaching in bed, of course, but when it comes to dating... Maybe he really is a bit awkward."

I couldn't imagine a man like Kaden making mistakes on a date. Quite the opposite, in fact. Whenever we had gone out together, he had behaved like a gentleman. Never for a second had it felt forced. We had never run out of things to talk about. But we had also known each other for many years and there was an undeniable chemistry between us. Everything was easier for me in his presence. I was sure he felt the same.

Irritated, I wrinkled my nose. "This would turn into role playing. We'd have to do the pretense of being strangers and..."

"Actually, I'd take a wager on how long it would take him to be annoyed by that."

Smirking, I shook my head. "I'm afraid he's not even going to get involved."

"Try it. And then report back to me. Or maybe I should be a fly on the wall."

"You probably should have done that on the last two dates," I replied, turning just in time to see Kaden lean against the frame of the patio door and give us both a disparaging look.

"I had no idea there would be a private party on my terrace. And that it would be so bad that there wouldn't even be music."

Kaia rolled her eyes. "We're celebrating, grumpy. Nika?"

Waiting, Kaden looked at me. He seemed curious, and I could barely contain the joy inside me. It was such a small thing, and yet I felt the need to hug someone again, to rejoice with them.

"I got promoted to restaurant manager today," I explained with a grin.

Kaden's eyebrow went up. "You'd think I'd know everything that's going on at my resort, but apparently that's a mistake."

His eyes darted to Kaia. I couldn't interpret it correctly, but it didn't matter because the next moment he was coming toward me to congratulate me on my success with the strong hug I had longed for just a moment ago.

I was afraid it would seem wrong. That it would feel wrong. But the opposite was true. Even though Kaden had everything under control, he seemed genuinely happy for me. It might have irritated him that Kaia had made the decision without his consent, but in the end it didn't matter.

Over my head, Kaden must have spotted the cake, because I felt him stretch out his arm. "We should make a rule. If there's cake in my flat, I want to be informed immediately."

He pulled away from me, only to take a knife to the cake. What he did to the cake could not be described otherwise. In the end, however, a plate with a slice of cake was in my hand, so I had no complaints.

With an indulgent sound, Kaia popped the first bite into her mouth.

"But before you make someone assistant manager, I want to be informed," Kaden said, pointing his fork at Kaia and then, without waiting for her answer, pounced on his piece of cake.

Smiling, I did the same, but not without enjoying the whole package. Kaden stood next to me, the lukewarm night hugged my body. The sea roared in the background. The scent of the countless flowers and trees wafted through the air.

Everything was more than perfect. I was in paradise in the truest sense of the word – I had been given a piece of the cake called a contented life.

I looked at Kaden with a sincere smile, gave him a quick sideways glance and then turned my eyes to Kaia.

If I had to choose a family, it would probably

always be the one on this terrace with me. I had never felt as comfortable with my sisters in Iowa as I did right now.

Kaden leaned over, took the champagne glass from my hand and raised it. "To you. It wasn't part of the plan for you to have a career here, but I can't say I have any objections. I'm happy about it."

Kaia seemed pleased with her brother's response, nodding in agreement and pouring herself more champagne. "To the *Honolulu Sun*. And here's to the sun shining again since Nika got here."

I snorted as Kaden rolled his eyes. Still, a grin tugged at the corners of his mouth and he had a hard time suppressing it.

I was already screwed, not even four weeks in. It was still eleven months to go. How I was going to get through them was beyond my comprehension.

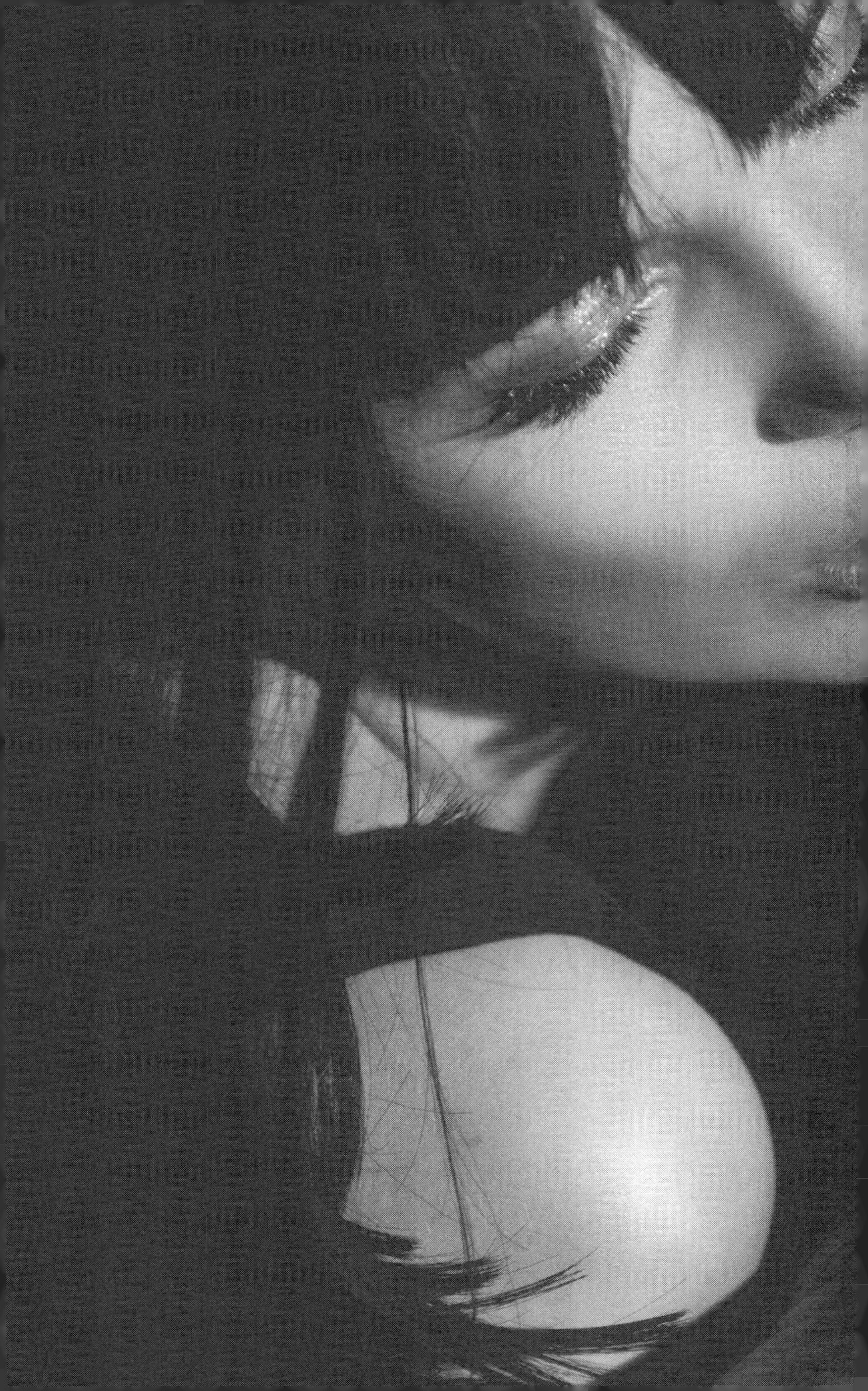

Kaden

"If you want me to do this, then you owe me a date on my terms," I growled, wrinkling my nose slightly.

I seriously wondered where she'd gotten this damned idea. Pretending I didn't know her – so we could practice dating, so she could judge whether I'd made enough effort on the other dates she'd sent me on... by God, did Nika really think I was sabotaging her? The exact opposite was the case. I was trying my hardest to see something in all these women that intrigued me. But I was just as fussy as ever.

If it became clear within the first twenty minutes of a date that a woman was no good, what was the point of getting to know her? And I wasn't trying to say that these women weren't capable of being in a relationship. Absolutely not! It was just that they were not capable of being in a relationship with me.

"Aren't we doing almost everything on your terms anyway, Kaden?" asked Nika, raising an eyebrow.

I clenched my hand into a fist under my desk. Not because I felt the need to hit anyone. But because she wanted to make a ridiculous fuss to find out what mistakes I had made on a date.

"You expect me to pretend I don't know you. I know what you like to eat, what makes you sick, how you sleep, how you shower, and how you stand in front of your wardrobe in the morning just to put on the same clothes you always wear. I know what you eat for breakfast and most importantly, I know what your pussy feels like inside. And now I'm supposed to forget all of that so we can pretend that we met by chance and go out on a date. In case it wasn't clear enough, I hate role playing." Our eyes met intensely, but Nikau didn't look away. She kept eye contact until I finally looked down. She shook her head.

"How do you think I act when I go on these dates? I don't fool around. I try really hard. But these women aren't…"

I didn't finish the sentence.

"I don't even want to hear that, K. We have a deal, and if you want me to do what I promised, you better try harder on the dates."

"I'm going to do that without you having to test me."

"What's wrong with that, huh?"

Whoever had put that idea in her head ought to burn in hell.

"Everything," I growled. "Or do I need to repeat what I just said?"

"No need," she hissed, "I understood exactly what you said. But that's not good enough to get a pardon. We're going to do this. Consider it fun. Think of it as practicing. I don't know. The main thing is for you to prove to me that you're not a complete idiot when it comes to dating."

She must have noticed in the last couple of weeks that this was not the case at all. The way we treated one another. The things we did together, even far away from what happened in my bedroom... all these were good indicators that I was not too stupid to get to know a woman and, above all, to make her happy.

"Fine. But in return, the next date is the one I want."

Nikau sighed. "Sure. A date according to your wishes. If it's not significantly different from what we usually do. I'll file a complaint."

I narrowed my eyes. "That won't be necessary. But it's good of you to emphasize it in this way."

Of course, I wouldn't tell her what I was thinking – and that I was clearly winning this deal.

"Anything else?"

"Yes. I want to know whose stupid idea it was."

She pressed her lips together. She seemed to be considering whether to tell me a lie or the truth. "Kaia suggested it as a joke when we were on your terrace. I haven't been able to get it out of my head since...

but after you came back so unsatisfied from another date, I thought it was time to test you."

Of course this idea came from Kaia. I should have guessed. Whenever she could, she pulled the strings. And mostly because she liked to annoy or embarrass me or make me feel like I was being taken for a ride. Not that I can say I haven't enjoyed teasing her before. But sending me on some sort of roleplaying date with the woman I knew to the core was a bit too much.

"Sure," I muttered. "I'll just have to do another night ambush."

So I could scare her and throw her into the pool.

"So you're going along with this, aren't you?"

"For my sake, please, let's talk about something else," I demanded. "For instance, it wouldn't be a bad idea to repeat the beach party."

Nika narrowed her eyes. "You're just saying that because you want to kidnap me again into some dark corner to…"

Unconsciously she bit her lip. Obviously, the memory was haunting her right now – and I didn't want to complain about it. Everything we had done together in the last few weeks was burning deeper and deeper into my memory. It got worse when she knelt in front of me and looked at me with that anticipatory look.

"Actually, I'm saying this because it's a good way to integrate the residents and get them interested. For people who aren't sure if this is the right place for them."

"Marketing," she interjected.

"That's right. So we're having the next party this month. It'll be run by the restaurant again."

Nikau told me she would start preparations soon. But something told me that the original topic of conversation had not yet been completely taken off the table.

WHAT NIKAU WAS ASKING ME TO DO WAS LUDICROUS AT best – and a disaster at worst, because I stood firm. We'd simply been friends for too long for me to successfully pretend I didn't know her. As I had already told her, I knew far too much about her. I knew all the details, had witnessed so many important events in her life, and we fucked. How much closer can you get to a person?

And now I was supposed to pretend she didn't look familiar as she entered the bar in a black cocktail dress. As if she was just another woman. But she was not – would never be. This was evident from the general reaction of the men in the bar alone, as she made her way toward the bar and thus toward me.

I saw a young man jump up and move toward her out of the corner of my eye. Our gazes locked. Two seconds later he was back on his ass, eyes lowered to the table before him.

It bothered me. Some random wanton was trying his luck with Nikau. She was not here to be the object of some idiot's advances. She was here to spend the rest of the evening with me. Only me.

Even though I was already getting annoyed that I couldn't talk to her like I normally did, but was forced to pretend like it was a first date.

I glanced at her as she came to stand next to me, deliberately looking straight ahead. She seemed to ignore that I existed.

Yet another thing that was driving me mad inside. Insane. It left a bitter taste in my mouth when she gave me the cold shoulder like that. I gritted my teeth. I wanted to end this spectacle right now. But Nika had no intention of interrupting what we were doing. She was simply too stubborn. Too eager to find some fault in my behavior that would give her the right to reprimand me.

But I would not allow it. I would prove to her that I was capable of dating other women and succeeding at it. The only thing I had to do was to forget my hatred of this situation.

Normally, an evening in a bar would go differently. I would have complimented her on her looks, ordered her a drink and tried to make her feel at home.

She looked striking. The black dress clung to her curves, accentuating her ass. The focus was not on the fact that it was a damn expensive dress, but that she knew exactly what she wanted to achieve with her appearance. Her long hair fell over her shoulders, curled at the ends, and the red lipstick almost magically kept my eyes on her mouth.

My mind was in a whirl. I wanted to kiss her – and then force her to wrap her sinful lips around my cock, to let me feel her tongue and then, after I had come in her mouth, to show me how much she enjoyed it. How much she loved that.

"So, what brings you here?" I asked, already feeling particularly stupid about it.

That's not how you talk to women. Was it? I usually didn't have this sort of trouble.

I noticed that Nikau raised an eyebrow and turned her head slightly to the side, giving me an appraising look. Somehow it had slipped my mind that she had spent years working in a seedy establishment in Iowa and probably had a lot of experience in keeping someone at arm's length when she wanted to.

But her lips curled into a grin, and she turned the rest of her body toward me.

It was no wonder that the young man had gotten up to try and catch her while she was still in the middle of the bar. He wanted to make sure he would be the first to lay claim to her in a room full of men. Too bad that she was already mine – no matter what kind of games we were playing tonight.

Only she did not know it yet. In fact, I had yet to prove it to her.

From under her lashes she sparkled at me with

amusement, as if waiting to hear more from me. But she hadn't even given me an answer to my initial question.

I told the bartender to serve us our drinks – ignoring the fact that in her scenario I should have asked her what her drink was first. I knew the answer. So why take a detour?

"Either you're clairvoyant or you have very good taste," she remarked as the drink appeared under her nose and – astonishingly – it was exactly what she usually drinks.

This was ridiculous. My skin felt far too tight. At some point during the evening, I would have a heart attack if she insisted on further playing this charade.

I forced a thin smile to my lips. "Don't worry, I know what I'm doing," I said.

"That sounds pretty chauvinistic."

"It's the truth, though."

Usually at this point I would ask the crucial questions. There was no time to waste, because whenever I returned to the resort from another failed date, I'd seek out Nikau to make it clear to her, one way or another, that she hadn't found the right girl for me yet again. It was lovely. Like playing a game where we both won because we ended up in bed together. Exhausted. Satisfied.

But now Nikau had a fixed script in her head and insisted on torturing me. So she basically left me no choice but to play along and later – for another failed date – make sure the end result remained the same.

The only thing that kept me sane was the thought that I was allowed to choose the next date and I already knew exactly where it would take us.

"Let's skip the small talk and get straight to the point," I finally said. That's how I'd done it with the other women. And that's what she wanted to see.

Didn't she?

"And what would this important point be?" she replied. I heard a hint of amusement. It didn't make it any easier for me to remain serious.

"Let's start with what experience you've had."

"That's a very indiscreet question for a first date, isn't it?"

"And extremely important. A deal breaker if the answer isn't right."

She narrowed her eyes a little. "I'm learning," Nika finally said.

Did my direct, brash way annoy her? Was it her annoyance that I was letting her say these things, even though I had a clear idea of how well she was learning?

"Is that so? If you already have someone to teach you all these things, then why are you coming on a date?"

She opened her mouth. "Because he's an idiot who doesn't deserve my attention."

The laughter that rose in my throat was impossible to suppress. "Is he?"

"Yeah. He's quite an idiot. And so terrible with women."

I looked at her intently. "Really? What's the problem?"

"He obviously doesn't know how relationships work, that they're not just about sex and kinks. Maybe getting to know the person before throwing other components in the ring would serve him better."

"Pretty presumptuous, isn't it? Maybe with just one look at these women, you can decide whether they are suitable partners or not."

"Oh yeah, and how am I supposed to imagine that?"

I shrugged. "Maybe they turn up and keep talking about the *Honolulu Sun*. Or ask indiscreet questions about how much you earn. Or maybe they don't have a clue what BDSM is, but they'll do anything without a second thought as to what's behind it and what it entails."

"It sounds as if these women are very simple minded." A deep furrow had formed between Nikau's eyebrows. It could only mean that she was seriously worried about what was going on with these people.

"Indeed. So maybe you should be a little more forgiving of the fact that this guy is so quick to be sure of what he can take and can't take."

"Or maybe he's just really picky," she added.

"And that's a bad thing? To want to keep up a certain standard? Not taking anyone who crosses your path? In my opinion, it's a very wise thing to do.

And to my knowledge there are other people who do it that way too."

With a thoughtful sound, she turned to her drink. "What other questions do you want to ask?"

"Would you say that you are more of a submissive or a Dominant?"

Her gaze met mine. Insistently. "I think there's only one correct answer to that. You should be aware of that by now."

"Do you have any ambitions for a taste of the other side as well?"

She pressed her lips together before deciding to answer my question. "Yes. But only for a very specific purpose."

I decided not to probe any further. "And would you go to the press at any point in time to air your dirty laundry?"

"No. But I would tell them who you really are."

And there it was. The first crack in the facade of our shared roleplaying.

"And who am I?"

"I've read all the articles. Every single one of them I could find, Kaden. And the things they write about you couldn't be further from the truth. It kind of makes me sad that they say all these things about you and there isn't anyone to stand up and tell the truth."

"I don't care what the press say. As long as the people around me know it's all a lie."

"You don't think it affects everything you do? These women read who you say you are online. They try to appeal to that side of you. If you ask me, that's called manipulation."

"And it would also happen when I get to know the women for the first time and then ask them what they have in mind in terms of sex."

The bartender gave me a look I couldn't interpret. Maybe it was one of the stranger things he'd overheard. Who could say for sure?

"Don't take this the wrong way, but I want to feel like when I'm with you I don't want to have to worry about making a mistake. I want to be with someone who is like my best friend. Someone I can laugh with, but also feel comfortable talking to. I want the kind of sex that is hard and I'm the one dominating. But I also want the kind of sex where I'm half asleep in the morning…" I stopped myself and shook my head. Nancy had been the best example – none of that was possible with her. She spent hours in the bathroom in the mornings, long before I even woke up. When I told her to do something, she would only do it because she was thinking of my money, which might reward her later in the day if she got it right. She hadn't paid any attention to my talks about the problems at the resort, and her interest in doing anything else had been low.

Accordingly, the time she'd managed to survive with me was also very short. Every woman I had dated in recent years lost out to Nika when I compared all this and drew the immediate parallels. Nika came out on top easily.

"Do you realize that guy over there keeps staring at you?" I asked abruptly, looking over my shoulder.

She raised an eyebrow. "Is that really important now?"

"Yes. Because he thinks he can get his hands on you, even though you're already in very good company."

"Well, maybe I'd rather have a conversation with him than with you. He might want to talk about something other than sex."

I snorted. "So this is the subject that bothers you, isn't it?"

"Perhaps it's not appropriate for this place and occasion." Nikau attacked my boundaries. She leaned against them and tried to tease me with all her might. She challenged me.

"Oh, so you'd rather talk to him? Did I get that right?"

She didn't answer, so I put a hand on the back of her neck and leaned closer to her ear. "How about I take you to the back and you scream so loud that everyone here knows how hard you're getting fucked? Maybe they'll turn green with envy. But more importantly... you won't have any desire to talk to him afterward. Do you have any idea why? Because that bastard would never get the same reaction out of you."

Really, I'm sure it was just a bit of fun on her side, and yet I felt I had to make it clear to her that she was here with me – and there was no question of her diverting her attention to another man.

I knew my words had made her wet almost instantly as I saw a delicate blush spread across her cleavage. She squeezed her thighs together and looked straight ahead with that glazed look. Was she wondering if doing this was really a possibility?

"Do you really think this is an empty threat? That I wouldn't show you just how much I detest the very words that come out of your mouth? Entertaining another man... do you think I would let you get away with insulting me like that?" I straightened a little more and pressed myself against her side. The fact that she stubbornly continued to look straight ahead amused me. But she wasn't able to ignore me. Her body was incapable of that. She responded to me, even when she didn't want to, or when she felt it was an inappropriate moment.

"Let's go to the back. Be a good girl and come along. Pretend it's the most natural thing in the world. Maybe try not to blush quite so much?" I slid my hand down her arm and closed my fingers around hers.

It only took a slight nudge for her to follow.

"Don't look like I'm about to fuck your brains out and you're looking forward to it. We don't want anyone following us and seeing you like this," I murmured, leaning back in her direction. "Do we? Do you want anyone to see how much fun you're having with me?"

I saw the barely perceptible nod out of the corner of my eye as we stepped into the dimly lit hallway that led to the toilets. The back of the bar gave me absolute peace. I stepped up behind her, grabbed hold of her upper arms and pushed her through the first door that we came to.

Fortunately for me, it gave way without an alarm going off – and without any other people behind it. We entered another corridor which was not even properly lit. It was probably used to transport the liquor coming in from the yard. That was fine with me.

A grin automatically spread across my face as I noticed that goosebumps had already formed on Nikau's arms. They spread down her neck as I made her feel my hot breath. Her body pressed against mine in search of support, but I only pushed her forward and against the cool brick wall.

Just in time, she turned her head. Showing me what I wanted to see. The corners of her mouth turned up slightly, as if she couldn't hide how much she was into this. How much she wanted it. She was waiting for me to make the first move, and there would be no turning back until I was completely satisfied with what she had given me.

"If I hear you say one more time that you prefer talking to other men..." I started with a warning undertone.

"Then what?" Her answer was as breathless as it

was surprising – she usually played by the rules. Tonight, different rules seemed to apply.

Was she trying to rebel against me, to add a bit of thrill and make sure I punished her all the more? That I took out all the anger on her I'd felt since she'd suggested this stupid?

Oh, I was going to enjoy teaching her that lesson. I pushed her dress up over her ass without warning. Roughly. She wasn't wearing any underwear, so what had just happened was no spontaneous accident!

I swore as I looked down and saw how wet she was already. Her wetness shimmered between her legs, ready to be tasted and spread.

The urge to drop to my knees and bury my face in her pussy was strong, but I resisted – and instead let my hand whip across her ass. So hard that I saw an imprint as soon as I pulled back and repeated it on the other side.

Panting, she pressed her torso against the wall, her ass thrusting provocatively at me. Fuck. In the last couple of weeks, the things she had given me had gotten so much worse. Nikau had discovered her dirty side, her filthy self, and there was no longer any shame in her acting out that side of herself. Like now, when I whispered in her ear what a slut she was, she replied with a moan, completely lost in paradise.

"What do you think your little friend from the bar would have to say if he could see you right now? The dress around your waist, no underwear, a red ass and so wet that it's running down your legs. Do you think he would be able to handle you? Would he make you feel the same way that I do? He wouldn't be so happy to have you in front of him like that.... not the way I do. Do you understand?" I found it harder to concentrate on the punishment with each word. Still, the praise in my statement was nothing but pure seriousness.

Every time I had Nika in front of me, it was a moment of gratitude. For her unconditional surrender and her trust in me, so much so that I could humiliate her in such a public place. The fact that she accepted it all with a smile was just another incentive for me to take the game to the next level. To go much, much further.

But I didn't give her time to form an answer through the mist of her pleasure. Instead, I pulled her around and forced her to her knees, right at my feet, one hand already on the strap of my belt.

"Show me how much you want my cock," I growled, watching as she put her hands behind her back and spread her legs a little further apart, settling into the position we'd spent weeks perfecting.

For me, she had been on her knees for hours, and yet each time it sent a new feeling of power through me – that Nikau gave me. No one else.

She licked her lips before I released my cock from its prison. I looked at her immediately. I had no choice but to brace myself against the wall with my hand as her mouth closed around the tip and she gave me a first suck. With a deep rumbling in my chest, I closed my eyes.

The deeper she took me, the harder it was to control my breathing and reactions.

"Fuck, that feels so good," I hissed as I put a hand in her hair and pulled her face closer to my stomach. "This is exactly what I'm talking about when I say prove it to me."

The enthusiasm with which she slid my cock into her mouth, her tongue teasing me, her moans vibrating through my body... Fuck, nobody had perfected blow jobs like Nika.

She'd been good to begin with, but since she spent almost every lunch break in my office, under or on my desk, busy providing us with much needed distraction... she paid attention to how my body responded. To what made me feel good. To what was driving me crazy... and she systematically used it to my disadvantage.

She may have been made human by God, but her mind, mouth and pussy were made by the Devil himself. And I was into it. I was a sucker for what she had in store for me.

"Let me just..." I announced my next move, grabbing her head and starting to fuck her mouth as I pleased, claiming it for myself. As if it wasn't her mouth, but her fucking pussy...

Her moaning, the wet sound of my cock sliding over her lips, the vibration where we met and the danger of being caught at any moment made this experience so much better.

"Stand up," I commanded less than five minutes later, pulling her to her feet and pinning her back against the wall. "Now tell me who you enjoy spending time with best."

"You," she gasped.

"And whose cock do you wish you had inside you?" Not Bar-Boy's. That much was a given.

"Yours."

"Damn right. And who does your pussy belong to?" I asked, the head of my cock pressed against her entrance.

She was almost howling, longing to finally feel me inside her.

"Yours. My pussy is yours, Kaden. God damn it. Now, fuck me already. Please."

But instead of sliding inside her and doing us both a favor, I held back. Frustrated, she thrust her hips at me, but I kept leaning back, tormenting both of us. "So you want me to fuck you, do you? Just a few minutes after you'd rather go home with some other man? It's not very convincing, don't you think?"

"I didn't mean to…"

Roughly, I put my hand on her ass and cupped it. "You didn't what, Nika?"

"I was teasing you. Irritating you. To get a reaction out of you. So that we could…"

"That's it? That's how desperate you are? You crave my cock that much?"

She nodded. There were tears in her eyes. From the blowjob? From the overwhelming lust that gripped her? Either way, this was the reaction I had least expected, but somehow was in need of. With a powerful thrust I slid into her. Until it was no longer possible to go any deeper.

And then I stopped for a moment. I rested my forehead on her shoulder, breathing in her aroused scent and feeling her pussy tighten around me. Holding me captive. Making sure I felt every sensitive throb. She was so wet. Warm. Actually, a quickie in the bar wasn't enough – I wanted to spend hours inside her and this was just the beginning of a long night of punishment and pure ecstasy.

Punishment because she thought it was necessary to make me fuck her out of jealousy. Had she asked... I probably would have had her on the bar in front of everyone and made sure that all those buffoons had a taste of what real sex was like at least once in their lives.

Nika tried to create friction between us, pressing her ass against my loins, but I was stronger and held her still. "On my terms, remember?" I murmured in her ear before I braced myself against the wall next to her head again, pulled halfway out of her and then slowly entered her. Slowly. Almost so slowly that it was torturous.

My eyes slid between our bodies to watch my cock sink into her pussy. Again and again. At first just a few inches, then deeper, and finally so deep that her wetness spread over my stomach.

Eventually I dropped my hands to her hips, gripping and guiding. Pressing into her, pulling her toward me, adding more force to the movement.

If we'd remembered we were in a public place when we first started, that thought was completely forgotten now. Her moan went right through my bones. Mine, right into her ear, gave me even more goosebumps. As she trembled, almost imperceptibly, her pussy held me tight. I lost myself.

The only purpose of my existence was to fuck her to orgasm and then cum in her mouth. I wanted to see her swallow my cum and how she thanked me for it afterward.

"I want you to come for me... and maybe you should make an effort not to be too loud. Or is everyone supposed to know what we do?" I whispered to her. "Not that I would mind. Far from it. But they wouldn't understand..."

My sentence caught in my throat as Nika suddenly and unexpectedly came so hard on my cock that she almost knocked us both off our feet. With all her ferocity, her muscles contracted around me, making it harder and harder for me to fuck her properly. Still, I fucked her right through her climax, before withdrawing and forcing her on her knees again.

Completely dazed, she looked up at me and when I brought my cock to her mouth this time, it was much gentler. Nevertheless, she took it as eagerly as before. Sucking and licking, she let me slide down her throat, doing everything she could to bring me closer to my own peak.

I put one hand on her cheek, stroking the soft skin with my thumb, completely absorbed in the sensation she was giving me. Normally this would be the time when I would let my praise flow into all the degrading words, letting her know what a dirty little slut she was – my dirty little slut – but right now I was at a loss for words.

My head went blank as my orgasm hit me as unexpectedly as hers had hit her. All I felt was a brief tingling at the end of my spine. Then my cock twitched in her mouth and I poured out onto her tongue.

It felt like half an eternity while the orgasm swept through me, completely taking over my brain and making me feel high as hell.

If I was calling her my dirty little cum slut in my head, then she had more than earned it. As much as I loved to watch her cum, I loved to see how she got off on making me cum even more. She was so perfect. As if she was made for me.

She withdrew only a few seconds after I had filled her mouth. Nika licked her lips, took up the position she had been in and opened her mouth just to stick her tongue out. A mixture of her own lust and my cum gathered on it. But the mischievous twinkle in her eyes was what made the gesture so insanely sexy.

"Swallow," I commanded and watched as she promptly did as I said. And as if she had perfected it to finish me off, she stuck out her tongue again to show she had followed my request perfectly.

I looked at her, shaking my head. "Every time I see this, I could get hard on the spot, only to abuse your mouth again." I held my hand out to her. "Now stand up."

She reached for it and let me pull her to her feet, and I set about adjusting her dress so that, at least from the looks of it, no one would notice that she had spent the last few minutes on her knees.

Then I ran my hand through her hair, cleaning up the mess I had made in it. Meanwhile, Nika took care of tucking my cock back into my trousers, fastening the zip and belt, and cleaning up any traces she had left.

"Perhaps you'd find other women more convincing if you did the same thing to them," she murmured after a few seconds, her hands resting on my chest.

At first I growled something unmistakable. Then I gave her an answer that I was sure she didn't want to hear. "No other mouth could hold this power over me. And I'm not just talking about my dick."

She slapped my chest. "Idiot. There are plenty of women out there who would suit you. You just have to give them a chance."

And refrain from corrupting her for my own purposes? Never.

I had mistakenly assumed that the charade would end after this little encounter, but no sooner were we back at the bar with new drinks in front of us than Nikau turned back to me, that look in her eyes that told me I had better brace myself because she was going to make another one of those statements that made me livid.

As if to keep me guessing, she first sipped her drink, then slowly and deliberately set it down. I could tell by the hunch of her shoulders that she was thinking far too much, even though some of the tension that always seemed to hold her body captive had gone. She was thinking about everything.

About the dates, about the women, about the contract that would only run for a few more months. Was she afraid of not succeeding in that time? If she'd only asked me what I thought, I could have told her that I didn't think it would be bad to marry her after all. At the time, it seemed like the best decision I had ever made.

Nikau and I worked so well together. It seemed only natural to try and keep that going and to make sure we were both living lives that made us happy. But I could only speak for myself. I knew that Nikau would do everything in her power to keep her end of the bargain. So far she had consistently failed, but perhaps one day she would present me with the perfect woman – if she was looking for me and not to complete the deal.

"Are you satisfied? With the way things are right now, I mean," she finally asked.

This was a question I had not expected to be asked. Had I given any indication that I was not? Had I given her the wrong signals? Had I unconsciously made a mistake that made her think I didn't feel better than I had in years?

Irritated, I leaned back a little to get a better look at her, but her face gave no hint that the origin of this question was negative. So I just narrowed my eyes slightly before nodding hesitantly. There were just some slips one did not want to make.

"Do you feel different about that?"

"No. I just want to know if we're on the right track. That's all."

"On the right track?"

"Well, I don't want any sudden misunderstandings, you know?"

"So are you satisfied?"

"You mean apart from the fact that I still find it hard to believe that all of this had been lying dormant inside of me without me even realizing it?"

I shrugged. "Sometimes it just takes a certain trigger."

And for her, I had been that trigger. Fortunately, I didn't need to experience how I would have felt if some random Dom had gotten his hands on her just to give her all the wrong values. There were so many people out there who had this idea that they were the best in this kind of relationship. In the end, though, they were just taking advantage of other people who put themselves in vulnerable situations where they needed to be protected – not further exploited and manipulated to get what they wanted.

"I'm glad you didn't give me a choice."

"You could have said no at any time."

"But I didn't want to. This part of me might be new, but it's at least as exciting. Besides... it changed some views."

Even though she didn't specify, she didn't have to. I knew exactly what she meant. Finally, she took a deep breath and let it out, as if that hadn't been the difficult part of the conversation.

"Kaden, do you really think you are incapable of loving someone?"

Clearly this was something she was thinking about, so I decided to address it – even though I was reluctant to talk about it, and to work out with myself what it all meant to me.

"I just don't think it would be healthy. The lines could blur, and before I know it... you know where I'm going."

"But aren't you closing yourself off to happiness? I mean, if there was a woman out there with whom you could have the perfect relationship, it would be silly not to get involved just because all the possibilities scare you."

"It would be safer for everyone involved," I

replied. "Besides, it's all theory. All the failed dates prove it's a good and sensible approach, don't they?"

"Sure. For now, maybe. But what if, when you're fifty, you realize you made a big mistake and missed it all?"

"Do you think I would ever neglect or abandon my principles like that, Nika?" Even though Kaia was young at the time, she had witnessed enough of my parents' arguments to be damaged. Tears would suddenly well up in her eyes whenever someone got louder in a conversation. Even if she had nothing to do with the conversation, even if she wasn't involved. Our parents' fucked-up relationship had permanently destroyed us both, and even though we had become reasonably capable adults, there was no denying that our childhood had a huge impact on who we were today. Neither Kaia nor I had ever been in a healthy, loving relationship. In my case, it was all about sexual preferences, without the fulfillment of which I was never happy, and in Kaia's case… well, we didn't talk about what went on behind closed doors most of the time. But I knew that she had gone through a similar process as me.

And we had accepted the way things were. How we had developed, what it meant for us in the future, and how we would deal with it. So why would I ever want to deviate from that?

"Maybe it would make things easier for you. Or it might help if you worked through what's bothering you so much."

"You want to send me to therapy?"

I had expected Nikau to roll her eyes at this point. But unwilling to look at this with a little more humor, she just kept staring at me seriously. "I want you to acknowledge some of your problems and not pretend they don't exist. Wasn't the whole point to grow together and face problems we can't face alone?"

"But there is no problem. And therefore no reason to deal with anything."

I expected her to continue, but my last sentence drew only a nod from her, and the conversation seemed to be over.

"Does that mean we can drop all this nonsense now and I don't have to pretend I don't know you to prove something?"

She grinned. "Not that we've been pretending for the last few minutes," she murmured. "But don't get the idea that I have a satisfactory outcome to report. You should rethink what happens on your first dates and what conversations you have."

"You think I should tell them about my parents' problems and the importance of kinks in my life?"

"Or try telling them about your hobbies and who you are outside of the media."

Which was basically wasted energy when, within the first few seconds of a conversation, it became clear that the woman sitting opposite me was only interested in the number on my bank account. Whichever way you looked at it, it all boiled down to the fact that I clearly preferred a purely physical relationship.

"Or, in the future, you can just leave it to me to worry about my dates and concentrate on finding the right woman instead." What I said sounded harsher than I meant. But our agreement was not based on us giving each other therapy. We had an agreement about sex and our friendship. If I really thought I needed to deal with the traumas of my childhood, I certainly would.

Nikau nodded. "Fine. Then get ready to go on more dates in the next few weeks. I'm going to find so many women for you that it's almost impossible that the right one won't be there."

The thought amused me, even though I dreaded spending a lot of my time getting to know complete strangers who, after five minutes, turned out to be the same as everyone else. But for the sake of Nikau and our deal, I'd put up with it. As long as she held up her end of the bargain in ten months' time.

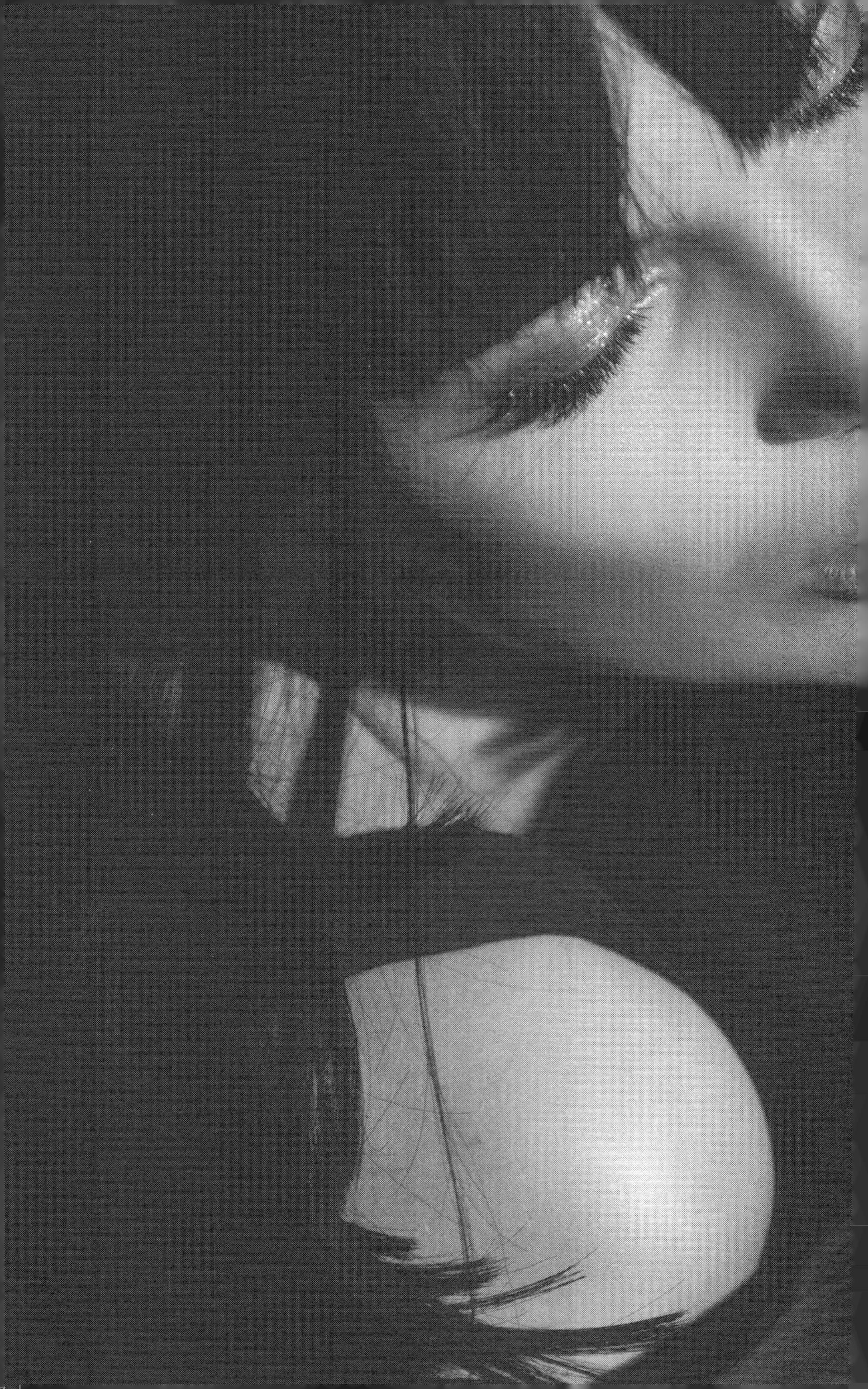

Nikau

I lay on one of the sun loungers by the pool with my eyes closed. The guests who were not taking a midday nap were spending their time in the water, soft music playing in the background. So there was a lot of activity, but I didn't let it distract me. Instead, I enjoyed the commotion, listening with half an ear to what was going on.

Working in the restaurant was exhausting. Both physically and mentally. So I was all the more grateful for the quiet moments, the days when I didn't have to work. They were at my disposal. That's why I always ended up on the beach or by the pool when I wasn't on an excursion around the island, meeting up with old acquaintances.

It all felt like coming home. I even visited my old neighborhood and drove past the high school where I lived for a brief glimpse into the past. O'ahu held so many secrets and memories, and they were still right where I had left them.

I couldn't dwell on my thoughts for long though, because soon a shadow crept across my figure. When I carefully opened one eye, I realized that Kaden was standing directly above me.

"Remember that date you promised me?" he asked almost nonchalantly.

I rolled my eyes. "Really? Like now?"

"Well, more like tonight, but I want you to be able to give yourself enough time to get ready for it."

"I need to prepare?"

"Choosing an appropriate outfit and all that stuff…"

I immediately raised an eyebrow. "Where are we going?"

But Kaden shrugged, unwilling to give me a proper answer. "You'll find out when we get there. A date on my terms. Those were your words."

I had agreed under duress, knowing that I would not get what I wanted if I did not. Not that the date had been a complete success. On the contrary. Things had come to light that I would rather not even think about. Kaden had always been stubborn, but his inability to see how much he was hurting himself surpassed that original stubbornness. Still, I couldn't blame him. But I couldn't force him to do something he didn't want to do either, so I decided to ignore the subject.

I groaned. Whatever he had come up with would

surely make me regret it later – having made him this promise in the first place. Getting involved in something when I knew exactly where it would end up.

"Why don't you just tell me what to wear?"

The answer came faster than I had expected. "Something that emphasizes your assets. And something that makes it clear who owns you. But I'll take care of that myself."

I looked up at him skeptically, shielding my eyes with my hand. "Kaden... where are we going?"

But he just shrugged again. "You'll find out soon enough. Tonight at eight, you're mine."

As if I did not belong to him at any time of the day or night...

But I nodded, feeling a strange anticipation that couldn't even be justified.

I STILL DIDN'T KNOW WHAT KADEN HAD PLANNED FOR the date, but at least he seemed to like my choice of a red dress. At the back, the neckline went almost to the end of my spine, while at the front it stopped just above my navel, emphasizing all my assets as Kaden put it.

As I looked in the mirror and imagined how others would perceive my appearance, I immediately realized that their gaze would not be able to decide. My skin, which shimmered golden, or my breasts, which were set off perfectly by the dress. My collarbone, which blended elegantly with my shoulders, especially when I drew them back a little. My back... or my ass, there were so many possibilities and I agreed that the red dress was a damn good choice. Combined with the high heels that wrapped around my calves a bit, the look seemed perfect.

Things got even more interesting when Kaden drove up in his car – an absolute luxury car that I would never have expected him to drive, and yet I thought it suited him better than anything else I could have imagined.

He was wearing a suit I had never seen him in before. It fit better. Seemed more elegant. And made him even more handsome than he already was. Every time I looked at him, I felt my pulse flutter and shoot up.

We looked like one of those power couples in the glossy magazines. Either he wanted us to look like that, which would mean the press would be there tonight, or it was one of those coincidences that showed once again how well we harmonized.

I felt the tension of the evening even as I slid into the car beside him on the cool leather.

"Are you going to tell me where we're going?"

A grin tugged at the corners of his mouth as he shook his head. "Afraid you'll have to show a little more patience to know."

"Are you worried I'll want to go back to the resort if you tell me where we're going?"

"No ... I just want to see the look on your face

when you find out what it is I'm going to do with you."

Somehow I had a feeling this wasn't about food. Or anything a normal person would have called dating.

I HAD AN INKLING OF WHERE THIS WAS GOING AS WE turned into the road that led into the industrial estate. Part of me felt the same anticipation as before, and another part was seriously worried about whether this was the right thing to do. Whether Kaden was serious about what he was doing – and whether he knew exactly what he was doing.

He stopped the sleek sports car right in front of the entrance to a massive brick building that looked out of place amongst all the warehouses and companies. Even from the outside it was obvious that the windows had been tinted. An inconspicuous facade which surely held a secret not fitted for everyone.

"Is that what I think it is?" I asked, my fingers digging into the seat. Unfortunately, if he had any intention of sharing me with anyone, I would have to hastily remind him of our contract and everything we had talked about.

I swallowed as the excitement was now joined by nervousness. It was an emotion that I wasn't quite as good at handling as the others.

"What do you think it is?" asked Kaden amusedly,

his hands still gripping the wheel. Nevertheless, he looked at me curiously.

"A swingers' club, isn't it?"

I didn't expect him to laugh out loud. "God, no. This is more exclusive. Not everyone gets invited, and just because you've been invited doesn't mean you automatically get in. The bosses here are careful about who their customers are – and it's a safe place where everyone can act as they please. It's a sex club, not a swingers' club."

"What's the difference?" I demanded, because in my eyes there was no difference at all. I studiously ignored everything else he had said. At least for now, until I was sure what to make of it.

"The difference here is that it's not about finding other people or couples to have sex with."

"Then why have a club?"

"Because many people like to talk about it. Or like being seen. Some of them also like to watch. But the bottom line is you have opportunities you might not have at home."

"You can afford anything you want," I groaned irritably.

Kaden didn't need a strange sex club to have fun. If he felt like it, he could have all that at the resort.

"I could. But it's not the same. Besides, there's no need for a dungeon in the basement of the *Honolulu Sun* when I can have fun here."

"And you thought it was fun for me to watch

other people? Or that the thought of others watching me is a turn-on for me?"

"I thought it was time I had a go at you and what you've learned. I'm not going to make you do anything you don't want to do. I will never give you to anybody or watch as anybody tries to get you."

Soothing. Very reassuring. Or maybe not. Just because he didn't like this one thing didn't mean there weren't hundreds of other ways he could get us both into previously unknown situations.

Situations that could be as fulfilling as me getting involved with Kaden. So far, at least, I have had no regrets about it. If anything, I made the most of it...

"Unless you want to back out..." he teased, looking at me sideways.

"What are the rules?" I asked instead of answering his provocation.

"You will wear a collar and act as my sub. If I tell you to do something, you will do it – no ifs, no buts. Your safe word still stands. I will not force you to do anything that makes you uncomfortable, but I will take every opportunity. Your body is at my disposal. Whenever I see fit," he explained in a dark voice.

My body knew exactly what he meant. It reacted with this telltale heat between my legs that would not subside anytime soon. In fact, it only increased as he continued his efforts to embarrass me.

The first thing I thought about was getting collared. The collar. I had read about it – and so far I had regarded it as a form of humiliation. Not as a way to identify myself as Kaden's property. Even so, I didn't know if I would feel comfortable with being put on a leash like a dog. That was the next step, after all. Wasn't it?

As if Kaden had read my thoughts on my face, he continued his explanation, "Most of the other subs here have a dress code. Nothing – or a hint of nothing, if their masters are generous. I don't approve of you walking around the club naked if you don't want to. I wouldn't do it either, so I don't think I can ask you to do it. Besides, you'll be by my side the whole time. No going off alone. Otherwise I might feel compelled to try out the whip collection. Of course you're free to talk to whoever you want, but you should remember who you're representing."

I swallowed. As if his reputation was an extension of my behavior. Shit, there were so many rules and things to follow that my head was already spinning – and we hadn't even entered the club yet.

"Do you have friends in there? Business associates?" It could be embarrassing if I bumped into people at work. The more I thought about it, the more I dreaded it.

"Some of my acquaintances might be there. But the club's rule is that nothing is said outside about what goes on in there."

Although it made sense, I didn't like it at all. What if someone got the idea to use what they had seen as intel against other members? "And if you were to meet them in real life, would you still be able to look them in the eye?"

"Why shouldn't I, Nika? Your tongue was on my balls and I can still make eye contact with you without thinking about it every time."

I opened my mouth, but the heat rising in me forbade me from saying anything. I would regret it and I didn't want to risk that. So I nodded as if I understood what he was saying and decided to take the evening as it came.

It was probably not the reaction he was expecting, but we had not entered the club yet. Maybe my mind was changing. And my reaction.

"Well, have we cleared up all the loose ends, or is there something else keeping us from going in?"

"You mean other than the nervousness that is making my throat tighten?"

Kaden stifled a laugh. "Yes. Exactly. Except for the nervousness."

"No," I squeaked. "Everything's fine. I think."

"Wonderful." He leaned in my direction and reached into the glove compartment, only to pull out a black leather collar. It was discreet. Like a chain. With a small ring. If worn in everyday life or in public, I don't think anyone would have given it a second glance.

Kaden's gaze shifted to me as he threaded the band through his fingers. His expression changed. Without further ado, he looked around, checking the surrounding buildings and the street. Then he nodded toward the pavement in front of the club.

"Out of the car and on your knees by the driver's side door," he ordered.

I lost control of my jaw. My common sense told me to laugh before I flipped him off. Kneeling on the tarmac where everyone could see me? How fucked up was that? And how crazy was I for seriously considering it because I was interested in what his next move would be?

I swallowed my rising anger and reached for the doorknob to let myself out. Clenching my fist, I walked around the car, watching Kaden's face through the windscreen before kneeling down on the pavement next to the car. Sharp pebbles dug into my knees – and suddenly it didn't matter that I was wearing a dress. I still felt exposed. Watched. Humiliated. Weak. At the mercy of someone else's will.

And Kaden made me wait too... until I was in the right position and my hands were relaxed on my thighs.

Only then did he open his door and step out. The fact that he towered over me, that we were in the middle of an industrial area, sent shivers down my spine. The anger was still there, but with a hint of excitement.

I swallowed because the thin collar was still between his fingers. He was playing with it, watching me. I knew it. Felt it without even looking at him. I lowered my gaze. I wanted him to move and get me out of this situation.

As he came closer, his scent hit me with full brunt. A flutter of my eyelids, then a surge of pure pleasure in my loins. Fuck. It hadn't taken Kaden more than three months to corrupt me. To turn me into someone who responded to primitive sex and a power imbalance that feminists the world over protested against. But didn't they know how liberating it could be to confide in someone who knew exactly what you needed? Who could give you everything – and more than you wanted? That there could be someone who knew the most secret places, who knew which boundaries could be easily approached and which could be crossed to make the experience even more special, even better? And at the end of the session, when the magic was over and the mind was clear, the soul balanced and the body satisfied, you returned to the life you had led before. It was simply a mistake that the power was with Kaden. I still possessed it – he just borrowed it to give me all these wonderful things, because I could never do them on my own.

After a few seconds, my breathing was shallow. I was tense, and the realization that I liked doing this, that I enjoyed it, and that it was of my own free will didn't make it any better. I felt dirty, but in the best way possible. In fact, when Kaden got down on his knees in front of me and slowly slid the collar over my neck, I felt in every touch how proud he was of me. How much it meant to him that I could trust him like that.

I swallowed, feeling the tightness of the band, and allowed him to close it around my neck. As his fingers touched my already sensitive skin there for a few seconds longer than was absolutely necessary, goosebumps crept up my shoulders and down my arms. I held my breath, blinking against the emotions that suddenly surged through me. It was all so unexpected.

Kaden moved even closer until his lips were pressed against my ear. "Good girl. Now you're going to wait for me right here."

Wait? Here? What did he mean...

But before I could raise my head to ask, he had pulled away, got back into the car and closed the door without looking back at me. I felt panic again, but this time for a different reason.

He liked to test boundaries. I just shook hands with my panic, laughed, and it whispered to me that someone would show up at any moment. So it was down to two possibilities: I would get laughed at, or they would exploit me. Maybe even both.

The temptation to just get up and stand in the doorway was strong, but that would also mean breaking the rules and letting Kaden down. Unless it was an absolute emergency for my safeword, there would be punishment, and as much as I liked the feel of his hand on my ass, I didn't want to find out how many different kinds of whips and floggers this club had.

So I swallowed my fear and reminded myself that I had enjoyed serving Kaden in this way. That I damn well enjoyed sharing his dirty little secrets. In a way, I was even his secret, and nothing he'd made me do so far had caused me any shame in retrospect. The pleasure prevailed and for that I simply could not be embarrassed.

Caught up in my thoughts, I didn't hear the sound of approaching footsteps until I felt Kaden's fingers against my cheek. "When we leave later, I want to see you like that again."

I nodded to signal that I understood. Only then did he pull me to my feet. His hands slid to my hips as he gave me a proud smile. His eyes reflected it. "You look stunning no matter what position you're in," he said quietly, knowing exactly what he was doing to my panties.

Today I wore panties but only because I was afraid that someone might have a glimpse at them.

Kaden led me to the entrance, rang the bell and the door opened. A nondescript man let us in. He checked what Kaden was holding and waved us through.

If he had seen what had happened outside, he didn't show it. Maybe he was used to such sights and had lost interest in them long ago. Whatever it was, it reassured me enormously.

The background music could easily be categorized as 'music for sex'. I quickly realized that the club was not trying to cover anything up. In fact, at first glance, it all looked like a slightly more luxurious kind of club. But then you looked closer, discovering that some people were completely naked, kneeling on the floor or having sex on one of the surrounding seats.

You could smell it too – the lust and excitement of those present. Pheromones were in the air, kicking in as soon as we took five steps into the chaos. Even though it was largely civilized, it was obvious where we were. Kaden had been acknowledged by some. Over the years, how many times had he come here? How many women had he brought?

A man in a suit approached us from the left and tapped Kaden on the shoulder. It appeared that they knew each other. Until they hugged, and that was a definitive.

"Kaden? Have you come to grace us with your presence once again?" I noticed his gaze fell on me. "And first time escorted? What have I missed?"

"Lei, this is Nikau. My…"

"Sub," I muttered. Because that was exactly what I was, if we were being honest.

Lei raised an eyebrow, but nodded. "Then I guess you've got some explaining to do, Kaden. Let's have a drink."

I followed the two men to the bar. My first instinct was to blend in with the crowd and not stand out – if I didn't attract attention, there wouldn't be any weird situations to avoid. The only bad thing was that, with the sinful red dress, I had a flashing light arrow above my head, which automatically attracted glances.

Lei scrutinized me for a few moments. At least it was not Kaden's gaze I felt on me. That much was certain. And even though I kept my eyes down, I couldn't help but take a closer look at my surroundings. Behind the bar was a huge, tall, wide glass wall with hundreds of bottles of expensive alcohol shimmering in every color imaginable.

But that wasn't what really caught my eye. It was what was behind it. For this glass was not a mirror showing me what was happening behind me. No, I could look through it and see a couple enjoying themselves on some kind of sex swing. Everyone in the room could see the spectacle, but no one seemed as fascinated as I was. My mouth went dry. I would never have described myself as a prude. But now that I was face to face with these people, all of whom were openly living out their sexual preferences, I realized I had missed out on a lot over the past few years.

Why was I content to have five minutes of fun with a semi-attractive man who couldn't even bring me to orgasm? He probably didn't even care as long as he got off. When I could have something else? Something much more fulfilling? All the needs I hadn't known about until Kaden had shown up?

At first I had scoffed at it, but now I saw him in a completely different light, and I believed that sooner or later this would be my undoing. I still believed there was a woman out there who was perfect for him, but in the two weeks since our conversation in the bar, I had let the search slip. For no particular reason, just because I didn't want to leave this world any sooner than I had to.

Still, I stared at the couple behind the glass, absolutely certain that while we could see them, they could not see us. I continued to stare until Kaden cleared his throat softly and I... just like that, dropped to my knees right next to his feet and took the position I had taken outside on the pavement.

Fuck. That was called conditioning, wasn't it? I read his body language so casually that I was just reacting instead of thinking about what I was doing. So it seemed natural to slide to the ground when he cleared his throat, because that was exactly what Kaden wanted. The sound of satisfaction he made signaled exactly that to me.

And Lei? He still seemed to be impressed by the fact that Kaden had shown up with company. Whatever that meant.

"Well, I'm all ears, my dear," Lei began. I had to prick my ears to understand him at all.

Kaden's posture remained calm. Relaxed. As if this was his natural environment and it was perfectly normal to have a conversation while several feet away a woman was being fucked by three men, announcing her pleasure to the whole club.

"Nika and I have known each other for a long

time. Since we were kids, to be exact."

Somehow I expected him to tell about our bargain. He would lay all the sordid details on the table to show off for his mate. Instead, that was all he said, and Lei didn't seem to feel the need to probe any further.

Had Kaden given him a look? Was that all there was to say? We just knew each other – so it was natural that we would find ourselves in such a dynamic?

Even though it was only in my head that I was exaggerating, I felt a sharp sting.

Nothing we had done had been obvious. It had all been like a small battle. A battle we had fought with each other, only to end up in a situation that somehow benefited both of us.

"She's looking for the right woman for me, by the way," Kaden interjected a few seconds later. I heard the smirk in his voice.

Lei laughed. "We've been trying to set you up for eight years. Did you tell her that?"

"Only indirectly," he replied. "But she's stubborn and self-confident. So I dutifully go on every date she sends me on."

It all sounded like another tabloid headline. The next time they wrote about Kaden, they might say that his best friend had tried unsuccessfully to get him married. That this time, instead of Bridezilla, it was the groom who mutated into a monster. They would come up with something.

The carpet under my knees started to get uncomfortable, as was the motionlessness, but soon there would be a point where my body wouldn't care, as long as Kaden kept paying attention to me. And he did, just like now, when his fingers slid over my cheek. Tender and loving, just the kind of touch I was craving before the next time he tested or humiliated me without warning.

"What shall we start with? You don't deserve the whips after how well you behaved... so how about a little reward?" Kaden's voice sent shivers down my spine. Whenever he spoke to me like that, my brain shut down.

It wouldn't take long for me to start salivating just because of how he sounded. But it would probably not stay that way, because the moisture between my legs was already dripping. Kaden had my body under his control. I had wrapped myself around his little finger so successfully that the slightest hint of fun with him made me react like this.

Other women would have been disturbed by the power I gave him. It made me smile, knowing I had a similar effect on him. When I looked at Kaden in a certain way and gave a verbal cue, I could see his cock pressing hard against his trousers. Just like that. All because I had irritated him a little, without even having to take my clothes off.

"Lei, would you excuse us?" Kaden stood up and motioned for me to do the same.

So I got up, straightened my shoulders, and

enjoyed that Kaden put his hand on my lower back to guide me through the crowd. Even though they didn't see him coming, the others automatically moved aside, leaving a small path for us to walk through.

It was only then that I noticed the whole room was hexagonal in shape, with corridors leading off in all directions. For a brief moment, I wondered what other secrets were hidden in this building, but Kaden had already led me on, depriving me of the chance to turn my head in the various directions and spy clues telling me what was happening elsewhere.

"We've never talked about how you feel about other women," Kaden murmured in my ear as he pushed open a door. I kept my eyes down, but only until he grabbed my chin and forced me to look up. His body was firmly pressed against mine from behind as I drew in a sharp breath and watched as one woman fucked another – with a strap-on much longer and thicker than any cock I'd ever seen. Kadens included.

I opened my mouth, blinking, only to close it again. I couldn't have told him if he'd asked me what the sight was doing to me. On the one hand, it excited me to see a woman in the dominant position taking what she wanted. On the other hand, I was completely heterosexual and could not imagine making out with a woman.

It wasn't until I looked again that I realized the woman lying down had been tied up. Her wrists were attached to a pole and the ankles were in a spreader bar – even if she had wanted to, she couldn't close her legs. She was left helplessly exposed.

That was something I had a lot more sympathy for.

"They don't know each other, by the way," Kaden murmured, nodding toward the corner of the room. A man sat in an armchair, watching the spectacle unfold. "He's their Dom. And anyone who wishes to do so may make use of them as they see fit. There is just one rule. No orgasms for her." His rugged cheek brushed against mine.

"How do you know that?" I drew a breath and immediately heard him chuckle softly.

"Because that's the way they are whenever they are here."

So he had his fill of it, too. And even though we just fucked, even though it had happened before I came here, even though I had no right to, I felt the slightest pang of jealousy.

Kaden's hand slid down my body, pushing the dress up a little. His fingers pushed my panties aside, sliding through my pussy and sinking two of them into me without warning. I gasped and reached for his arm. Searching for support.

I would not have an orgasm while the woman he had already fucked was also in the throes of orgasm. I would not...

A soft hiss escaped me as Kaden matched the rhythm of his fingers inside me to the woman's thrusts. Every time the dildo sank into her pussy, his thumb brushed over my clit. It was useless to resist. I leaned back against him and tried to close my eyes. It wasn't what was happening that was making me so aroused. That was Kaden's fault, fucking me with his fingers.

A moan escaped me. The scent of my arousal surrounded us both, and I felt his erection pressing against my back. It was still just his fingers that drove me crazy, but he would make me lose my senses again in not too much time. Maybe then I would forget that he had fucked that woman over there.

Kaden's fingers slid into me with no resistance at all. They went harder and faster. I heard him inhale sharply. A deep rumbling went through his chest as I automatically lowered my head against his shoulder. The next moment, had he not held me upright, the orgasm would have swept me off my feet. But he didn't stop there. He continued to tease my twitching, pulsating pussy until the glistening ball of lust in my abdomen exploded once more.

Cursing, I clawed at his arm and bent forward a little, trying to escape his fingers as he drove them further into me. But he didn't pull back until my legs were shaking and all my weight was on him.

My dress fell back into place. Kaden raised his hand to his mouth. Out of the corner of my eye I saw him licking them with pleasure. He tasted my wetness and twisted his mouth into a smug grin.

Fuck. Why was it so fucking sexy, having him possess me like that?

"Let's do it again," he murmured, grabbing me and throwing me over his shoulder as if I weighed nothing. His hand landed on my ass to ensure I didn't fall to the floor. He crossed the corridor with long strides before pushing open another door, stepping inside and locking it behind us.

I couldn't see much of the room upside down, and when he finally sat me down on a soft bed, he didn't waste any time before reaching for a blindfold and pulling it over my eyes. His hands slid down my neck before resting on my shoulders. Affirmation.

By now, my pulse had risen to unimaginable heights, throbbing so hard in my throat that I almost couldn't breathe.

"Spread your legs," he ordered, and I did just that.

I heard him pacing around me. Then, all of a sudden, my underwear disappeared and the hum of a vibrator filled the room. I almost flinched, so intense was the unexpected touch as he ran it up my leg.

The next moment he pressed it against my clit. It was only for a second, but it was enough to make me squirm.

Did it feel so intense because he'd blindfolded me or was it because he'd already made me come twice?

He let the vibrator slide into me on a low setting before I heard him stand up. I had a picture of him rolling up his sleeves and looking at me, pondering what to do next.

"You ticked off the box on your questionnaire that a threesome with another man would be all right. So would having anonymous sex."

I swallowed. Then I nodded.

"Today's your lucky day. Because that's what we'll be doing. And don't worry, you won't see the second man again. In fact, you won't see him at all. You won't hear him either. He may be there, but your attention will be on me all the time, do you understand, Nika?"

So this is what it felt like to be in heaven and hell at the same time. More than surprised, I nodded again.

"If he gives you any instructions, you are to ignore them. You do what I tell you to do, nothing else," he continued. "Nothing else," he continued. "He has no rights. He can't punish you. Unless I tell him to, he's not even allowed to fuck you. When you come, it will be on my cock – and yes, I will make sure you know the difference."

I knew exactly what Kaden's erection felt like. It was nothing like what I had felt before. However, his reiteration of all these basic conditions and rules made me feel more secure. It was so easy to forget them in the heat of the moment. And in the end, one of the boundaries that had been set before might have been crossed without a consensus.

That way, it would most likely not be the case.

Kaden had proven this to me time and time again. He had shown me how responsible he could be and that my peace of mind was paramount. None of this would happen unless I agreed. As soon as I told him, he would draw a line in the sand and make sure I was all right.

Being able to rely on that – one hundred percent – made it so much easier for me. I'd only ever been in relationships with men who had no regard for the value of their promises. But Kaden... Kaden took them all seriously and made sure I was aware of that at all times.

"What else?" he mused. "Put yourself out there, Nika. You want to make a good impression... and make sure I can be proud of you. Repeat the rules for me."

"I'm not allowed to see him."

"Go on."

"I won't listen to him and I won't pay attention to him."

"And who do you pay attention to?" he continued.

"You alone."

"Exactly. What else?"

The excitement shooting through my body made it incomparably difficult to keep my thoughts together. "He has no rights over me. He cannot give me orders. Only you can. If you are inside of me, then I am allowed to come. Otherwise, not."

A sharp pain exploded in my cheek. He had slapped me, just like that. But the shock turned to excitement far too quickly. He hadn't slapped my face before, and now that he had...

I wanted him to repeat it. Although my lower lip quivered in reflex, a grin spread across my face.

"What was that for?" I asked innocently, in full knowledge that I didn't actually have permission to do so.

My head snapped in the opposite direction. I instinctively clenched my teeth, still grinning. This was a whole new level of bittersweet torture, the adrenaline coursed through my veins from the hit I hadn't seen coming.

"You missed the point, my love. Think carefully. Otherwise, I'll have to slap you again to jog your memory." I squirmed inwardly at the harshness of his voice.

Normally you couldn't tell who Kaden was behind closed doors, but in those moments when he let his dark side out, I couldn't help but reach for it and rejoice when he did.

He pulled me into his dark world, into his inky black abyss, and I willingly followed him to the farthest corner. Kaden had me in his grip. He truly had me.

"Um," I said, trying to remember what else he had said.

But that wasn't good enough, and Kaden promptly made good on his threat. My cheek grew hot and my adrenaline levels rose to the point where I felt like I was flying. The pain, coupled with the gentle vibration inside me, made me clench my thighs. No more orgasms for me, but I could use the feeling, this plateau of pleasure. It was not something he had forbidden.

"Try again, Nika," he brought me back to reality. His warning undertone told me this was the last chance he would give me – before taking harsher measures.

Part of me, as always, wanted to know what other punishments he could think of. Another insisted that we remember immediately and return to the original plan. Namely, being fucked by two men.

So I moistened my lips and squared my shoulders. "If you don't allow it, then he is not allowed to touch me at all."

Satisfied, he hummed. "There you go. I was beginning to have my doubts about how good your memory really is."

I heard him move away from me and at the same time felt the tension return to my shoulders. What would he do next? Had he been waiting for this day to implement some of the points I had written on the questionnaire? How cleverly he had arranged this. A date on his terms. Because he had guessed that I would have backed out if he'd told me what he was up to. But it didn't matter now that I was in the middle of it, where my fear was history.

"Hold out your arms," he suddenly demanded.

The next thing I knew I felt something close around my wrists. Then he lifted my arms up and back until I was forced to lie on my back. Metal banged against metal, but that wasn't what I was concentrating on. His leg was pressing against my pussy as he knelt between them. And the fabric rubbed so gently against the irritated skin that I had no choice but to moan softly.

But just as quickly as he had touched me, he pulled away. Except now I was lying down – unable to move my arms an inch.

"If at any time your hands feel numb or cold, let me know immediately," he said. You might think that would have pulled us out of the scene, but the opposite was true. I sank deeper into it, knowing there was a safe way out if necessary.

Shortly afterward I felt his hands on my thighs. He pushed them further apart until he had fastened something around them. Before I knew it, my legs were fixed in a position of his choosing. Until now I had always been allowed to move. Today he took it away completely.

I could barely feel his fingers as they trailed over the sensitive skin inside my thighs. It sent a pleasant shiver down my spine. I got wetter with just the touch.

But then I heard the door open and close, the tension in my muscles changed. I couldn't assess the situation. I didn't know what was going to happen next. That made my pulse race even faster, but this time for different reasons.

Verbally, at least, the two men didn't seem to

communicate with each other, but I had no doubt that it was with looks or that they had discussed the details beforehand to be on the same page.

"Let's start with something simple," Kaden announced.

In the next instant, the vibration inside me grew stronger. Surprised, I gasped and threw my head back, still trapped in absolute darkness. Strangely, I didn't mind being at the mercy of a stranger.

"Give me the knife," Kaden demanded.

Knife?!

He seemed to sense my momentary shock, for his amused laughter filled the room. "I have to get you out of your clothes, Nika."

At this point, I would have liked nothing more than for some kind of endearment to come out of his mouth. Something to make it clear that I was not just an object to be shared between the two men, but more than that. His.

Kaden placed the blade between my collarbones, right in the hollow. I felt the tip bite into my skin and then move deeper. Immediately his full weight was on me and his tongue ran over the spot he had just knowingly injured.

A muffled moan escaped me. I wanted to beg for more, but he was already straightening up and the knife came back into focus. Fabric tore where it went, and he slid it across my skin more than once, only no longer with the intention of hurting me.

"I don't usually play with knives and blood,

Nika," he murmured in front of me. "But the night we made this deal, I tasted you. And all these years, I couldn't help but think what it would be like to have you lying helpless in front of me so I could do it again. I know, it's sick, isn't it? It's the weird sex stories you used to bring up. But the truth is... I wouldn't want that with anyone else. You're the only one who twists my mind like that."

Fuck.

FUCK.

Fuuuuuuuuuuuuck.

A shudder ran through my body as the words dug deeper than the knife ever could. Even if I wanted to call him a sick pig, I couldn't. For the depraved part of me, the part that only existed because of him, had its answer. All that I had called strange and categorically rejected not so long ago was now moving into an entirely different perspective. Preferences differed. And if I could find it attractive and hot when Kaden licked over a wound that he had inflicted on me, then it was no longer so difficult for someone else to become aroused when he behaved like an animal.

How much deeper would I fall into this hole? Alice's fall had come to an end, but I felt like mine would never end because Kaden kept challenging me in new ways.

I exhaled heavily as his knife slid across my stomach. It passed over my hip, I felt his hot breath on my sensitive breasts before finally landing on my mound of Venus. He paused there.

"Our friend here has a slight taste for sadism, Nika. And maybe I told him you'd scream for him before we went any further." That was the only warning Kaden gave me.

With a loud crack, a whip landed on my thigh. I jerked, instinctively wanting to close my legs to protect them from the attack, but the restraints held me in place. Open to the blows.

Another followed. This one brought tears to my eyes, though I was immediately seized by a new wave of lust, the vibrator inside me still doing its job and successfully distracting me. At least until the whip came down again.

This time it did not stop at a single stroke. A hand closed around my breast and teased my nipple. A sound escaped me. A sound that could only be described as a mixture of pain and pleasure.

"That's not enough, Nika."

A warm hand ran over the irritated spot on my thigh and I knew it was just a distraction. To lull me to safety before the next blow hit me.

And it hit me. Hard. Unexpectedly. And right on my already pulsating pussy. I cried out, leaning against the restraints and cursing, which immediately earned me a blow to my torso. The whip ate nastily into my skin.

My second scream was lost in Kaden's mouth as he kissed me wildly, one hand on my throat. My pulse pounded against his fingers, and the need to scream faded. It was replaced by the need to moan into his mouth and deepen the kiss. After a few seconds, though, he pulled away from me.

"Is that something you miss about what we do, Nika?" he murmured, and I shook my head. "Words. Or do I have to hit you again?"

But it had not been him who had been the one with the whip. I knew that for sure.

"No. I'm not missing it."

"But you can bear it?"

"For you," I replied breathlessly.

"Good girl."

I squirmed. Inwardly and outwardly, as the vibration inside me increased. Again there were hands on me, toying. But it was the head between my legs that demanded attention.

A tongue slid through my folds, touched my clit and traveled back down to my entrance. The vibration continued, making me breathe harder.

Only Kaden's cock.

Never before had I such a hatred for his rules.

"Oh, did you think I would bring you to orgasm already?" It sounded like he was mocking me. "I'm just teasing you. I want you to be sensitive… to make your pussy tighten around my cock like never before."

I swallowed. If that was his intention, we were on the right track. My skin felt tight. I was sweating and so wet between my legs that I could almost taste my excitement in the air I breathed.

Kaden paused for a moment before returning his

attention to my pussy. I was on the edge again. So skilfully, the pain exploding in my left breast was delayed. And dull. Nipple clamps.

I suspected it because the next thing I knew he was flicking against it and I was thrusting my hip against Kaden so roughly that he had to push my ass back onto the bed.

I mumbled something – what, I didn't know myself. A curse. A plea. A request? I don't know, but it made him laugh. The vibration shot straight to my center and made me moan. How else could I make room for the tension and my feelings? I was bound, unable to move except to dig my fingers into the restraints.

"You're doing such a wonderful job," he praised as he licked my pussy again, almost driving me mad. "I wonder what it feels like for you when I leave the vibrator inside you?" he asked, not a second before the tip of his cock pressed against my entrance.

He would drive me wild. Feral. Like an animal. I knew it. My eyes rolled back as he entered me painfully slowly. Inch by inch… until his cock pressed the vibrator against a spot that made me scream.

It almost felt like an act of violence when the orgasm unexpectedly tore me in two – and Kaden began to fuck me just as ferociously.

But it turned out to be a mistake to open my mouth, because no sooner had I let out the sensations which were raging through me than there was a cock in my mouth. Deep in my mouth. I gagged, all my muscles contracted, but the sudden intrusion didn't diminish my orgasm. If anything it made it more intense.

There were so many things going on inside me, I didn't have a clue what to do with them.

"Show him what I've taught you," Kaden growled. My body went on autopilot to pleasure the stranger with my mouth and tongue. Still moaning, still in the bonds, still fighting for control of my body that I simply did not have.

But Kaden's orders were clear and I was in no position to argue. I didn't want to, because I liked what was happening so much that I kept thinking I had arrived in paradise. In between, I also wondered if I had accidentally swallowed a particularly good drug that put me in that ecstatic state that made me feel everything twice and three times as intensely.

The excitement, the hormones, the fact that Kaden had appropriated my desires and put them into action without me having to worry about it – all these factors made this session all the better.

If there had been any lingering skepticism in my body, it was gone now, replaced by a complete willingness to enjoy it all. They gave me everything they had to offer, right down to the last minute. And there was no question that the two men had thought this through.

In fact, as soon as I started to move my head – as much as I could – Kaden began to fuck me with exactly the same rhythm and intensity as I did with the stranger's cock.

My own enthusiasm determined how he treated me.

Hands were on my legs, sliding over my breasts, closing around my neck. He tugged at my nipples, twisting them until I let out a moan of pain, which was immediately soothed as Kaden's cock pushed the vibrator deeper into me, bitter sweetly hitting my cervix or changing the angle in which it entered me sending new waves of pleasure through me.

I could no longer think clearly. In those moments, I existed to be used by Kaden and the stranger in any way they could think of. They used my body, my arousal, for their own pleasure, doing exactly what they felt like. It was all about sex – and not necessarily about me having the most fun. That was just a nice by-product, but certainly not the main focus of these two men.

The stranger clearly had a taste for sadism. It was he who continued to inflict pain on me. He slid so deep into my mouth that I had to gag, tears welled up in my eyes and I couldn't breathe. But as long as I played with my tongue and felt him getting harder and harder in my mouth, I loved every second of it.

The way my chest tightened and my brain felt even lighter the more he played with my breath. And Kaden, who fucked me incessantly, never for a moment deviating from the pattern he had chosen for tonight.

Even when he wasn't speaking, when his voice wasn't in my ear, I could hear him. The praise for how well I was doing. How proud he was of me. And then he started praising me with names. Calling me all the things that came so easily to his lips, that would surely have hurt other people, but that did only one thing for me in those minutes: a flutter in the pit of my stomach that took over my whole body and validated me in what I was doing.

I wanted to be his filthy little whore. His dirty slut. The one who swallowed his cum and thanked him afterward. I wanted him to press me into the mattress and use me to live out all his dark fantasies. Fuck, even if he wanted to run a knife across my flawless skin or watch someone else beat me, I wouldn't mind. I would kneel on the pavement, waiting for him, ready to offer my throat if he wanted to close the collar around it. All it would take was a word from him and my legs would fall apart, giving him access to the place where he loved to be the most.

All the feelings, emotions and sensations he made me feel, no one else had ever brought to light before. And Kaden did it so effortlessly – as if it was simply the most distinctive trait he possessed.

Outside of our dynamic, he would never get me down on my knees, but inside.... Fuck, one look and I willingly got on my knees and waited for him to give me the first instruction to set me on the right path. The path at the end of which I fell back into a hole and plunged down like Alice, over and over again, until there was a sign on my pussy that said "Eat me."

My heartbeat accelerated the longer Kaden fucked me and the stranger used my mouth according to all the rules. Meanwhile, one of his hands was on the back of my head, moving it for me. I was no longer in control of what was happening – he was. And he made me feel that I was nothing more to him than an object to be used for his pleasure.

There would be no emotional connection between us. This was not because I neither saw nor heard him, which in itself was an enormous act of self-control. After all, my own moaning could not be ignored, and Kaden did not seem to be quiet either, but simply because he was not the man who interested me and held me captive masterfully.

From a woman who wanted nothing to do with kinky sex, Kaden had turned me into an obsessive who couldn't get enough. It had happened in just a few weeks of him giving me his full attention. Unexpectedly. Without warning.

"Remember my rules?" Kaden broke into my thoughts. "We switch places. Your mouth is mine now, so I can watch you fight not to come on his cock."

Not a moment later he pulled out of me. The vibrator stayed in me, the cock also disappeared from my mouth, and I could hear the two of them changing places.

Kaden put a hand on my neck and moved my

head into a different position. Then his cock pressed against my lips until I let him in and he slid over my tongue and into my throat. Similar sensations raced through my head, only this time they were spurred on by Kaden and pushed to new heights. On and on until I felt his hand slide through my hair, over my head.

In my mind he was the only one in existence. The sounds that escaped him every time he pulled away from my mouth, only to enter me again. The smell of his arousal in my nostrils. The way his cock pulsed and twitched, tasting like me and almost driving me mad in more ways than one.

But how ever long I tried to ignore the stranger, as soon as he sank into my pussy with one fluid motion, grabbed my hips and began fucking me hard and relentlessly, my self-discipline ended. Heat surged through me, spreading from my center to my whole body, making me forget to breathe. His cock was so hard that every time he penetrated me, he hit the spot inside me that made me see stars. What he was doing was not only rough, but downright aggressive. Probably led by negative emotions he had accumulated inside him and had not let go of for a long time.

"If you hang in there, I'll reward you in a special way," Kaden murmured, barely audible. But it was the anchor I needed to hold myself together – and most importantly to keep me from chasing the orgasm that was building inside me, that wanted to explode so badly it was almost painful.

The movements of the two men were in perfect unison. Whenever the stranger entered me, Kaden would pull back, only to slide into my mouth with full length and hardness as the stranger withdrew from my pussy. My body was in constant motion, pulled back and forth between the two men and the pleasure they gave me.

Although it was only Kaden who was in control of my body, the other man had an undeniable influence on me. Kaden used this to his advantage. Again and again, as if he were an absolute master in this discipline that had been unknown to me.

I never thought I would end up in bed with two men. Even one who fulfilled my needs seemed to be an absolute phenomenon. I had Kaden as well as a stranger who had been so well trained by him that he might as well have been a clone of him – one even darker than Kaden himself.

I groaned, letting out my frustration at being forbidden an orgasm and trying to hold myself back. Kaden had been practicing this with me for the past few weeks, magically managing to make me come at the right moment with nothing more than a command. The words in and of themselves triggered something in me, but to hear them coming out of his mouth when he was deep inside me, fucking my breath away, always gave me absolute peace.

Now he did not want to say the words. For it was not his cock that was deep inside me. With subtle touches, Kaden let me know again and again that I had to pull myself together. To be just a little bit longer good for him so that he could take everything to an even higher level.

My body was reaching the limits of what it could take. The longer the two men tortured me, the faster I breathed and the more the muscles inside me contracted painfully. They wanted nothing more than to let go. I wanted nothing more than to let go and come, to explode and be consumed by the sensation that would follow, catapulting me to cloud nine and keeping me on a high of pleasure from which I would not soon come down.

Kaden always fucked me thoroughly and left no wish unfulfilled. But this? This was more. So much more that I didn't know what to call it.

Suddenly the stranger pulled out of me, but there was Kaden with his mouth right next to my ear, telling me what would happen next.

"You know what I would like? The sight of your pussy tightening around two cocks. I want to see you so full that your breath is gone and every movement, no matter how minimal, every friction brings unspeakable pleasure," he murmured.

I swallowed, unable to fully comprehend his words.

"Tonight we will take you apart, Nika. You will come again, but it will undoubtedly be so hard that your body won't have much choice in how it reacts..."

Two strong arms lifted me up; less than two

seconds later, Kaden was underneath me. His chest pressed against my back, supporting my full weight. Still bound, I could hardly react the way I wanted to. His hot breath hit the back of my neck as his hands closed around my thighs. He held me in place, even though I couldn't have escaped if I'd wanted to.

I gasped as he pulled the vibrator out of me and then penetrated me, surprised to find that this angle felt completely different.

His cock had already filled me perfectly and I had no idea how I could take a second, but at first it was just fingers sliding into me along with Kaden's cock, at a steady and unhurried pace. I rocked my hips, trying to get more, but the dark laughter from Kaden's chest told me all I needed to know.

I was getting wetter and more aroused, and when the fingers finally disappeared and the tip of another cock slid over my pussy, I knew the two men were about to destroy me – in the best possible way.

Fingers played around my breasts as a sharp burning sensation spread through my center. Without warning, he had pushed the first few inches into me and it already felt like I was going to burst at any moment.

I let my head fall back, unable to give the sensations room and air.

"You're doing so well," Kaden murmured to me. "If you could see what I see... Shit, that's fucking hot. I can feel you getting tighter and tighter. What do you think it will feel like when we move inside you together?"

Like hell. Or like heaven. Maybe both, because there was no point where they would not stimulate. All the sensitive spots, all the movements that gave me pleasure, I would get them all at once. At the same time, as soon as they both buried themselves inside me and found a rhythm.

More and more the stranger pushed into me, and more my pussy felt full, although it gradually got used to it, and the initial pain turned into arousal that spread inside me.

It was a constant cycle I found myself in. Whenever I came down from a high, the two men were there to spur me on and make me feel even more pleasure.

"Kaden," I moaned as he moved his hips against mine from below, welcoming the second cock deeper into me. From that moment on, there was no going back. It had just been the first and only warning that I now had no choice but to let two men fuck me at the same time – in the same hole.

How spoilt Kaden had made me.

At first they moved together, but soon they each fell into their own rhythm and that was all it took for an invisible force to take control of my body.

I might have sounded like one of the actresses in a porn film, but with each thrust and each glistening flash of excitement that shot through me, I just had to let my feelings out.

I felt full. Too full. The orgasm I had almost had returned with a vengeance, and the foreplay to it got stronger and stronger. My core throbbed. Pounded. Contracted around two cocks, making two men moan with strain at the same time. When I came, they would follow. I would pull them down with me.

The muscles in my body tensed. I squeezed my eyes shut, even though I couldn't see under the blindfold anyway... and then Kaden added to the whole thing his fingers playing with my clit with weeks of experience and finally making me lose my mind.

That was it. That's all it took.

I came jerking and screaming as they both fucked me like men gone wild.

Then what Kaden had mentioned happened. My body surrendered. It simply decided that the amount of pleasure it could take had been reached.

They had fucked me and brought me to orgasm so many times that I lost consciousness.

WHEN I AWOKE, MY BODY WAS STILL HUMMING WITH energy. The restraints were gone, I was lying in the middle of a bed, and the blindfold was history. As soon as I opened my eyes, I felt a rush of adrenaline coursing through my veins, making me feel more alive. I breathed in and out like a newborn, except for the almost painful throbbing between my legs. But that had already been taken care of. Kaden must have put an ice pack on it, because the cold radiated straight to my center. An unusual sensation – but I had plenty of them before my body had decided to pull the emergency switch.

A grin spread across my face. The sex had been damn good – so good that I immediately felt the high that had been with me all the time. But that wasn't the only thing on my mind. A part of me was expecting to wake up later with regrets. After all, I had not only been fucked by Kaden but also by a stranger.

But there was no shame. Instead, I felt something that could only be described as power. Because I had it. I got everything I wanted. And so much more, without even asking.

I sat up, the thin blanket slid down my naked body, before realizing that we were not in Kaden's apartment, but still in the sex club. Suddenly, I felt like Sleeping Beauty after her hundred-year sleep. The only question was, where was the prince who had kissed me awake?

I narrowed my eyes and looked around the darkened room. My eyes glided over all the devices that were undoubtedly designed to excite or satisfy a person in one way or another, until my gaze lingered on a second door that opened at that very moment.

I let out a sigh of relief when Kaden stepped out and looked at me with almost the same expression on his face. He was holding a bottle of water and something that looked very much like a snack.

"Are you all right?" he asked, a steep line of worry between his eyebrows.

"Fine," I assured him. "Honestly. I'm sorry I ruined the fun early on."

"Ruined?" He laughed before shaking his head and moving closer to hand me the water bottle. "Drink up," he ordered, "and you haven't ruined anything. Frankly, I half expected you to finish the game at some point. I'm more than impressed that you made it to the end. And fascinated by what your body has endured."

I could see in his eyes that this was not all he had to say on the subject. It had been fun for Kaden. And not just a little. It had probably been the interaction with another man that had made me helpless in front of him and a stranger. No matter what they had agreed upon beforehand, even without a preliminary conversation, they seemed to be in perfect harmony.

I was curious who it was, but I didn't dare ask. That was part of the deal. Part of the attraction. Having anonymous sex. At least in my case, because Kaden had made sure that this man met all his criteria and could not harm us in any way.

His words made me blush – a reaction I would probably never be able to shake, even though I was no longer ashamed. At least not where this matter was concerned.

"Thank you," I finally murmured, shifting slightly to the side and signaling for him to lie beside me.

Then I took the cap off the bottle and drank it in

one gulp before reaching for the snacks he had provided.

"How long was I out?" I finally asked, seeking his physical closeness by sliding up to him. Our legs touched. A start. But I needed more.

"Passed out? Only for a few minutes. But you fell asleep almost immediately afterward," he replied, looking at the clock. "Two hours."

His hands slid over my body, examining it. Every limb, every joint. He was looking for injuries or a point of pain from the restraints.

"I'm fine, Kaden. Really. There's nothing to worry. It was neither too hard nor too much. Honestly, I liked it more than I thought at first. Just…"

Alarmed, he looked at my face, which made me smile.

"Just a second man is not a necessity. I focused on you all the time, whether I wanted to or not. I could tell you apart instinctively, even though it was fun…"

"You wouldn't want to do it again?"

"I don't know."

"I would never lend you. But sharing? To end up being the one who goes home with you and owns every inch of you while other men long for it? I like the idea."

Of course he liked it. Kaden was dominant enough to find his pride in it. His honor. It turned him on when he could show me off, move me around like a steak in front of a carnivore. Because in that same second, he also knew that no one else had the same privileges he had. I would never give myself to anyone else in the same way. Another man may have fucked me, but he didn't own me. He did not know my secrets; my deepest desires and longings were hidden from him. Like me to him, the stranger was just a means to an end. Plain and simple.

I slid my hand up Kaden's chest to his neck until my fingers rested against his cheek. "You know I'd do almost anything for you, right?"

A few months ago, those words would never have come out of my mouth. Kaden may have always been my best friend, but the evolution of our relationship seemed to take things to a whole new level. Casually. The change had been gradual until we were suddenly faced with a fait accompli.

At least, that's how it felt. There was Kaden and Nikau before the deal, and there was Kaden and Nikau after the deal. Worlds apart.

"You at least made an impression, I can assure you."

I shrugged. "The only impression that matters is yours. It's your perception that counts. Not a stranger's."

Kaden grinned before running his fingers over my hand. "You blew me away, Nika. I didn't expect it to be so damn sexy to see you so relaxed. The way you surrendered and just let yourself go was beyond hot. When I think about it, I'm overcome with the desire to do it again."

Instinctively, I squeezed my thighs together,

causing the ice pack to make an odd sound. "I'm afraid that's not a good idea. For now."

I wouldn't be able to stay away from him for long anyway. In this place, with what had just happened... A yawn escaped me, so I took the liberty of sinking deeper into the bed and resting my head on his shoulder.

His arm slipped around my waist as if he had internalized that long ago, holding me tighter to him and giving me a kind of inner warmth that mere conversation and physical contact could never have produced.

I closed my eyes with a blissful sigh. "I'm really glad I signed this contract, K."

"You're only saying that because the sex is indescribably good," he murmured amusedly.

The problem was that I realized it wasn't just the sex that had me under his spell. Kaden had me wrapped around his little finger, and that scared the hell out of me. It was no longer just friendship and sex.

I was falling in love with him and I was afraid that tonight had been the turning point. In fact, it was this moment, right now, that had opened my eyes to this kind of physical closeness and what it did to me and my mind. I could no longer just blame other circumstances. There were feelings involved – and not ones I could bury deep inside and keep quiet about because they wouldn't go away no matter what I did.

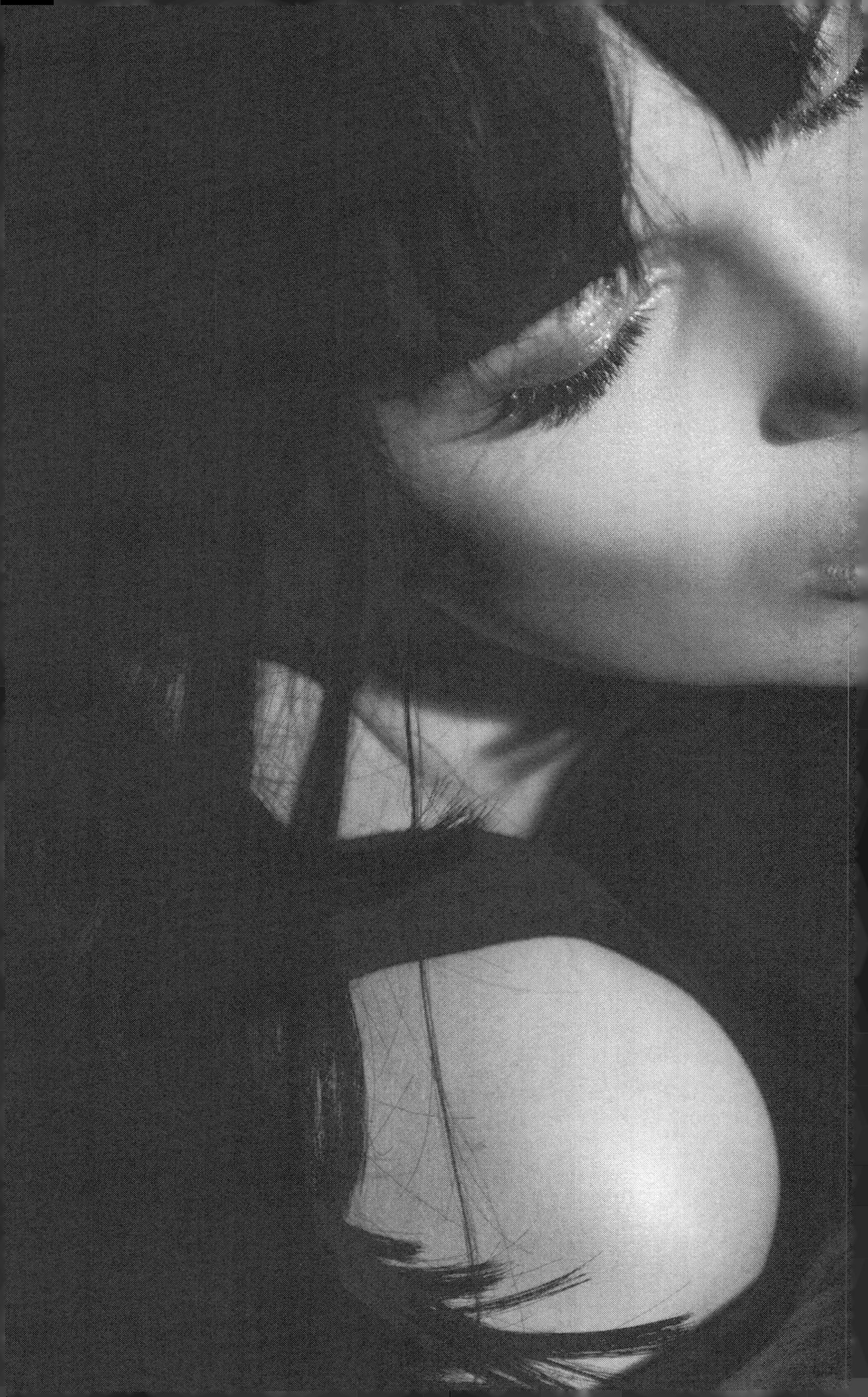

Kaden

Sex clubs like this had always been a part of my life. I'd visit, find a partner for the night and have a few hours of fun fulfilling my needs. It was after that night with Nikau that I realized just how different the experience could be. Not only had it felt better than ever before, but it was already seared into my memory. All the sessions I had here with other women had blurred into a grey lump in the back of my mind and I could no longer tell them apart. I had forgotten even the names in the days after the visit – simply because they had not been important enough to remember.

But when it came to Nika, to what had happened that night, every detail replayed almost automatically. The trust she had shown me. How she had lain blindfolded and bound in front of me, obeying every rule I had insisted on. How she had reacted after we had slowly introduced her to something new and then systematically used it against her...

I would never forget any of this, nor the relief I felt when she woke up after her nap and was in the best of moods. No one had ever fainted during the sessions, but then again, we had never fucked a woman at the same time before. But we had pushed them to their physical limits on several occasions.

It was like a miracle to see her get so carried away with her lust that her body couldn't take it anymore and finally gave in, for the protection of all concerned.

I didn't know where to start and where to stop. The knife, the slapping, her willingness to take care of more than one cock. What she said afterward, and how she fell asleep with her head on my shoulder, even closer than all those times in my bed.

The official part of the night was long over, but the party was still going strong, even though most of the guests had moved to more private rooms or gone home to continue the fun. The bass boomed throughout the building, shaking the floor and leaving no doubt as to where we were. Nevertheless, it was an excellent time to return to the *Honolulu Sun*. But not without completing the one thing I had announced at the beginning of the evening.

After Nikau's dress had fallen victim to the knife, I provided her with a replacement outfit that one of the staff had arranged for her. Like everywhere else in the world, money made the world go round, and to lure her away from her job I had offered her double her salary. Nikau wasn't going to walk out of here naked. As much as I'd enjoyed watching her lust being fuelled by another man, I had no intention of making her an exhibit in this godforsaken place.

Exactly five minutes ago, Nikau had disappeared into the bathroom and when she came out, much less conspicuously dressed, I crossed my arms and nodded.

She shook her head and looked at me. "I look like I'm about to go for a morning jog," she complained. What she was wearing was no comparison to the red, sinful dress she had donned earlier.

"No one will notice," I assured her. I knew the state the club was in at this hour.

In the front and main room, orgy-like conditions would prevail. Anyone leaving the party would be just as unnoticed as someone who had just joined. We could slip out unseen, get one last rush of adrenaline and then fall into my bed and probably sleep until noon, if Kaia didn't get the bright idea of using her key to my apartment.

I made up my mind quickly and held out my hand to Nikau. She looked hot, even in her shorts and top. Not because of the amount of bare skin, but because of the undeniable fact that she always had that effect on me. No matter what she wore.

With a sigh, Nikau finally took my hand and let me pull her closer. I opened the door and we stepped out into the hallway. A young couple came toward us, staggering a little, but otherwise it was comparatively quiet. Everyone was preoccupied with what they were experiencing.

When we arrived in the main room, it was exactly as I had predicted. People were lying on the sofas as if tied together. Some on the armchairs. Someone was moaning with pleasure, alcohol flowed in large quantities. Nika's eyes darted from one corner to the next, it seemed like something new was happening everywhere, something she hadn't seen with her own eyes yet.

After all, it was one thing to experience something first hand, but quite another to witness it.

At the bar, I spotted Lei, who raised his hand briefly to say goodbye and winked at Nikau before I ushered her out. The morning was dawning, the air was crisp, and a salty sea breeze blew through the industrial area, which was still asleep at this hour. It would wake up soon, for sure, but until then...

"Remember what I said when we first got here?" I murmured to her, holding her close to my side so I could feel her body shaking.

It brought an amused grin to my face.

"Kaden, I don't think that..." she started but stopped herself.

"Why? Do you think that throbbing between your legs is from before? Don't you think it's more likely that what you just saw has already arousing you again?"

She lifted her eyes to my face, a little stubborn and

perhaps a little annoyed that I was still not ashamed to offer her all the physical reactions she always so beautifully served up on a silver platter.

"You really want to destroy me today, don't you?"

I tilted my head. "That would never occur to me. It would be counterproductive, don't you think? I just want to see you hesitate. See if you can't take it. So that I can prove to you that the opposite is true."

"We don't fuck on the pavement, Kaden." She crossed her arms, ready to turn this topic into a discussion that would fuel the fire between us.

"But who said anything about fucking?" I looked at her almost innocently.

Surely she didn't think I would push her down on the asphalt to get what I wanted? I had some decency left. Even if it might not look like it sometimes. Especially when I fucked her without any morals.

I let my hand slide down her throat. That only irritated her more than my statement. This time I beat her to it. "Why don't you get on your knees, and I'll show you what I'm talking about?"

She gave me an appraising look. Usually it didn't take her more than a second to sink to the ground and get into position. She seemed to be struggling with this, she continued to hesitate.

"If you want to get out of this situation, you have to use your safeword, Nika. Otherwise I'll continue," I reminded her. A simple way to make sure we were still on the same page. Maybe her behavior was just a game – some kind of challenge. Although I thought she had been dominated, humiliated and praised enough already tonight, there seemed to be no end to it for her.

The realization left me inwardly astonished as I had not expected us to move in this direction again tonight.

I raised an eyebrow in warning. Nika didn't want us to stop. But she didn't want to obey me without protest either.

Suddenly, I let go of her and circled around her a little. "What's the problem? Are you suddenly too noble to get on your knees for me? Do you need a reminder of how it works?"

There was a particular amusement in my voice. Normally I wasn't a big fan of these brat fantasies, but whenever Nika acted like one, it tickled a particular set of reactions out of me.

Starting with the fact that I wanted to verbally push her to her limits before I physically showed her who she had just messed up with. She knew what was coming – yet she chose to challenge that side of me again. To tickle me until I couldn't help but punish her for her behavior in all the ways she liked. That was the thrill of it all, wasn't it? Crossing a line, experiencing the consequences and learning to appreciate the excitement and pleasure even more.

Nikau tilted her head, as if to consider what she needed. But I already knew the answer to that. I stopped directly in front of her and lowered my head a little to remind her that I towered over her and that it would be easy for me to force her to comply.

She looked at me resolutely. A faint grin played around her lips and her left eyebrow raised slightly. Challenging. Leisurely, she crossed her arms behind her back.

"What are you going to do, Kaden?" she asked casually as if trying to find out what was for breakfast.

Brat.

I had to laugh because her behavior was both a huge turn-on and a source of great anticipation. I had just wanted to fuck her again at the end of the night. Now I would not allow her this triumph. She would not even come if she continued to defy me.

"The question is, what do you want me to do? I want to do the opposite. Or make it five times worse. You know what you do a lot in training? You repeat an exercise until it's physically impossible to do it again. Until the body gives up and decides: this far and no further. But you already know that, don't you? Do you think you can do it twice in one night?" I raised an eyebrow in question, watching the lines on her forehead deepen as she pondered whether she could endure the same ordeal again.

"There are still enough men in there who wouldn't say no to another fuck. How do you like being tied up, lying in the middle of the room, on your stomach... blindfolded... and anyone who wants to can use you for their pleasure?"

She stared at me, eyes wide. "You wouldn't do that," she breathed.

I tilted my head and shrugged. "What do you do when you have to choose between that scenario and finally getting on your knees in front of me?"

A low growl escaped her lips.

"Don't forget to unbuckle my belt on the way down."

Her upper lip twitched as if her growl was about to be followed by a snarl, but what came out of her mouth were the sweetest words I had ever heard.

"Of course not, *Master*."

Words that instantly checkmated me, giving me an erection that was harder and more painful than anything I had experienced since Nikau had signed the contract.

I knew that if she put her lips around the head now, it would only take a few seconds and a few movements on her part for me to explode. But that was not going to happen.

I watched as she slid down my body, deftly unbuckled the belt, and finally sank to the pavement in front of me, her knees spread a little and her hands on her thighs.

Still, she looked at me stubbornly. As if she would not give up the reins voluntarily this time. My hand twitched, but I just closed it around my cock, letting it slide up and down a few times, watching Nika as I took over the task that usually fell to her.

"There are some women in there who would do

anything to kneel before me and feel my cock in their throat," I said.

"But for these women, it wouldn't get hard."

Now that was a bold statement to make. And one I didn't want to challenge. I wasn't sure if it wasn't true. Fuck. What the hell had this woman done to me?

Instead of hitting her with the flat of my hand, I used my cock. Not even the pain coursing through my cock was enough to make the erection disappear. Nika had put a curse on me, because now my dick seemed to listen to her more than to me.

There was that amused grin again that made me want to use her mouth so long and hard that she forgot to smile.

She would think of me for the next few days whenever she used a muscle in her face. And of this very situation. That she had disobeyed my command and that I had forced her to obey.

I hit her again before grabbing her chin and coercing her to open her mouth. Then, without warning, I thrust down her throat until she choked.

Tears gathered in her eyes and mingled with the saliva running down her chin. Messy blow jobs. My favorite. I pulled back just a few seconds to let her cough and catch her breath before I was so deep in her mouth that her breathing was cut off.

The tightness of her mouth and throat wrapped around my cock like a second skin, throbbing and pulsing, radiating warmth. With each gag she mastered, the sensations that shot through my erection and into my entire body increased.

A moan escaped me as she gasped.

"The look in your eyes, my love. You don't really hate me. Secretly you love it when I use your mouth hard and recklessly. I bet you're wet. Not just wet, but so wet that I could easily fuck you. But I won't," I began. "Because you don't deserve it. My cock will stay in your mouth until I come. And then you'll wait right here while I take my time getting the car. Then we'll clean up the mess you've made when I get back."

I held her head still and began to pound her mouth. The gurgling and gagging that escaped her, the wet sounds that came with every movement, drove me mad. Nika's cheeks were flushed, her whole face showing reactions to my rough treatment. But she was still grinning, as much as she could, with my cock between her lips.

I reached into her hair with one hand to gain even more control over her head and watched as my cock slid down her throat, causing a slight bulge, before sliding back out of her mouth.

"Master, then, is it? So you think I've earned that title? I control you and keep you on the straight and narrow enough to be called such a name by you." Our eyes searched and found each other. "And what if I don't allow you to do that?"

We both knew that would not be the case. I wanted to tease her. To elicit an even more emotional response from her. But Nikau turned the tables and before I knew it, her tongue was pressing against my erection from below. She sucked me, and teased me in places that only she could find.

With a curse, I held onto her head as I felt the orgasm brewing inside me at the end of my spine. I came down her throat, pulling out only when I had regained my breath.

My cum, her spit and tears were smeared across her lips and mouth. A small work of art that would remain until I returned, pushed it onto her tongue with my finger and made sure she cleaned up the mess herself.

I pulled my trousers up and buckled my belt before looking around. Not a soul to be seen.

"You wait here." I headed for the car park with one last look at her disheveled hair, smudged face and still labored breathing.

I wouldn't take long because I didn't want anyone but me to see her in this state, but a few seconds of waiting would undoubtedly send the adrenaline rushing through her body one last time.

That was what I wanted.

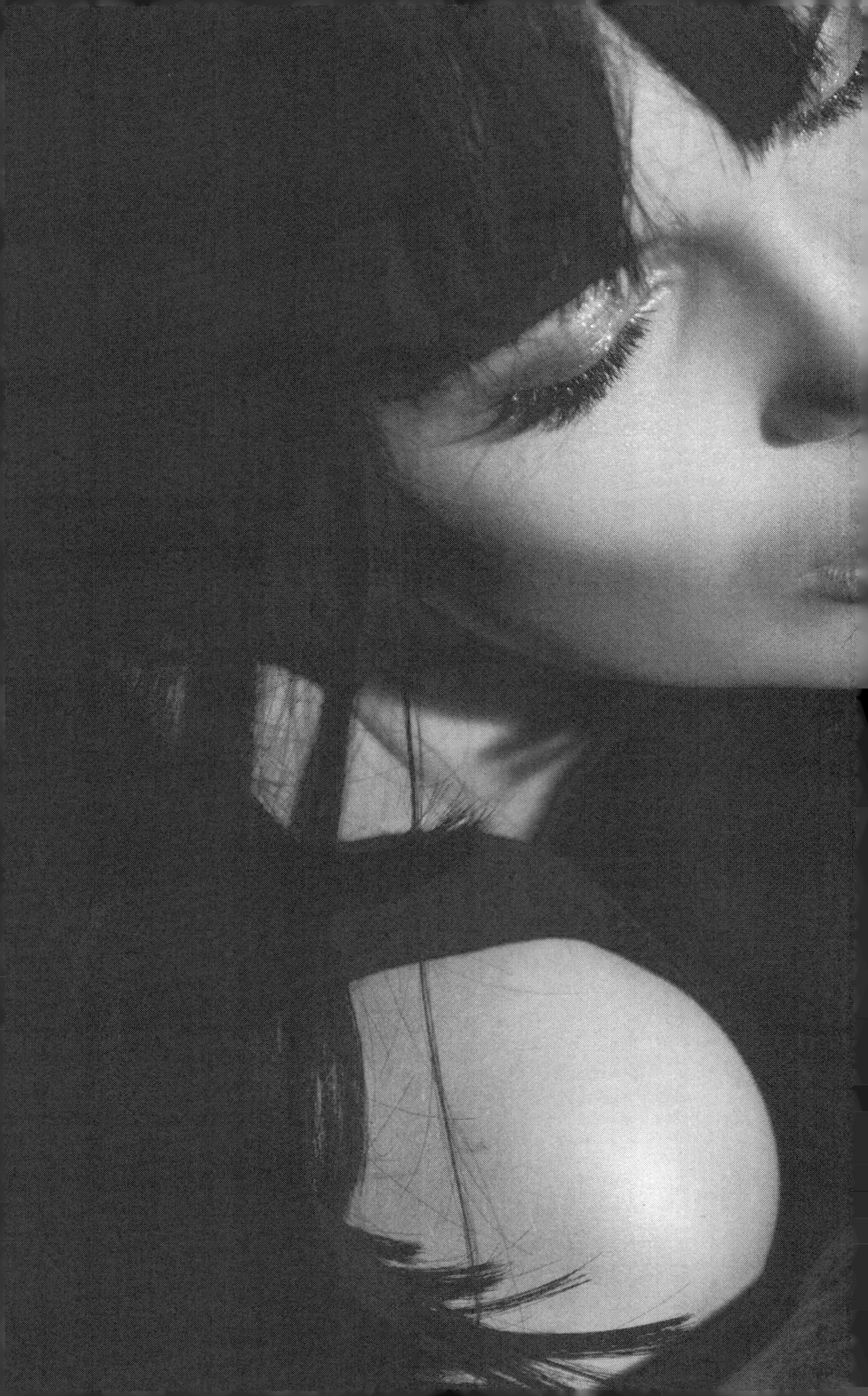

Nikau

My forehead rested on the cool surface of the surfboard as the waves lapped gently around me. I deliberately ignored the fact that a surfboard was not meant to be a bed, although every now and then water would splash into my face or down my back. All I needed was a pillow to bury my head in and a blanket to pull up to my ears. Unfortunately, the water would become quite a problem as the fabric would soak up quickly and become quite heavy. So my plan to relax in the shallow water right on the shore had a few flaws, but I could not complain.

It wasn't until the beach filled up and the sun rose higher that I had to give up my surfboard and forcibly face the day, even though I didn't want to.

I forced my brain to keep sloshing around like the water. Never to hold on to a thought, and certainly not to move in a direction that held danger. Above me a scattered gull screeched, the leaves of the palm trees rustled and the scent of the breakfast set out near the pool drifted toward me.

It would have been a perfect morning, except that the proverbial sword of Damocles had been hanging over my head for the better part of a week, and I didn't know whether it would go away if I just ignored it.... or whether I'd have to deal with it.

I didn't know if I could hold on much longer to the idea that everything was fine. Nothing was fine when you got right down to it. Nothing.

It was not only the night in the sex club that opened my eyes. Also the morning after. And all the hours that followed. Even before that, there had been a quiet foreboding in my mind, but something in the last few days had caused the energy to shift significantly. At least for me. Kaden was the same man he'd always been, which didn't make it any easier, but it did make it a little more complicated.

He didn't have a clue about anything. And he wouldn't, if I had my way. I couldn't tell him that I'd lost the game we'd played together. It had been dangerous from the beginning. A risk. I had taken it in stride. Until suddenly I stopped sending him out on dates with women I thought would be a good match for him. Then I'd cut back on the dates and got more from him instead. I had tried to have a conversation, to test the waters.

I'd told myself all this time that there was nothing to hang on to. It meant nothing.

But in reality that had been a lie. Maybe I had been lost from the moment he handed me the contract. Or maybe it was when he showed up at my door and made me an outrageous offer. It felt like a lifetime ago. Not just a few months.

From the very beginning, we were playing with fire. It was a hot and dangerous dance. And now, against all expectations, I had fallen in love with Kaden, even though he categorically ruled out love and had no plans to ever put himself in a vulnerable position with a woman.

A laugh escaped my lips. I laughed at myself. Cold and bitter. I had been stupid. So stupid. From the first second, Kaden had stood out from all the other men I'd dated. A small part of me must have realized what we were getting into.

I made a face, desperately searching for a solution to my stupid problem. If I kept my mouth shut, said nothing and went back to looking for the perfect woman for him, I could disappear in a few months. It didn't sound too bad in theory, but in practice it made me sick to my stomach to think that he could pay the same attention to another woman as he did to me.

The title I had given him that night had just slipped out. I had tried to suppress the word. To focus on the essential. But the feeling, the need to say it, had been so overwhelming that it had happened in a split second. And his reaction had justified it – catapulting me back into those higher realms, even though I tried to fight it.

Since then, this strange connection between us had only grown deeper. The title came to me as easily as his name – only one of them was reserved for a special time, had a special meaning...

Frustrated, I let my arms hang in the water and shook my head, causing the surfboard to wobble and almost send me over the edge.

This could not be true. How could I have lied to myself when every gentle touch on my neck, back, throat or cheek made it even more obvious? To nestle into the touch, to seek and find its support, to be strengthened by it, to feel like a better, more contented person.

That Kaden was incapable of loving anyone was a misconception on his part. He showed it in everything he did. Unconsciously. It had always been that way, and it hadn't changed until now; it had just become more intense. More focused because we were so much closer. A level had been added that had ultimately passed us by before.

Part of me even wondered if the same thing could have happened then. Not a deal, but a night together that started out as a mistake and ended up as the most incredible piece of luck. There was probably not much to be gained from thinking about it.

Kaden would use any confession as an opportunity to suspend our contract and get as far away from me as possible. I was almost as sure of that as I was that today would be unbearably hot.

In the end, my only choice was between keeping quiet and continuing to manipulate my own attempts to barter him away to another woman so I would end up marrying him but still taking my secret to the grave, or getting out of his life to give myself a chance at happiness. Though I wasn't sure who or what else I would find now that I was used to having him back in my life.

"If you want to kill yourself, try it without the board!" The female voice from the beach was Kaia's. And even though I was so scared I thought I would fall into the waves, I managed to stay on the board.

Killing myself as Kaden would not return my feelings was a bit drastic.

I heard a loud splash and less than thirty seconds later, a shadow slid in beside me. Out of the corner of my eye, I saw Kaia turn around, clasp her hands under her head and stare at the sky.

"You look like you are having an existential crisis."

Or a crisis in purpose. Kaia hit the nail on the head, no matter what you wanted to call it. So unerringly that it hurt.

"I don't know what you're talking about," I murmured, closing my eyes and wondering why I hadn't brought a pillow with me. Weren't there any waterproof ones?

"Let's see. It's early morning. Instead of lying in your bed – or Kaden's – you're floating on the ocean, all alone. Face down on a surfboard. That screams for desperation. I also found a bottle of wine in the sand. Looks like you wanted to have a drink before work too. You know who drinks at this hour? Idiots, students, the mentally ill, and the unhappy in love." Kaia groaned. "You don't look like an idiot. I doubt you suffer from depression; if you were to study on top of your job, that would be suicide. So... does Kaden know about this?"

Sure. Kaia came down to the beach with her glass ball and guessed what I had been keeping hidden from myself for half an eternity.

"No," I grumbled.

"And are you going to tell him?"

A snort escaped me. "Of course not."

Kaia made a sound of disappointment. "I was hoping your forced date would bear fruit."

Well, the previous date had only been one of the many reasons I had fallen for Kaden. That Kaia had hoped for exactly that was news to me.

"Maybe I shouldn't have come here in the first place," I muttered instead of reacting to her revelation.

"I don't think that's how we should approach this."

"We?" I repeated.

"Okay, maybe you are prone to spontaneous depression. After all, I seem to have made a mistake." Her sarcastic reply made me smile, at least. It wasn't much, but it was more than I'd managed since I'd been here.

"I'm sorry. I wasn't aware that my feelings had been released for general discussion."

"Why don't you tell him? Nika, it's not the end of the world."

But Kaia had no idea. At least not when it came to the contract and everything connected with it. "Because he has told me on several occasions that he has no plans to ever love a woman."

"But he loves you. That's more than obvious."

"He wouldn't call it that."

"What then?"

"I don't know. I guess it's part of our wonderful friendship."

This time it was Kaia who snorted. "Friendship. Exactly. That's why he's always looking at you like he's about to put a ring on your finger."

"Ironically, that's exactly what he plans to do. Eventually. When I haven't succeeded in finding the right woman for him."

I felt Kaia's gaze on me, but I couldn't bring myself to turn my head, open my eyes and look at her.

"If you ask me, he found her a long time ago and is just too much of a stubborn idiot to realize it."

"It's not that I haven't tried to bring it up. But Kaden is damn sure of himself. He doesn't want to end up like your parents."

"I doubt very much that you would hit him. Or abuse him. And I can't imagine the other way around. He's just too affectionate. And attentive. Loving, if you want to take it to the extreme." Kaia knew her brother well, but unfortunately that didn't change the fact that there was a difference between what you could observe when you focused on Kaden and the reality he created for himself. "He hasn't spent as long with any woman over the years as he has with you. He hasn't looked at them, treated them or spent nearly as much time with them as with you. He never missed a meeting because of these women. He has never been late. And he never saw them at lunch. There were no trips or dates, and I didn't have anything to do with them either."

"So we're a good match. But that doesn't mean that, when he's already told me that he'll never change his principles, I can stay by his side, keep quiet and hope for the best."

"I can talk to him, Nika," she suggested confidently, but I shook my head.

"That won't be necessary. I should quit. Run for the hills. Leave him without an explanation so he won't think about coming after me."

"We both know you won't do that." Kaia sounded serious. And she was right. I was an adult, not a character from a romance film.

"Fine. Then I won't chicken out and leave. What do you suggest instead?"

Now, if she was going to wax lyrical about some grand romantic gesture that would make everything all right, I would probably consider drowning myself in the sea after all.

If there was one thing I wasn't, it was romantic. I could make grand, sexual gestures – because Kaden had taught me that you didn't have to be ashamed of what you wanted – but beyond that, the air was getting really thin. Why affirm your feelings and the love you felt when gestures and actions said more than that anyway?

And they had said a hell of a lot over the past few weeks, whether Kaden wanted to admit it or not.

"Back to my original question. You should just tell him. Play your cards close to your chest and hope for the best. You could still lose, of course, but you could just as well win. It would be worth it, wouldn't it?"

It felt like we were going round in circles. Over and over again, only to return to the point where there was no way around telling Kaden the truth, knowing it wasn't what he wanted. It was selfish to hope that he would change his mind – or even demand it, or push him in that direction so I would have the advantage and get what I wanted. In the end it was just a small thing, wasn't it? The only difference was that he felt the same way and admitted it. If I didn't say anything and he couldn't admit anything, all that was missing was that one official title.

But in this case I was manipulating myself so masterfully that I might as well make up a clown face and laugh at myself in the mirror.

I closed my eyes, took a deep breath and held it. Even though it didn't solve my problem, the pressure that settled in my chest after a few seconds felt good. It didn't make my head any clearer, but in the end it didn't matter.

Kaia was simply right. I had to tell him. Be honest with him and myself, and then find out what it meant. Where it led.

"What do you want me to say?" I asked aloud. She laughed. "Hey Kaden, stupid story, somehow I fell in love with you?"

"Stupid should be removed from that sentence."

I finally found the motivation to turn around on the surfboard and sat up so my legs dangled in the blue water. Kaia did the same, but not without examining my face.

"How long have you been sure?"

"Since our date a few days ago," I replied.

"And today it still won't leave you alone?"

"Even the best efforts to ignore it failed." Because it was foolish to ignore something when it was right in front of you every day. I spent more time in Kaden's apartment than in my own. I woke up next to him or in his arms more mornings than I did alone. We ate lunch together. And dinner. Sometimes we showered together. What he said, how he acted... because I was clear about how I felt, the rest felt much more meaningful.

"How about you tell him you're in love with him –

and see how he reacts? You don't explain it. You just say it like it is."

"Has that ever worked before?"

"I don't know. It's never happened to me. But I know Kaden well enough to know that he appreciates directness way more than some hoo-ha that's far too pompous for such a profound matter." Only Kaia could managed to downplay the matter in such a way.

I shook my head and looked at her. "I don't have a good feeling about this. You realize that, right?"

"Then you should probably get it over with quickly so that feeling goes away. And if you need support, I'm here. I can tell Kaden off if necessary."

"I don't want to force him to do anything. Or talk him into something he doesn't want."

She shrugged. "It's a good thing you're not me. I saw it then and I see it now. If he continues to resist, I'm afraid I will have to tell him that he's not entitled to any woman's attention in the future."

At least that made me smile. Kaia was right. But it was easier for her, as an outsider, to say and do all this than for me, who was far too deeply involved in a relationship with Kaden. I didn't want to hurt him, I didn't want to force anything on him, or leave the impression that I had similar traits to his mother.

If he didn't take my confession well, he would grasp at any straw. Even if it meant demonizing me and turning me into someone I was not. That's how any person who has resisted something for years would react, not wanting to admit they could feel anything. It could be that the idea of feelings disgusted him and he believed he was incapable of trusting anyone on this godforsaken planet, but he was simply wrong.

He trusted me. He showed it to me every time we came close to each other, physically and mentally naked. Kaden was capable of more than he let on.

Determined, I looked at Kaia after she had said nothing more. "Fine. I'll tell him. But if it goes wrong, you book me a flight straight off the island. Deal?"

Kaia held out her hand. "Deal."

MY HEART LITERALLY JUMPED INTO MY THROAT AS SOON as I entered the part of the hotel where Kaden's office was located. I could have chosen any place, any time, but before I got in my own way again and talked myself out of telling him, I preferred to get it over with now.

Kaia's words slipped through my mind, but they didn't do anything to calm my nervousness. On the contrary, they caused more anxiety and a sinking feeling in my stomach.

"Kaden has an appointment," the secretary called when she saw me in the corridor. Just a friendly hint, but I ignored it anyway. As far as I was concerned, he could be in a meeting with five of his business partners; I needed to see him now. Not tonight or tomorrow. I needed to see him now.

A strange reaction, actually, considering that I had been carrying this knowledge around with me for a few days and had not been able to say it out loud until now. Until Kaia came around the corner and recognized it without any words from me.

To my surprise, the door to Kaden's office was open and when I turned the corner, I saw him sitting behind his desk – with a woman in a loose summer dress in front of him.

I automatically raised my eyebrows until I was close enough to see that it was not a guest or some business associate, but the woman from the club. The one he had already fucked.

For some completely incomprehensible, irrational reason, I felt jealous. It made me walk nonchalantly into the office. Kaden's eagle-eyed stare did not escape me as I walked around the desk and sat on the glass top next to him.

"Like I said you really should leave." Kaden sounded like he had said that sentence more than once and had been ignored repeatedly in the last few minutes.

"I thought the club had a rule about discretion," I interjected, my eyes fixed strictly on Kaden. The nameless woman didn't see anything but my back, which almost surprised me a little.

Usually I had no interest in jealousy because I had always believed there was nothing to stop a person who really wanted to be unfaithful, but in Kaden's case…

For my own sanity, I interrupted the train of thought and focused on what was happening in the office. I heard the other woman get up with an indignant snort. Her high heels clicked on the tiled floor as she headed for the door.

I could see on Kaden's face the exact second she left the office. Behind her, the door slammed shut as if she had to reiterate her point.

Kaden shook his head and I couldn't help but laugh. Not because I had found it so funny to spy on this woman in his office, but because she had made that cinematic exit.

"How did you know I could use your help?" he asked as his hands tightened on my thighs, pulling me further to the left with a strong jerk so he was between my legs as soon as he moved closer to the desk.

I shrugged. "It was just a coincidence, nothing more."

"Did I see jealousy on your face?"

Damn, that was a quick change of subject. And suddenly far too close to the topic I had come here for in the first place. There's no such thing as jealousy if you have no feelings for a person. If I admitted it, would he draw the right conclusions? Or would it take more than that?

"To be honest, that's exactly what I felt back at the club when I realized you'd had a thing with her."

He twisted his mouth into a grin. "Doesn't mean I'd touch her a second time. Or was particularly happy about what happened."

When he said it, it sounded damn normal, like the truth. But my brain was focused solely on the fact that he'd just been with her, and seeing her in his office now made me do things I didn't want to say out loud.

"Yet she felt the need to come here and try to do just that. And she didn't like that you turned her down either."

"That's not my problem, is it?" He looked at me urgently. He had no idea. "All those dates didn't bother you either, did they?"

"Because that was different," I countered, knowing full well that I had been manipulating them for some time. Besides, he hadn't screwed any of the women, and he wouldn't, because he was far too choosy for that.

He had proved it time and time again, and when I compared his statistics over the last few years with how long he had put up with me.

"Why this jealousy? It doesn't suit you at all. Besides, there's no reason for it."

I narrowed my eyes. There were a lot of reasons, all having to do with my stupid fear that in a few minutes this could develop in a direction that would catapult me back into my old life.

"I'm missing something here, aren't I?" asked Kaden with a healthy dose of skepticism.

Slowly I nodded. But instead of answering right away, I bit my lip and looked up at the ceiling. Why did it have to be so damn hard to talk about your feelings?

We could have endless discussions about sex and what we did in the bedroom. I could show him how I felt with subtle gestures. All that was no problem. But looking Kaden in the face and saying the words, standing naked in front of him and hoping he didn't laugh at me, took it all out of me.

"I'm jealous because..." I started and immediately stopped myself. Jealousy was not what this was really about. "I don't know how, Kaden, but somehow you've become important to me. And I'm not talking about our friendship. I'm talking about how the sex, the dating, the time we've spent together, and what you've made me realize has made me develop feelings for you. I can't send you out on any more dates because I don't want you to find someone else. You've already found me."

He stared at me as if I had suddenly started speaking Klingon. This was not good. Was it?

"I love you, Kaden," I managed to say, even though the words almost choked me.

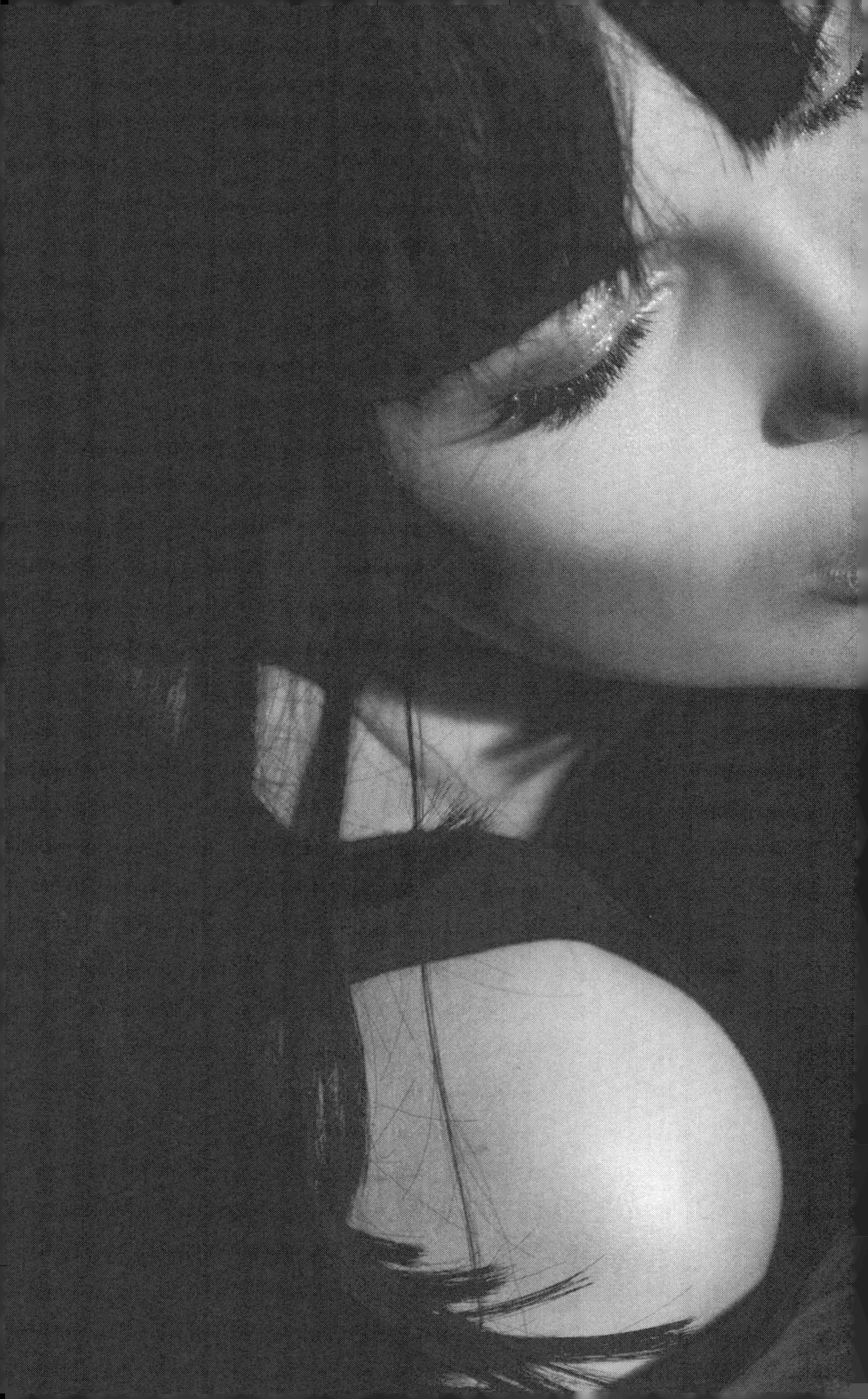

Kaden

The words ate into my brain like acid through a surface. Suddenly, it was no longer Nikau sitting on the desk in front of me. Suddenly, I was no longer a grown man, but a child who had seen too much.

"Don't you understand I'm doing this for love?" I saw her fist flying toward his face. He didn't even raise his arms to defend himself. A split second later I heard her fist do damage.

The scene played over and over in my mind's eye, mixing with reality and making it hard for me to stay there and give Nikau the answer she deserved.

My body was going crazy. My heart was racing. I was getting hot, only to feel cold coursing through me immediately afterward. I clenched my hands into fists and pushed my desk chair back half a foot to get some distance to her and the source that had brought the memory to light in the first place.

I swallowed and shook my head. The rational part of me knew Nikau would never do such a thing. But the irrational part... it only saw my mother using those words as an excuse to justify her violence.

So it was not the meaning of the words that almost made me jump and run, but the memory I associated with them.

It took me a few moments to see clearly again. Until Nikau's face moved into my field of vision and was no longer overshadowed by my parents, who had not even noticed my presence on so many evenings.

"You should go," I groaned.

If I could just get them out of my sight and regain control of my senses, I could handle this.

"Go? Did you hear what I just said?"

"Yes, and I don't want to hear it!" The answer was too harsh. It was too harsh because I already knew we were both completely lost.

But I just couldn't hear the words. Not from her mouth. Not from anyone's mouth, really. All this time I hadn't thought I might find myself in this situation. It hadn't worried me. But apparently that had been a mistake. A bloody mistake that was now catching up with me.

My ears were ringing, so I blinked. I also remembered Kaia – and how much she'd heard about our parents' problems, though I'd always tried to make sure she didn't notice. At some point, my limited ability to lie to her had failed.

"Do you really want me to go now, Kaden?"

I nodded. "Yes. Leave me alone so I can... forget this."

If I could erase the memories of my childhood and what my parents had done to each other with the push of a button, I would do it right now, because then I wouldn't feel the way I did.

I could not even look at her properly. Again and again my gaze blurred as the memory came to the fore and demanded my full attention.

How sick was it that this one word of all things had triggered me so strongly that I would probably soon see the room from the side if things continued to go crazy like this?

"Can you please talk to me, K?" The pleading in her voice made me grimace. My eyes narrowed. How was I going to explain this to her? Talk to her when I could barely think of anything other than what her words had brought out in me?

I would have much rather reacted directly to that than to what it had done to me. I didn't want her to think it was her fault. That she was the cause of my body reacting with panic instead of joy. Or whatever you wanted to call it.

"Please, let's talk about this," she continued. "Or at least tell me what's wrong with you. I'm worried."

Whenever we had talked about it before, it had never been a problem. So I had no idea where this reaction was coming from. I could not justify it. All I knew was that Nikau had to disappear from my office so I could breathe more freely. So I could regain control of my body and my mind.

If she didn't leave voluntarily, I had to get out. Outside. Preferably to the other end of the resort, or at least far enough away that it no longer felt like there were weights on my chest.

"No offence, but I need to put some distance between us," I groaned, rising just enough to brace myself against the desk, push past it and head for the door.

"Kaden!" she screamed. Desperate. Outraged. A little angry.

But she didn't follow me. That was good. Wasn't it? On the way out, I realized it was not good. It felt wrong. Running away felt wrong. But I had already taken the first steps. Turning back was out of the question.

Besides, the physical distance would help me. Even out in the fresh air I could breathe more freely again. But the memory still danced at the edge of my vision, even when Kaia came toward me.

Another angry woman in my life. Wonderful.

"Have you lost your mind or why are you acting like a lunatic?" she asked, grabbing my upper arms and preventing me from walking away, leaving her standing there.

"Nika…"

"Loves you, I know. That's why you shouldn't be

out here. You should be in there. Kissing her. Or fucking on your desk, whatever the right answer is."

I shook my head. "I shouldn't."

"You should. Because you love her too."

"I know."

"You... know? Then there's all the more reason to be in there."

"I can't do it."

"Sure you can. And you will. Because if you don't, I'll kill you myself." The threat made me snort.

But her use of the word also triggered the memory again. Again I heard my mother justifying her violence against my father. Again I felt helpless because there was nothing I could do to stop it.

Kaia's fingers dug into my upper arms as she realized something was terribly amiss. "Tell me what's wrong."

I stupidly found it hard to focus on her face. She had to know. About herself.

"As she said it, I could only hear Mother shouting at Father as she hit him. 'I'm doing this out of love. I love you, don't you understand? How can this be violence when I love you? You're the most important person in my life, so you'd better put up with this for me if you want to show me that you love me too.' I remember every single word and her voice overrides everything else." I wanted to put my hands on my head to make it stop. "I can't explain it to her. Do you know how ridiculous that sounds? I feel the same way, but I can't say it because it makes me think of our parents."

"Is that why you've never said it before?"

"Maybe I've loved her for over a decade, but my brain automatically associates love with domestic violence, so I'd rather ignore it than pay attention to it." But how could I ignore it when she was sitting right there in front of me, about to give me a future that I hadn't persuaded her to give me through a deal or a contract?

"I think you'll come with me for now," Kaia murmured, still not taking her hands off my upper arms.

MAYBE IT HADN'T BEEN A GOOD IDEA TO JUST FOLLOW Kaia, because somehow she seemed to have the glorious vision of going straight into confrontation therapy. At least that's what it felt like when I looked out of the car at the house we'd grown up in. It was now overgrown, most of the windows were smashed and the front wall was sprayed with graffiti. Once it had fitted in perfectly with the friendly neighborhood. Now it was just an eyesore. It was ironic that the exterior now resembled what had gone on inside for years. The neighbors had never noticed, so the outrage was all the greater when the beautiful facade cracked and the truth was revealed.

"I guess you don't want to end my agony. You

want to make it worse and make it last for the next ten years, or how should I interpret that?" I gave Kaia a questioning sideways glance because she was leaning loosely on the steering wheel and didn't seem to be as upset as I was.

Then again, she had not received a declaration of love from the woman who played one of the most important roles in her life.

"Actually, I just want to prove something to you."

"And what is that?"

"That you can either decide to put the past behind you… or that you should consider making an appointment with a psychologist to work on your issues."

Like a bull at a gate. Wonderful. "I don't need a therapist."

"I went to one. He helped me."

"Because of our parents?"

"Among other things, yes."

I looked at her skeptically. "And you never told me?"

"Because you were always sure you didn't want or need anything like that. But since you had a panic attack after Nika told you she loved you, maybe you should think about it…"

The word *love* rang in my ears again. I made a face. I was disgusted by the memory and the fact that my body reacted like this. Unnecessarily. This was justifiably inappropriate.

"Can you please not keep repeating that?" I grumbled, looking directly at her instead of continuing to look out the window.

"Why? Love isn't a bad word."

"Kaia."

"Look, a normal person wouldn't react like this. You should be happy. Come on, Kaden, you've known each other since you were little. We've been through so much together, and I've seen how close you are more than once. You never wanted to admit it, but you loved her when you didn't even know what the word meant. And that was long before you attached a false definition to it."

It felt like I was on a spinning top, going round and round, repeating the same insights. If Kaia was aware of all these things, why had she always held back and never spoken about them? I already knew the answer to that. I was the problem because I would probably always have stifled such conversations. Blocked them because I couldn't talk about it.

"So you're a master of observation, but the rest of the time you just sit back and see what happens?"

"Suggesting that you two go out came from me."

"Of course. From whom else?"

"So don't tell me I didn't do anything."

"We almost had a fight on that date. You realize that, don't you?"

"And you know you left her, right? In your office. Alone. After she confessed her feelings. After she chose not to just walk away because she was afraid you would push her away."

I narrowed my eyes. At first she had wanted to build me up – had we already got to the part where she would beat me up for my decision to run away? I slowly opened my mouth, but Kaia shook her head in warning.

"You know how you were always there for her? I remember the panic the first time she got her period. You handled it beautifully – even though you had no idea and had to sneak around and read up on everything. After every high school fling that went wrong, you built her up again. This could go on forever – and vice versa. You love each other and have for a long time. Why should there be a problem now just because this one word comes into play? Basically, you already have a relationship. Nothing has to change."

So why exactly did it feel like everything had to change?

"I don't think the problem is that you've witnessed domestic violence. You're just afraid of being so close to it. It makes you vulnerable. And that makes you afraid because we all live in a time where it's so damn easy for people to hurt someone else. Intentionally. Unintentionally. No matter what. There's hardly any human relationship that doesn't end with someone losing faith in everything."

"Kaia…" I started, but she shrugged.

"You know I'm right. And you also know that you won't let her go."

"What if the press does what they've been doing for the last few years?"

"Drag you through the mud? Put you in a bad light? Or try to sabotage your relationship?"

"All of the above."

"That won't work as an argument. Nika knows what the press has said about you over the last few years, and it didn't stop her from coming back to Hawaii with you. Or from putting up with you these past few months. She knows better. And so do you. This is just a stupid attempt to get you off the hook."

Did she not know I had only used my dark side to lure Nikau home? To wrap her around my little finger and make her fall in love with me without her noticing. So in the end I would have to keep her for myself and never let her go, because it was impossible to find a woman who could fulfill all my needs. I had known her for a long time and had got it into my head that it was either her or no one else?

"I've heard that line about your priorities too, so you might as well save it." She looked at me warningly.

So Nikau hadn't just hinted, she'd told her more. That was good, because it also meant that Kaia knew exactly what she was talking about – and wasn't just using some platitudes to make me feel better. Or make me decide to do the right thing.

Even though I had known what it was for a long time.

"What doubts do you still have?" Kaia asked after a few seconds, as if she was ready to draw the sword again and fight against my thoughts.

"To be honest, I don't know. Maybe a small part of me didn't expect it to come to this and now has no idea what the next step is."

"Maybe you should have had a relationship that lasted longer than two weeks. To get practice, you know." Her ironic undertone made me narrow my eyes.

Kaia sometimes had no filter. Between her thoughts and what came out of her mouth there was supposed to be a checkpoint that prevented statements like the one she had just spat out.

"I haven't even felt the need to get rid of her in the last few months. You know that, don't you?"

"I do. I just wanted to make sure that you were aware of it as well." Kaia grinned. And was getting on my nerves even more than she already was.

"Instead of doing it in this weird way, why don't you just tell me everything straight out?"

She shrugged. "Would be boring, wouldn't it? Besides, it's a learning process. I can't chew it all up for you."

Which in turn sounded like I was emotionally and mentally challenged and would be a total wreck without my sister's help. It was a wonderful conversation, as only siblings can have.

"When did you get so annoyingly bad?" I muttered.

"Oh, you'd better shut up. You'd be lost without me. Let's talk about how you're going to justify your little meltdown. You'll have to apologize."

"You make it sound like I behaved like an absolute monster." She hadn't even been there, and I had just described the broad outlines of our conversation without going into detail. Kaia simply had too much imagination, which she always used at the wrong times.

"I mean, we both know how you can be sometimes, Kaden. You should just grovel and hope for the best. I'd be pissed as hell if I were her."

I rolled my eyes. "Point taken."

Kaia was probably right about more than just that. If I was going to have a semi-panic attack every time someone used the word love in the proper context, maybe I needed to see a psychologist to fix the broken part of my brain. Or whatever a therapist's job was.

I looked back toward the house. As much as I would have liked to say that I only had bad memories of this place, it was not true. In fact, there were just as many good ones. Most of them had to do with Kaia and Nikau or my father, but they had existed. And without all that history, I probably wouldn't be where I was today. I wouldn't have a luxury resort and I certainly wouldn't have fulfilled this dream... I didn't want to sugarcoat it. But the experience I had seemed to have had a positive effect on me.

"Kaden... I think there's a problem."

I turned my head, taking in the pale expression on her face, already sensing trouble. "What kind of problem?"

"When Nikau and I spoke this morning, she said that if the conversation with you failed, I would have to buy her a plane ticket."

"But it didn't fail," I replied irritably.

"You told her to go away so you could forget all about it. I wouldn't exactly call that successful." Why did she sound angry now?

"My mother's voice covered everything else. Yes. I wanted to forget her."

"But you didn't tell her that."

"Of course not."

"Wonderful. Then you better hope she's not on a plane yet, because when she couldn't reach me, she just went to the airport herself."

"She what?"

I reached for Kaia's phone, wishing for her to drive at last. Although I didn't call Nikau from my mobile, she didn't answer. Either she didn't want to talk to Kaia or she was already on a plane. I hadn't thought about my choice of words and had made another mistake that I would regret once I got her home.

"When you were asked how much you wanted to do wrong today, you just said yes and nodded, right?" Of course, Kaia still had a stupid line on her lips.

But at least she did me a favor and took us to the airport by the quickest route. Nikau was not to leave the island under any circumstances – because I would not survive another trip to Iowa. Culturally, and because she would probably strangle me with her bare hands if she found me on my knees begging on her doorstep.

AT LUNCHTIME THE AIRPORT WAS A LIVING HELL. Not only was it taken over by tourists, and the shuttles to the hotels were waiting everywhere, no. The very active islanders were also ready with leis to welcome the new arrivals.

All this did not make it any easier for me to find Nikau. Especially as she was not answering my calls or those of Kaia.

A glance at the departure board reassured me that the next flight to Iowa wasn't for a few hours, but as I understood Kaia, Nikau didn't care where the flight went this morning – the main thing was to get off the island. Away from me.

For the first time since that moment in the car, I felt something like desperation rising in me. If she'd really left, I would have to drag her back to O'ahu, no matter what. There was no way she would leave me now that we were on the same side. I just had to explain it to her.

But to do that, I had to find her. Kaia was also trying to find her. But we ran into each other again before we got close to Nikau.

And the fact that Kaia shook her head as soon as we were in sight didn't seem to be a good sign either.

"She's not here," she began as soon as we were close enough. "But she hasn't left the island either. She still doesn't want to see you."

"Did you tell her that?"

"You can tell her yourself."

"You just said she doesn't want to see me."

"Not at the moment. Maybe she'll change her mind and you'll get a chance. And if you don't take it, maybe you should consider letting the vet…" She left the sentence unfinished and shrugged. "You should have just stayed with her. That would have been the best thing for all of us." Almost motherly, Kaia patted my shoulder. "Let's go home."

I gritted my teeth and started to move. But the feeling that spread through my chest took my breath away. This bottomless abyss that threatened to swallow me was worse than the panic attack I had felt earlier.

Not even when I had watched her leave Hawaii with her family had it felt as bad as it did now. It didn't help that Kaia was trying to comfort me.

I didn't even know what to be angry at. Myself for using the wrong words and leaving her in the dark? Nikau, because she just wanted to run away? My parents, because they were responsible for the problem that had led to the situation in the first place? Or just the universe, because it had dealt me these cards and was laughing at the way I had handled them?

ON THE WAY BACK TO THE RESORT, ONE THOUGHT followed the next. Not for a second did I have any peace from what was happening in my head. Back then, when Nikau had gone to Iowa the contact between us had come to an abrupt end because I didn't want to make things any harder for both of us. Everything had become easier as soon as I had started suppressing her existence and forgetting what I had suddenly missed in her absence. Irretrievably, because she would not just come back. I had to wait almost a decade for her to return. But the situation was different now, and a second time I would certainly not endure waiting for her, or sitting on my hands until she found a reason to come back to me. That was out of the question. I may have made a mistake with what I had said – but then I would make a whole lot more of them if it meant she would eventually come back and we could talk about the issue in a way that worked for both of us. All these thoughts were nothing more than a pathetic attempt to keep my bottomless panic under control. Because it was spreading further and further inside me, making it hell to breathe properly again. It had been out of affect. The only question was how we were going to solve this problem if Nikau did not want to see me. Part of me understood how hurt she was by my choice of words. Part of me wanted to slap her for being so stupid, but another part of me was just annoyed at the whole situation. We had been in such wonderful harmony for so long, never arguing and making each other feel good. Only to have it all fall apart because of a stupid misunderstanding, fuelled by the unrelenting panic inside me, my mother's voice still playing on a loop, trying to convince me to make the next mistake? But burying my head in the sand, throwing in the towel and giving up was not the answer. I just needed a few hours to collect myself and then I would find Nikau. Whether she wanted to or not. Kaia seemed to be an advocate of giving her the space she needed – but if her brain worked anywhere near as badly as mine, she'd run through hundreds of scenarios so far, and in none of them had I come out well – because she didn't know the truth, only the version she'd made up in her own mind. And by God, that was certainly not the version I would let her leave the island with.

That's why I was so surprised when I smelled her familiar scent as soon as I pushed open the door to my apartment and stepped inside. I frowned because that was not what I wanted in my nose. Not when she was hiding somewhere else and avoiding talking to me. To look me in the eye.

At least that's what I wanted to fixate on until my eyes fell on the open patio doors – and the woman sitting on one of the chairs. Waiting.

"You're here," I stated in utter disbelief. It wasn't my imagination, was it?

My legs carried me to the door, and when I

stepped out, I wanted to grab her in my arms and apologize for what I had said, without thinking about how it might look.

"I am," Nikau replied, looking up at me and keeping her expression neutral.

That freaked me out even more than the fact that she was even here. "I thought you didn't want to see me."

"I don't. Because you just walked away and left me standing there," she muttered. "I hope the drive here from the airport was enough to teach you not to do that again."

"Because it feels like shit. I get it," I replied, grabbing the back of my neck.

Actually, we were just dancing around the issue that was bothering us both. But we didn't seem to have reached the point where we could meet in the middle and make sure we liked each other again.

She wrinkled her nose. "I never should have told you. Then this wouldn't have happened, and now I wouldn't have to worry about returning to Iowa or… I don't know. I haven't had time to think about it yet."

I raised an irritated eyebrow. Back to Iowa? Had this woman lost her mind? "You're not going anywhere, Nika," I growled, taking a step toward her before crouching down to be at eye level with her if she avoided looking up at me.

"I'm certainly not going to stick around and take all the emotional damage that would come with it."

I closed my eyes, took a deep breath and tried to

calm my frayed nerves. In a voice that was far too calm, I finally answered her, "You're not going anywhere, Nika. You're not getting your ass off this island, off this resort, and certainly not out of this apartment. You're staying here, with me, by my side. And if that's not clear enough, then... I don't know. I need you to be with me."

"But you don't love me."

Instinctively, my fingers twitched, but I clenched them into a fist, swallowing the sensations threatening to rise again inside me. "You're wrong. I just can't say it because I keep hearing my mother's voice using it to justify everything she did," I explained. "And I certainly don't feel that way because you allow me to corrupt you and make you my perfect mate. These feelings have been there for a long time – it's just that I've always suppressed them so I wouldn't risk ending up in a similar position to my parents."

Which was ridiculous. I knew that now.

"I don't understand... we've always been best friends. You never seemed to be interested in me." I understood all the words that came out of her mouth, but they were still like a riddle.

"Asking you out would have meant losing you. Making myself so vulnerable would have meant that I probably would. Seeing you move to Iowa when we would have been anything but friends would probably have destroyed me. But making a deal with you to marry me one day.... That's as close as I could get."

"But you couldn't have known if I liked what you were into."

"Remember what you said then? Maybe I'll find someone who doesn't suit me at first sight. But the attraction is so strong that we develop into the people we need to be to have a future together."

She nodded hesitantly, "And you said I was your plan B."

I let out the breath I had been holding. "Actually, I didn't want to find anyone else. Secretly."

Every word I said cost me so much to overcome, because I was just waiting for the moment when my childhood would knock on the door again and take its toll.

"And at first glance, we weren't really a good match. But then you showed me that there was another side to me and who you could be; sometime between the day you showed up in Iowa and the date at the sex club, I fell in love with you," Nikau replied. "And then I got scared, because all this time you've been so vehement that nothing will ever change in your principles and love doesn't exist for you."

She was right, of course. Because I had said all that because it had never seemed like there was a realistic chance for us. In my world, I had done everything I could to ensure that she would end up being my wife and that I would get everything from her that was somehow possible within that framework. She fell in love with me and suddenly new ways opened up, just because I had drawn her into my darkness. I had never expected that.

"I'm an idiot, okay? We can agree on that if you want. But I don't think we would have made it this far ten years ago, no matter the circumstances." After all, we had both been young. Inexperienced. Wet behind the ears. And that being seperated for a few years hadn't damaged our friendship became clearer every second. We had picked up where we had left off and not a second had felt wrong. So there was nothing to regret. "So are you going to stay here or do I have to tie your ass to my bed and wait for that to convince you?"

Nikau made a face, a little annoyed at my choice of words. "And you didn't mean that you had to forget what I said?"

"I would never want to forget." Only what my brain had subsequently served up and made of it.

"Then I'm sorry. I didn't know it could affect you like that. I thought of a lot of things, but this wasn't one of them."

"It's not your fault. It never was. It just had a massive effect on me," I explained. "That's why Kaia made me think I should see a psychologist. Not just for me, but for both of us."

She shook her head. "A few hours and everything changes again. Can we record for the future that we are no longer looking for ways out?"

"I'll at least try."

"Good, because I'm still not over the fact that you

never said a word, and everything depended on whether or not I happened to fall in love with you."

"I want to write idiot on my forehead."

In the last few minutes, the invisible weight had been lifted from my shoulders. I had not expected the conversation to go like this. I had thought we would argue. Loudly. A little over the top. And in an unnecessarily hurtful way. But the conversation we had was proof that we had both grown as people, and in the way we treated each other. The unnecessary drama didn't exist, at least not when we managed to talk to each other and get rid of what was weighing us both down.

It may be that not everything went well right from the start. But the last few minutes clearly showed that I was capable of being the dominant part of her submissive side and the man who could find a place at her side if I stood up for what was happening inside me. It wasn't difficult. I just had to get into the habit of not burying everything down deep and hoping it wouldn't bother me anymore.

I held out my hand to Nika in a sort of final peace offering. Without hesitation, she put her hand in mine.

"Promise me that nothing will change," she asked, looking directly at me. I wasn't sure if she was saying this for herself or out of consideration for what I had revealed to her.

"Nothing will change," I confirmed, after thinking about what was really going to change. We had already dealt with each other as a couple before. We didn't need to adjust that, nor was it new. And all the other elements already had the same baseline. So why change something that has always worked? "But I would definitely like to introduce you as my girlfriend in the future. Or as my future wife, because I won't deviate from the deal."

"And the dates?" she snorted amusedly.

"Are history. If I go on any again, it will be with you. And no one else. So are we agreed?"

"More than clear," Nika replied quietly, leaning forward.

I placed a finger under her chin, pulled her closer and took possession of her mouth, knowing that the rest of her body would follow. Her lips pressed against mine until our tongues met and the kiss became much deeper in a fraction of a second.

We had never kissed like this before – only when we were in a session. So there were probably things that would change. But they would probably be changes that no one would have any complaints about.

Slowly I pulled her closer until we sat together on the terrace floor, lost in each other and busy making the unspoken apology clear.

I let my hand slide down her back, the other on her neck to hold her in place. A tiny part of me still feared that Nika would get up and walk away and that I had simply imagined this conversation and everything that went with it – in my desperation to create a level where we could meet and talk.

But Nika didn't disappear, and holding her in my arms didn't turn out to be a hallucination. She stayed there until we got up at some point, because we couldn't spend the rest of the day on the terrace, and Kaia was definitely waiting for an explanation, wasn't she?

"Did my sister know you would be waiting for me here?" I asked abruptly. One look at Nika's face was enough.

Still, a grin spread across her lips. "I told her when we spoke. And also that I wanted to let you sweat it out a bit."

"Do you know how many thoughts I had on the way here?"

"Many?"

"A whole lot."

"But you didn't have to worry about it?"

"I would rather have it if I didn't have to chase you all over the island to talk to you," I muttered.

Nika shrugged. "You were the one who taught me that certain behaviors can sometimes have consequences, and it's best to learn from them."

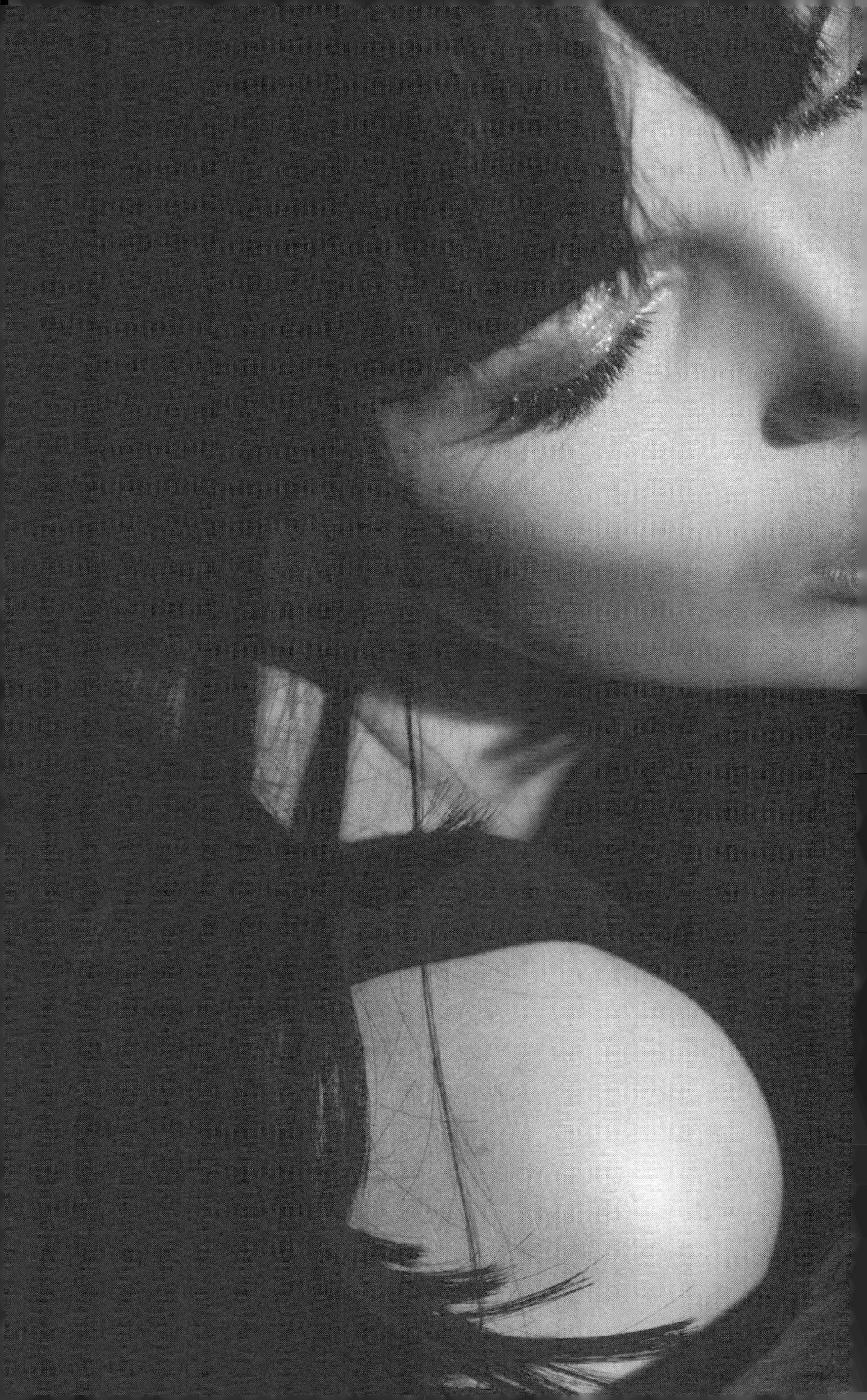

Nikau

Drama ruled the world. And so did the tabloids, they bent over backward to get a headline and build it up until there wasn't much left of the original story. It was a shame because by the time the journalist had intercepted me at the supermarket to talk about my relationship with Kaden Haoa, I had already chosen the perfect statements. He had asked questions that were more than indiscreet, but I had answered them all truthfully – only to see a picture of us on the front page. Together on the beach, after surfing. But the photographer had come onto the private property of the *Honolulu Sun*. With this photo, he had probably put together the last missing piece of the puzzle to give his story a glamorous finish. Or one that distorted the core of the story so Kaden was now the evil of O'ahu, seducing innocent women and raising them to be monsters.

I had never laughed as much as I did that morning when I discovered the newspaper on the breakfast table and read the headline. It also made me realize that it didn't matter what you told the press – in the end, they would always make up a story that wasn't the truth, but rather the image they wanted to portray of Kaden. Which was funny because he was right next to me during the interview, making sure every word made sense.

I had thought it was necessary to be on good terms with the press so they would finally clear up the false assumptions about Kaden, but when it came down to it, it really didn't make any difference. He could probably move to a convent and make a vow of chastity, and they would still write about him screwing the nuns on the altar. The reality and what they wrote about him were so far apart that I was very amused when a new headline appeared.

It was probably what Kaden needed as a reaction from me. Since he had understood that all the negative, slanderous words about him had no influence on me, he was much more relaxed when the newspaper arrived. He also stopped trying to keep the press away from me. This was probably partly because I had taken to teasing them. If they twisted our words anyway, you could start with a lie, couldn't you?

While the press spread false information, more and more locals came to our parties on the beach and got to know the real Kaden. The one who not only made money from the luxury resort but also created good jobs and ensured that the island kept its untouched places among the many tourists.

Four weeks ago I almost left the island, only to change my mind at the last minute. A decision I have never regretted because if I had left, I would not be waking up in Kaden's bed today. I wouldn't be happy to see him for lunch, and we'd spend the afternoon and evening on the beach before meeting Kaia and some friends for dinner. The contract was history – but only because it had been superseded by an official relationship that covered all the points we had already put in writing.

Kaden and I had taken the plunge, only to find that we didn't sink. On the contrary, we were floating on the water and had the best view.

I felt at ease. I felt an inner peace I had never known before and believed, for the first time in my life, that everything was falling into place perfectly and that the end result could only be better. Kaden was seeing a therapist – for me, but more importantly for himself. So I decided to do the same and work through the issues I had ignored for years.

As we grew together and left behind the parts of our childhood and adolescence that still affected us negatively, we soon became the best versions of ourselves – all while sharing our lives and having fantastic sex.

Sometimes I found it particularly ironic that all these issues had been with us almost ten years ago and that the solution was so close at the same time. Because back then I had only seen Kaden as my best friend, not as the man I could fall in love with because he suddenly turned out to be the perfect match for a version of myself I had never even met.

Ultimately, I couldn't even blame him for being silent and repressed. I didn't have to pretend to myself that I would have handled it any differently because in the few days between the realization and my confession to him, I had played out so many scenarios and was still firmly convinced that there was no future for the two of us together. At least not in the way my heart longed for.

And yet, life had proved me wrong – and made me realize that I needed to have a little more faith because everything fell into place as it should have all along.

By the time I returned to O'ahu, I had made rules for myself and broken them one by one. I had fallen in love again with my home and the man who had brought me back. Our deal had fallen through because I didn't want him to have another woman by his side and with his quirks and preferences, he had corrupted me in such a wonderful way that I couldn't even imagine life without him. Kaden's hand and voice had more power over me and what I felt than anyone else had ever had. He could bring me to my knees with the tip of his finger and make me tremble with a murmur in my ear.

Kaden had gone from being my best friend to my

master, only to claim the place at my side for himself, not just for a limited time, but forever. The original deal remained. We would marry – the exact date was still to be determined. My birthday, the day we made the deal, or something in between.

Whenever it was, I would let it come to me. Just like everything else that had come up since my return to Hawaii. The job at the restaurant, the management, Kaden, none of it had been actively sought, but somehow it had found me. I was grateful for that. More than that, I appreciated the obstacles fate had overcome for me to make it all happen.

So when my eyes fell on the article in the newspaper, I wiped a few amused tears from the corners of my eyes and thundered the newspaper into the wastepaper basket. Kaden had already read the report on his phone, as he received all of them by email, and I did not want to see the rubbish in my presence any longer.

It wouldn't be long before he returned from his therapy session. There were more important things to discuss than the existence of a journalist who knew no boundaries and would have been better off writing fairy tales than trying his hand at something as ambitious as journalism.

I sat back with a grin. I wondered what the reports would be like when the first information about our wedding leaked. Would they turn it into a Beauty and the Beast story? That Kaden had kidnapped me to force me into marriage? At least that would be entertaining.

As soon as I heard the key in the door, I turned. After therapy, Kaden seemed happy to be back in his own four walls instead of lying on the proverbial red couch and revealing his most intimate thoughts.

He came over to me, put a hand on my neck and pulled me to my feet for a kiss. It didn't last long because a second later he pulled away with a grin.

"I have a present for you," Kaden announced, almost a little proudly.

Skeptically, I raised an eyebrow. We both knew that surprises were not my favorite thing. "What is it?" I asked, hoping he wouldn't keep me guessing.

"My submission."

I tilted my head, not sure what he meant.

"We exchange roles. For one night. You dominate me so I can prove to myself that I can trust you blindly and there's no reason to fear a similar disaster as with my parents."

"Was that your psychologist's suggestion?"

He nodded. "As you know, she works with these things and has experience of the scene herself. She said it might help. Provided, of course, you feel comfortable with it."

If I hadn't seen myself in a role before, it would have been as a dominatrix. I was supposed to dominate someone else – and Kaden? Where would I get the finesse to do that when I had no experience whatsoever and wasn't even sure if I had a spark of dominance in the bedroom?

I felt like I was back in the early days, except I didn't feel the need to read everything the internet had to say about it.

"Do you think I'm cut out for this? I mean... I wouldn't even know where to start."

"Think about it, Nika. Just once, I would allow it – to completely give up control and be at your mercy." To my shame, I found those words alone were enough to make it more palatable.

The way Kaden said it, and that he dangled it in front of me like a juicy steak, made it easier to digest. And he knew it, because all the times I'd wished I could get back at him in kind, this time they could come true.

Just as little as I was dominant, Kaden had no spark of submissiveness in him. This could be interesting.

"What if I do something that makes things worse for you instead of better?"

"The same protocols apply as always. And you know what's okay for me and what's not," he replied. "Besides, I trust you. You wouldn't abuse that power any more than I do."

Although it didn't seem to cost him any effort to say that, I knew that he secretly had problems believing it. There was a small voice in his head that said the opposite. He had been working on this for more than four weeks. It would probably take him a while to get it under control and reach a state where that voice didn't have the power to send him into a semi-panic attack at the mention of the word love. This wasn't even about me and what we shared. It was all about what he had experienced in his childhood and youth.

In spite of everything, we had agreed not to avoid it. What good would that do? It wouldn't go away just because we never talked about it.

"Give me some time to prepare. Okay?" I finally said. After all, I had to figure out what to do with him without it looking like a beginner's pathetic attempt to feign dominance.

THERE WAS A FILM PLAYING IN MY HEAD. AN OUTLINE OF what would happen every second I dominated Kaden. I had lain awake for hours at night, running through every possible scenario.

I had thought about what I would say, how I would arouse him and make him willingly submit to me. I didn't want to make a mistake, to embarrass myself because I didn't know what to say, or to falter. I wanted to seduce him – to show him that even in this scenario he could let himself fall. Even if it was a one-off, I didn't want him to regret it. For more than one reason, it was not only about the trust between us but also about what was bothering him. And a little bit about me. For as easy as it had been for me to feel comfortable in his hands and to trust him blindly. It was now difficult for me to break out of these bonds and to accept that it worked differently and that, for once, I was not in the submissive role, but that everything was in my hands and that Kaden relied entirely on me. On what I had to show him and give him.

In my head, however, the film did not consider that we were not just any actors working to a script, but two living beings making decisions. That became clear when I realized I hadn't warned Kaden in my scenario – that I would drag him into a submissive role. Just like he always did with me.

Sometimes he would appear, and the next he would have his hand around my neck, muttering the dirtiest things I had heard that day. It was pretty clear that it wouldn't work the other way around, because I was physically incapable of subduing him.

I had to seduce him mentally, and the first step was to make him speechless at the sight of me. So it wasn't the usual outfit I wore when he came home from the office. Latex and leather were not and would never be my favorite, but I had to admit it sent exactly the message I intended.

There was a dark side, a dominant streak I hadn't seen in myself before. And apparently Kaden hadn't either, because when I turned toward him by the light of the candles, the bag fell out of his hand.

"Fuck," he cursed. Whether because of me or the bag...

Kaden was on the verge of bending over. I clicked my tongue. "Leave it."

I watched with satisfaction as he clenched his hand into a fist and slowly stood up, his movements stiffer than before.

I let my eyes glide slowly over him as I gently slapped the palm of my hand with the riding crop. I had no intention of hitting him with it – but it would be great fun to use it to tease him.

As I looked at his face, it was clear that his previous curse was mine alone. Good – because that meant I had found the perfect start for what was to follow.

I took a step toward him, just to see what effect it would have on him. Whenever he put me on the spot like that, I felt nervousness rising because I had no idea what was coming next. I wanted him to feel the same and to not know what was coming. What I had planned…

Kaden looked at me and held his breath. Tense. Until an amused smile spread across my lips, I tilted my head and let him know with a movement of my chin that he should get on his knees.

As I watched him sink to his knees, automatically assuming the position he had practiced with me for weeks to perfection, I felt a surge of power. As I took in the sight, I felt excitement spread through me. To see him like that, to see him fall into that submissive role and look up at me, waiting, full of trust and ready to let whatever I had planned wash over him.

God, I couldn't even describe how it felt to me. If it was similar for him, I understood more and more why he enjoyed adding this component to our sessions. There was nothing quite like the rush of power that came from the realization that you are in complete control.

After a few seconds I moved closer until I felt the warmth of his body. But I did not touch him, still too fascinated to explore the differences. As soon as he ordered me to get on my knees, I felt calm. It seemed to make Kaden nervous – either because it was not his usual role or because he could not read me.

To be honest, I still had no idea what I was doing here, and the scenario I had imagined was long gone. There was no place for the feeling I was experiencing. I liked seeing Kaden on his knees in front of me. But I had never expected to find pleasure as a Dominant, even for a short time.

Normally I only felt the need to submit to him, but there was something else in that moment. And it told me to savor the moment.

I squatted next to him and watched with satisfaction as he had to force himself to look straight ahead. It was so hard for him not to look in my direction that I leaned forward and grinned until my lips touched the sensitive spot under his ear. I let my tongue shoot out, teasing him a little until my mouth was next to his ear. The hairs on the back of his neck stood up automatically without me saying anything.

Shit. Seeing an otherwise dominant man on his

knees, just because I told him to... did something to me.

"Look at you. Such a pretty boy. Obedient. Let's see how long you can keep this up," I muttered before sliding the tip of the whip across his back. Very lightly, but enough to send a shiver through his body. This was followed by a growl that inevitably referred to the words I had addressed to him.

I stood up, circled him, and then leaned forward to remove his shirt. My eyes slid over his naked torso and the tanned skin and muscles beneath. Kaden was an imposing sight in any case, but on his knees before me... I suddenly knew exactly what I wanted to do to him.

Determined, I walked over to one of the chairs and sat down, spreading my legs a little to give Kaden the best view of my already wet pussy. I leaned back before slipping my hand between my legs. Normally, he wouldn't let me touch myself without his permission – but tonight, I was the one who made the rules, and he had no choice but to follow them. Even if it meant me masturbating in front of him.

As soon as I played with myself, his gaze became more intense. From my face, it fell directly on my hand, which I was skilfully teasing myself with. I bit my lower lip, stifled a moan in my throat and threw my head back.

I could hear him mumbling something. Probably his protest at not being allowed to take part in this action. I studied his face through almost closed eyes and let my gaze slide down. Satisfied, I noticed that he not only liked the sight, no. He was so turned on that his cock was pressing hard against his jeans.

Just before I came, I stopped and stood, and picked up the whip. I made my way to the bedroom, tapping the whip against my lower leg in a gesture that he had better follow me.

When he tried to rise, I shook my head. "On all fours."

On so many occasions he had made me crawl across the floor and I had never understood what he saw in it. But it was just an extension of the power structure. Knowing that your partner was doing everything you told him to do, and that it had this wonderful effect on you, that it seemed so sexy… it made a hell of a difference.

I stopped beside the bed and waited until Kaden was back at my side. "Sit on the bed," I ordered, watching as he did as asked.

Then I sat on his lap and pushed his shoulders into a lying position. I adjusted my position so that he could feel my pulsating center through the fabric right on his cock.

He looked up at me from below, that glint in his eyes I always saw just before he was about to fuck me. Only today he wasn't the one setting the pace. I moved my hips against him, feeling the friction building up between the fabric of his jeans and my skin, spurring me on and driving him crazier.

His hands landed on my thighs, his fingers digging into my skin. Desire.

"Is that desperation I sense in you?" I asked. "But let's not be hasty, shall we? I know you'd like nothing better than to be inside me, but I fear you'll have to be patient. Or do you have a good reason why it should be otherwise?"

I raised an eyebrow and moved my hips against his erection, watching as he searched for words but couldn't find them. I knew that feeling. When your thoughts were so empty, you suddenly couldn't even form a proper sentence.

He was always the verbose one, turning me into a person who only functioned according to his most basic needs, unable to communicate through the fog of lust. So it served him right when I did him the same favor – this one time.

"Don't you know what to say? Is the need so overwhelming? You want to be inside me so badly, don't you? Let's see what you have to offer in return…"

I lifted my hips slightly and reached between our bodies, sliding my hand over the fabric still covering his rock hard erection. A jolt went through his body as he threw his head back and moaned.

Slowly, I leaned forward, running my fingernails over his exposed throat. Kaden dropped further, prompting me to undo his belt and pull down his trousers so there was no barrier between us. I sat down again, but in such a way that he could feel my wetness but not penetrate me.

I could tell it was torture for him. It was an exciting development because normally he had no problem teasing me for half an eternity. But when it came to him, he suddenly became impatient.

My hand moved from his neck down over his chest and abs, which tightened under the scratch of my fingernails, making his erection press harder between my legs. I continued to rock my hips back and forth, feeling him twitch. Kaden looked frustrated.

I leaned forward, sliding my lips over his bare skin until I reached his chin and looked straight into his half-closed eyes. "Let's have a little competition. I'll fuck you. But if you come before me, I'll sit on your face afterward and you'll make it up to me."

He could only win. Kaden knew it. I knew it. And he didn't have a choice anyway, because not a second later I lifted my hips, wrapped my hand around his cock and slid onto him in one smooth motion.

Kaden inhaled sharply and I closed my eyes to get used to the sensation. He was deep inside me, filling me completely, and that alone made me almost explode with pleasure. Still, it wasn't enough, so I began to move on top of him. I propped myself up on him, lost in the fact that he couldn't even use his hands – simply because I hadn't allowed him to.

A moan escaped my lips as I could control the angle and depth of his penetration. Again and again I stimulated and teased the points inside me that made me almost see stars – only to tense my inner muscles and watch as he found it harder and harder to control himself from thrust to thrust.

I loved to watch the way it all began to slip away from him. How hard it was for him to lie under me. Idly. When he would have loved to have thrown me onto my belly and taken me so hard from behind that I would scream out his name. But not today. Or at least not now.

As I rode him, I picked up the whip again and slid it across his thighs, hinting that I might hit him with it at any moment – but I did not. The knowledge that it could happen was enough to keep him balancing on the edge.

"Did you know I can feel when your orgasm is coming?" I moaned. "You're getting harder. The movements of your hips are getting more erratic. And your cock…"

A sound of rapture escaped me, because for once I had taken it all in, instead of neglecting the last few inches in favor of speed. That's exactly how I continued: slow, deep and hard.

Once again Kaden tried to grab my hips, but I caught his hands, pushed them back onto the mattress, and kept on fucking him. I didn't allow him to fuck me from below, forcing him to stay still under me while I enjoyed every second of controlling how he penetrated me.

It would have been easy to bring him and myself to orgasm at the same time, but this time I wanted him to lose. I wanted Kaden to fail and experience a punishment that involved me sitting on his face and him bringing me to climax over and over again until I decided enough was enough – or he finally had enough and took control, only for me to regret my desire afterward.

With a grin I brought him to orgasm, feeling him pour into me, desperately trying to thrust deeper into me but unable to as I sat on top of him, moving my hips gently. I tensed my muscles as he came, lost in his cursing, and as soon as the pulsation subsided, I lifted my hips and let him slide out of me.

"Looks like you lost..." I murmured. That's as far as I got, though, because he freed his arms from my grip, grabbed me by my hips and lifted me right onto his face in one fell swoop, burying himself completely in my middle.

I grabbed the headboard as his tongue slid through me almost aggressively. Surprised, I gasped as he continued the assault, taking in my pleasure as well as his own. The satisfied humming that vibrated through me did the rest. Within seconds I came on his face for the first time, trembling legs included.

And Kaden did not stop there. He continued seamlessly, teasing and stimulating me further. I could feel the balance of power shifting and control slowly but surely slipping from my hands and back to him.

But he had trusted me – for the briefest of periods he had relinquished control and allowed me a first glimpse into his world, learning that he could rely on me.

Of course, I could have whipped him and spanked him like he always did with me. I could have put a collar on him and made him beg and kiss my feet. But none of that was in my nature. I needed a level where I felt comfortable, and apparently I had found it, only to be brought back to the world I was used to.

A second orgasm ripped through my body. Kaden's dark laughter reached my ears, giving me goosebumps I would not soon forget. Shudder after shudder ran through my body, making me tremble and forget what had been the plan a moment ago.

"You really should be careful about the desires you express, *Neyla*," he murmured darkly between my legs, and I knew he was going to make me come so often that I would end up regretting even talking about it.

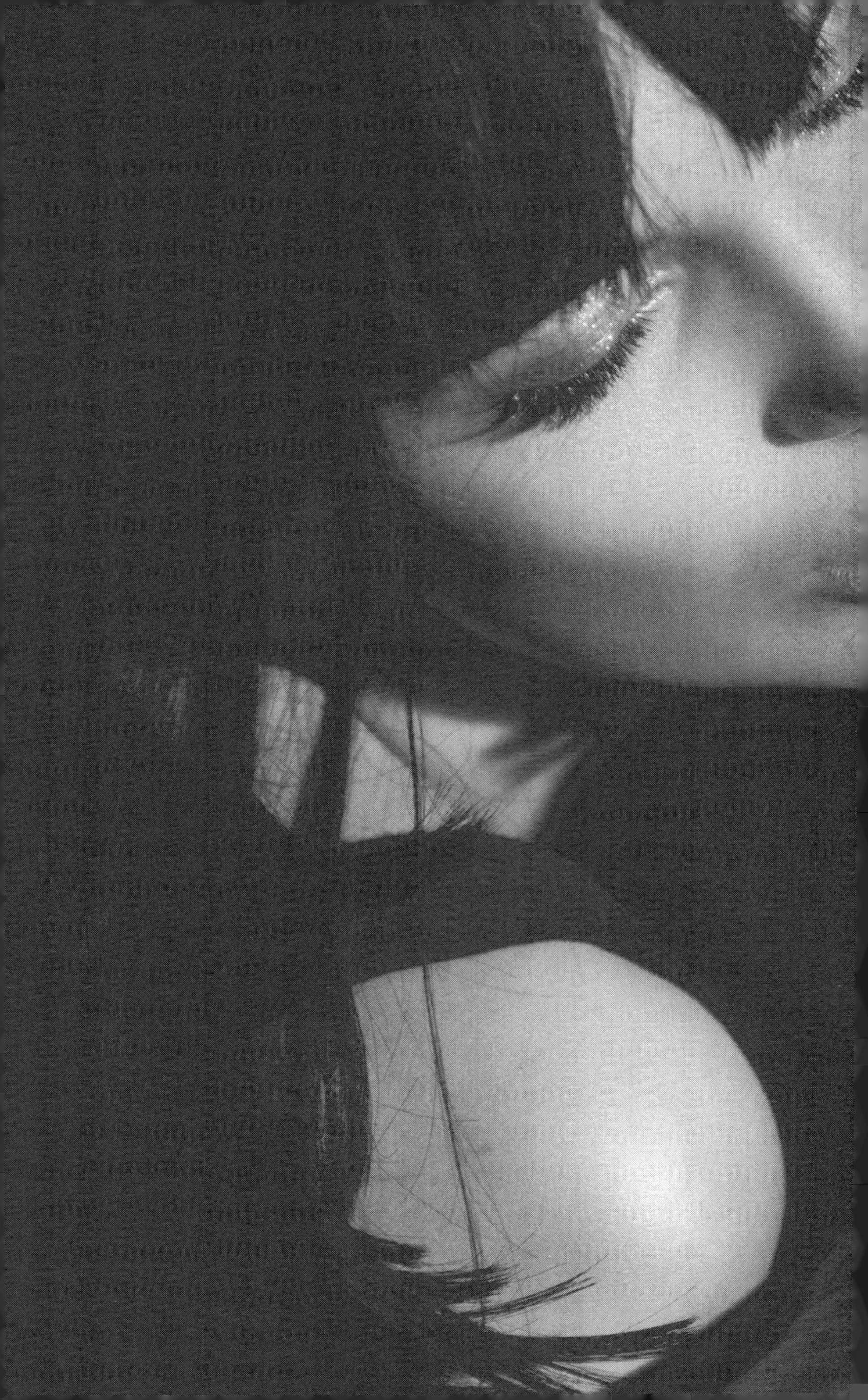

Epilogue

At some point, every little girl started thinking about the perfect wedding day. In most cases, there wasn't even a specific trigger, apart from the fact that it felt like a magical, fairytale event that was somehow part of growing up. In fact, that moment never happened to me. Either because I had been far too realistic as a child, or because I had spent more time with boys than girls – even though I had sisters. In any case, I had no idea of the perfect wedding, so I could now say that what was unfolding before me was more than perfect.

In the background, the blue waves of the ocean lapping at the beach, its white sand warming in the evening sun and resting comfortably between my toes as I stepped off the wooden jetty and paused to take a deep breath and enjoy the amazing view.

Torches were buried to the right and left of the path to the altar. They led directly to Kaden, who was waiting for me next to Lei – the man he had chosen to be our priest.

Apart from the two men, there was only a singer. No guests. No family. No press. Even if they were lurking outside the resort, they wouldn't steal this moment.

I felt tears welling up in my eyes, the moment was overwhelming. It had all started on that beach. With a deal that I had vehemently rejected almost a year ago, because I didn't believe I could ever be on the same wavelength as Kaden when it came to anything other than friendship.

But here I was, in a short white wedding dress, about to marry my best friend.

I swallowed and started to move as soon as the young woman began to sing. A touchingly gentle song. As the words *"I just want you to know who I am"* floated through the air, accompanied by the sound of the sea, I finally reached out my hand to Kaden, for a second completely captivated by how handsome he looked in that suit.

Almost casually, he ran his finger over the wound on my forearm that he had inflicted on me last night. A reminder of the blood oath we had sworn – and a promise for the future, because we had to spent it together, or… no, there was no other option.

Finally, I turned my gaze to Kaden's face, touched

by all the emotions I recognized there. Usually he kept them under wraps, rarely showing what was really going on inside, but after all the months we had spent fighting his demons, he could now proudly say he was no longer afraid to accept the love I had to give him.

We trusted each other blindly. No panic attacks, no fear, no worries that the past would repeat itself and I would be the one to hurt him. We would face the future together, even though in the beginning it looked like there would never be a "us" for us.

Lei said a few words that almost went unheard because I was busy looking into Kaden's eyes and reading what was written there. But when he finally opened his mouth to say something himself, all my focus was on that.

Not on the fact that my hands were barely perceptibly shaking and my pulse was pounding because he was about to murmur things in his velvety, dark voice that were only meant for my ears.

"We both know I've been lying to myself for a long time, Nika. I've always told myself I didn't feel anything for my own good. For you. Or for anyone. That felt safe. But it was a lie and, looking back, a stupid decision I made when I didn't know any better. To be honest, I always felt lost without you. Like a part of me was missing. I was able to survive and make a future for myself, but since the day you left the island, nothing has been the way I wanted it to be. I could live without you, but I'm glad I don't have to. I don't even want to, because it would mean giving up so many things I've gotten used to over the past few months. I know we found each other because of sex. But at the end of the day, there is something else that keeps us together. And I know I haven't said it before, but…" He was about to destroy my make-up for good. I could see it in the damned look he gave me. "I love you, Nika. And as of today, you're officially wearing not only my last name, but also the one that lets everyone know at a glance that you belong to me."

I looked down at the gold bracelet on my wrist. Cartier. Expensive. It was even more expensive because he'd had the original design altered to his liking so that it fit each of us, because he wore the same thing – and neither of us could take it off without the other. It had been there since I signed the new contract last night that sealed our future and bound us together forever.

This was only the official part – everything else was already sealed.

Still, a pleasant shiver ran down my spine, for what Kaden had just said was something he had not uttered even once in the past few months. I had felt it in so many ways, but he had never said it until now.

With that, he finally let my tears fall. "I love you too," I replied. "And if Lei doesn't make it official now, he'll be the one to feel the knife next time."

The two men laughed and then Lei sealed what had been brewing since Kaden's and my childhood.

… I really hope you liked the story of Kaden and Nike. There's also good news if you took a liking to Kaia. Her book will be the next one, and you can already preorder it right here: Love on my brain

Made in the USA
Las Vegas, NV
23 December 2023